'Lord St Claire.' She snapped her indignation as she attempted to pull away from him. 'At this moment I can think of nothing I would enjoy more than to see you consigned to the devil, where you so obviously belong!'

He gave a husky laugh, refusing to release her despite her struggles. 'You believe my past misdeeds serious enough to send me to the pits of hell?'

'You do not?' Juliet gave him a scornful glance.

'It is a possibility, I suppose,' he conceded consideringly. 'Drunkenness. Gambling. Debauchery. Hmm, it does seem more than a possibility, does it not…?' The lowering of his head towards hers slowly blocked out the moonlight overhead.

Juliet became very still as she stared up at him. 'What are you doing…?' she breathed huskily.

He gave an unconcerned shrug of those broad shoulders. 'As you seem to believe I am going to the devil anyway, I cannot see that one more indiscretion is going to make the slightest difference to my hellish fate!'

Carole Mortimer was born in England, the youngest of three children. She began writing in 1978, and has now written over one hundred and fifty books for Harlequin Mills & Boon. Carole has six sons: Matthew, Joshua, Timothy, Michael, David and Peter. She says, 'I'm happily married to Peter senior; we're best friends as well as lovers, which is probably the best recipe for a successful relationship. We live in a lovely part of England.'

Recent novels by the same author:

In Mills & Boon® Historical Romance

THE DUKE'S CINDERELLA BRIDE*
THE RAKE'S INDECENT PROPOSAL*

*Part of *The Notorious St Claires* mini-series

In Mills & Boon® Modern™ Romance

THE INFAMOUS ITALIAN'S SECRET BABY
THE VIRGIN SECRETARY'S IMPOSSIBLE BOSS**

**Part of the *International Billionaires* mini-series

Carole has now written
over 150 books for Mills & Boon.

Don't miss any of the magic.

Look out for Carole's next book
in Modern™ Romance in March 2010!

THE ROGUE'S DISGRACED LADY

Carole Mortimer

First published in Great Britain 2009
Large Print edition 2010
Harlequin Mills & Boon Limited,
Eton House, 18-24 Paradise Road, Richmond, Surrey TW9 1SR

© Carole Mortimer 2009

ISBN: 978 0 263 21151 1

Harlequin Mills & Boon policy is to use papers that are natural, renewable and recyclable products and made from wood grown in sustainable forests. The logging and manufacturing process conform to the legal environmental regulations of the country of origin.

Printed and bound in Great Britain
by CPI Antony Rowe, Chippenham, Wiltshire

THE ROGUE'S
DISGRACED LADY

For Karin Stoecker
Thank you for listening to me
when the idea for the St Claire family
first entered my imagination!

Prologue

Banford House, Mayfair, late July, 1817

'It *is* you, Sebastian!' his hostess greeted him warmly as he was announced into her drawing-room. 'When Revell informed me that Lord St Claire had come to call I thought… But of course Lucian is newly married, and most probably still upon his honeymoon. It is so good to see you!'

Sebastian, Lord St Claire, was, as usual, dressed in the height of fashion, in a perfectly tailored brown superfine over a gold brocade waistcoat and snowy white linen, with fawn pantaloons and brown-topped black Hessians. His fashionably overlong teak-coloured hair was shot through with natural streaks of gold.

He gave a roguish smile as he crossed the room

to where Dolly Vaughn reclined graciously upon the raspberry-red sofa in the drawing room of her town house. Except she was no longer Dolly Vaughn, of course, but Lady Dorothea Bancroft, the Countess of Banford.

Eyes the colour of warm whisky laughingly met her teasing blue ones as Sebastian took the hand she offered and raised it to his lips. 'Please do not shatter all my illusions and tell me that you were once acquainted with my brother Lucian,' he drawled.

'Intimately,' Dolly assured him mischievously. 'Stourbridge too, on one memorable occasion. But that is another story entirely…' She gave a delighted laugh as Sebastian's eyes widened at this mention of his eldest brother Hawk, the aristocratic and aloof tenth Duke of Stourbridge. 'Poor Bancroft has the devil of a time pretending not to be aware of the names of any of my past lovers,' she added with an unrepentant smile.

William Bancroft, Earl of Banford, should, and did, consider himself the most fortunate of men in having Dolly as his wife for the last three years. Before her marriage she had been the discreet paramour of many a male member of the ton—both of Sebastian's older brothers amongst them, apparently!

Sebastian's own relationship with Dolly was based purely on a platonic friendship that had developed when he first came to town at the tender age of seventeen, still a virgin. Dolly had found Sebastian a less experienced young lady than herself to introduce him to all the carnal delights.

'Please do sit down, Sebastian,' she invited warmly now as she patted the sofa beside her, still a golden-haired beauty, though now aged in her mid-thirties. 'I have ordered tea for us both. It is a little early as yet for me to offer any stronger refreshment, I am afraid,' she added derisively as he raised dark brows.

Sebastian could remember a time when it had never been too early for Dolly to take 'stronger refreshment', but out of respect for her role as the Countess of Banford he did not remind her of those occasions. 'You are looking very well, Lady Bancroft,' he complimented her as he sat down beside her. 'Marriage obviously suits you.'

'Marriage to my darling Bancroft suits me,' she corrected him firmly. 'And I refuse to allow you to behave so formally with me.' She tapped his wrist lightly with her fan. 'When we're alone like this, I insist we be as we always were—simply Dolly and Sebastian.' She turned as the butler returned with a tray of tea things, informing him, 'I am not at home to any more visitors this afternoon, Revell.' She waited until the servant had vacated the room before speaking again. 'I am afraid, even after three years, the servants still find my refusal to follow the rules something of a trial,' Dolly explained airily as she sat forward to pour the tea, the blue of her high-waisted gown a perfect match for her eyes.

She had given Sebastian the very opening in the conversation that he had been hoping for. 'But the ton are a little…kinder to you now than they used to be, are they not?'

'Oh, my dear, I have become quite the thing!' Dolly assured him laughingly as she handed him one of the delicate china teacups. 'An invitation to one of my summer house parties at Banford Park has become famously exclusive.'

Sebastian nodded. 'It is concerning this year's house party that I have come to see you.'

She gave him a look from eyes that had become shrewdly considering. 'Surely you and several of your friends have already received this year's invitation, Sebastian? An invitation, if my memory serves me correctly, that you have always refused in the past.'

They were both aware there was absolutely nothing amiss with Dolly's memory. 'I am thinking of accepting this year…'

Her gaze became even shrewder. 'If…?'

Sebastian gave a husky laugh as he relaxed back on the sofa. 'You are far too forthright for a man's comfort, Dolly!'

She arched blonde brows. 'For *your* comfort!?'

When Sebastian had come up with the idea it had seemed perfectly straightforward. A simple request for Dolly to include another woman—a particular woman—in her guest list for the two-week summer house party to be held at the Banford estate in Hampshire in two weeks' time. Unfortunately, Sebastian had overlooked the sharpness of Dolly's curiosity…

'You wish me to add another guest to my list. A female guest,' Dolly guessed correctly. 'What of your affair with the widowed Lady Hawtry?'

'Not much escapes your notice, does it, Dolly?' Sebastian said ruefully. 'That relationship is at an end.' As any of his relationships were, whenever the lady began to talk of marriage!

'So who is it this time, Sebastian? Is your reluctance to tell me her name because she is a married lady?' she prompted, at Sebastian's continued silence. 'I assure you, after three years amongst the ton, I am beyond being shocked by anything any of them choose to do behind closed doors—even when it includes my own!'

'The lady was married,' Sebastian admitted. 'But is no longer.' Despite his attraction to the lady in question, Sebastian would never have considered seducing her if she were still married— after all, even a man who was considered a rake of the first order by both the male and female members of the ton must have *some* principles!

'Another widow, then. But which one, I wonder…?' Dolly looked thoughtful as she considered all the widowed ladies of her acquaintance. 'Oh, do give me some clue, Sebastian, please!' she begged a few minutes later. 'You know how I have always hated a mystery.'

Yes, this had all seemed so much easier when Sebastian had sat at home alone, considering how he might gain an introduction to a woman whose very reclusive behaviour this last eighteen months represented something of a challenge to a seasoned rake!

He grimaced. 'Her year of mourning her husband came to an end six months ago, but unfortunately for me—and every other man who relishes being the widow's first lover—she has not as yet returned into Society.'

'Hmm…' Dolly tapped a considering fingertip against her lips. 'No!' She gave a disbelieving gasp, her gaze suddenly guarded as she turned to Sebastian. 'You do not mean—Sebastian, surely you *cannot* be referring to—'

He gave an acknowledging inclination of his head. 'She was one of the few who were kind to you three years ago, when Bancroft first introduced you to the ton as his wife, was she not?'

'You *do* mean her, then!' Dolly breathed softly. 'I would never have thought…!' She eyed him speculatively. 'Sebastian, you must be aware of the unpleasant gossip that has circulated about her since the untimely death of her husband?'

'Of course I am aware of it,' he said dismissively. 'It only makes the lady more…intriguing.'

The Countess of Banford frowned. 'There is often some truth to such rumours, you know.'

Sebastian shrugged. 'And what if there is? I told you—I intend seducing the woman, not marrying her!'

She chewed on her bottom lip. 'I am just concerned for you, Sebastian…'

He gave a grin. 'There is no reason to be, I assure you.'

'Your intentions really are not honourable, then?' Dolly gave him another of those shrewd glances.

'I have just told you they are not,' he reiterated. 'I am a bachelor by choice, Dolly—and I assure you, no matter what a lady's charms, I intend to continue in that enviable state!'

Dolly nodded. 'You do realise this particular lady has not been seen at *all* since moving to the estate left to her in Shropshire?'

'I would not be asking you to issue this invitation to her if I thought there were any other way in which I might be introduced to her,' Sebastian reasoned wryly.

Dolly's eyes widened. 'The two of you have never even been introduced?'

'Not as yet.' Sebastian grinned wolfishly. 'Her husband and I, for obvious reasons, did not share the same circle of friends.'

'He was rather a pompous bore, was he not?' Dolly conceded. 'So, the two of you have never actually met….'

'I have merely gazed at her once or twice from afar,' Sebastian admitted.

'And now you wish to gaze at her more intimately?' Dolly teased. 'Poor Juliet will not stand a chance!'

'You flatter me, Dolly.'

She shook her head. 'What woman could not be flattered by the attentions of the handsome but equally elusive Lord Sebastian St Claire?' She eyed his roguish good looks and the strength of his leanly muscled body appreciatively. 'It so happens, Sebastian, that I have already issued an invitation to the lady in question.'

'Better and better,' Sebastian murmured appreciatively.

Dolly gave an elegant inclination of one eyebrow. 'We were friends before her husband's death, and despite the gossip I have decided she cannot continue to languish in Shropshire.'

'Has she accepted the invitation?' Sebastian asked eagerly.

'Not yet. But she will,' Dolly assured him with certainty. 'Really, Sebastian, how could you possibly doubt my powers of persuasion?' Dolly rebuked as she saw his suddenly sceptical expression.

Indeed…

'What do you make of this, Helena?' Juliet Boyd, Countess of Crestwood, finished reading the printed invitation she had just received before passing it frowningly to her cousin as the two of them sat together in the breakfast room at Falcon Manor.

Helena gave Juliet a quizzical glance before taking the invitation. Her pale blonde hair was pulled back from her colourless face, her figure thin as a boy's in one of the dull brown gowns she always wore. A frown marred her brow when she looked up again. 'Shall you go, Juliet?'

Ordinarily Juliet would have left the Countess of Banford's invitation, and its envelope, on the table to be disposed of along with the other debris from breakfast. She hesitated now only because there had been a letter enclosed with the invitation. A handwritten letter that she also handed to her cousin to read.

'"My dear",' Helena read. '"You were always so kind to me in the past, and now I take great pleasure in returning that kindness by the enclosed invitation. It is only to be Bancroft and myself, and a few select friends.

'"Please, please do say you will come, Juliet!

'"Your friend, Dolly Bancroft".'

'It is very thoughtful of her to write to me so kindly, but of course I cannot go, Helena,' Juliet said softly.

'But of course you must go!' Her cousin contradicted impatiently, the sudden colour to her pale cheeks giving a brief glimpse of the beauty that was otherwise not apparent in the severity of her hairstyle and dress. 'Do you not see that this could be your door back into Society?'

A door Juliet would prefer to remain firmly closed. 'I want no part of Society, you know that, Helena. As Society has made it more than plain this past year and a half that they no longer wish to have any part of me,' she added dryly.

Her time of mourning had been difficult enough for Juliet to bear when she felt relief rather than a sense of loss at Edward's death. But the cuts she had received from the ton as early as those who had attended Crestwood's funeral, had only served to show her that Society now felt well rid of her.

She sighed. 'It is very kind of Dolly Bancroft to think of me, of course—'

'And were you not kind to her before she became Society's darling?' her cousin reminded her tartly. 'Before Banford's connections and his prestige in the House caused them to forget that she was nothing more than a mistress who married her lover before his first wife was even cold in her grave!' Helena added, in her usual forthright manner.

It had been her cousin's down-to-earth practicality that had helped Juliet endure this past year and a half of virtual ostracism, and she smiled at Helena now. 'It was a good nine months after his wife's death, actually. And Society was not so kind to me either twelve years ago, when Miss Juliet Chatterton married the retired war hero Admiral Lord Edward Boyd, Earl of Crestwood, member of the House of Lords, and adviser to the War Cabinet. I felt offering my friendship to Dolly Bancroft three years ago was the least I could do if it helped to ease her own path into Society even a little.'

Juliet had only been eighteen when she had married a man thirty years her senior. As was customary, the match had been made and approved by her parents, but nevertheless Juliet had begun her married life with all the naïve expectations of lifelong happiness that were usual in someone so young and unknowing.

She had quickly learnt that her husband had no interest in her happiness, and that in the privacy of their own home he was not the same man his peers and the country so admired.

Juliet's only consolation had been that her parents had not been alive to witness such an ill matched marriage as hers had turned out to be, Mr and Mrs Chatterton having drowned in a boating accident only months after Juliet had married the Earl of Crestwood.

The unhappiness of Juliet's marriage had been eased a little when her cousin Helena, then sixteen years old, had escaped from France six years ago and come to live with them, becoming Juliet's companion. Crestwood, it seemed, had been coward enough not to reveal the cruelty of his true character in front of a witness.

'Then you must let her do this for you, Cousin.' Once again Helena was the practical one. 'You are still far too young and beautiful to allow yourself to just wither away in the country!'

'I assure you I am not yet ready for my bath-chair, Helena!' Juliet gave an indulgent laugh, re-vealing straight white teeth between lips that were full and unknowingly sensual.

Now aged thirty, Juliet knew she was no longer in possession of the youthful bloom that had once caught Crestwood's eye. Instead, she had become a woman of maturity—and not only in years. Her time spent as Crestwood's wife had left an indelible mark upon her.

Thankfully, she had borne Crestwood no children to inherit their father's cold and unfor-giving nature, and so her figure, although more curvaceous now, was still slender. The long darkness of her hair was healthily shiny, loosely confined now at her crown, with wispy curls at her nape and temple as was currently the fashion.

Her complexion was still as creamy and unlined as it had ever been.

But there was a lingering shadow of unhappiness in the green depths of her eyes, and Juliet smiled much less often now than she had been seen to do during her single coming-out Season twelve years ago. Before over ten years of marriage to the icy Earl of Crestwood had stripped her of all that girlish joy.

'Anyway, I will never remarry,' she added fiercely.

'No one is suggesting that you should do so, silly.' Helena reached out to squeeze her clenched hands affectionately, having been intuitive enough within months of coming to live at Falcon Manor to know of Juliet's unhappiness in her marriage. 'Two weeks at Banford Park, to gently introduce yourself back into Society, does not mean you have to accept a marriage proposal.'

Juliet had been softening slightly towards the idea of a fortnight spent in the congenial company of Dolly Bancroft's 'few select friends', but this last remark made her bristle anew. 'Nor any other sort of proposal, either,' she stated, only too aware, after years in their midst, of the behaviour of some of the ton at these summer house parties, where it seemed to be accepted that a man would spend his nights in the bedchamber of any woman but that of his own wife.

Helena shook her head. 'I am sure, as she has said in the letter that accompanied her invitation, that Lady Bancroft just means to repay your earlier kindness to her.'

Juliet wished that she could be as sure of that. Oh, she did not for a moment doubt Dolly's good intentions. She had come to know the older woman as being kind and caring, as well as deeply in love with her husband. Juliet only feared that her own idea of good intentions and Dolly Bancroft's might not coincide….

'Oh, do say you will go, Juliet!' Helena entreated. 'I can come with you and act as your maid—'

'You are my cousin, not a servant!' Juliet protested.

'But your cousin is not invited,' Helena pointed out ruefully. 'Think on it, Juliet. It could be fun. And you will be all the fashion, with your French maid Helena Jourdan to attend you.'

Fun, as Juliet well knew, was something that Helena had not had much of in her young life.

Her parents, the sister of Juliet's own mother and the Frenchman she had married twenty-five years ago, had been victims of the scourge that had overtaken France during Napoleon's reign, both killed during a raid on their small manor house six years ago, by soldiers in search of food and valuables.

Helena had been present when the raid had occurred, and reluctant after her escape to England to talk of her own fate during that week-long siege. But it had not been too difficult to guess, from the way Helena chose to play down her delicate beauty and dressed so severely, that she had not escaped the soldiers' attentions unscathed.

The two of them had lived quietly and alone except for their few servants this past year and a half, at the estate Crestwood had left his widow, and whilst Juliet had not minded for herself she accepted that at only two and twenty Helena would probably welcome some excitement into their dull lives.

The sort of excitement a two-week stay at Dolly Bancroft's country estate would no doubt provide....

Chapter One

'I have no idea why you felt it necessary to force me from my bed at the crack of dawn—'

'It was eleven o'clock, Gray,' Sebastian pointed out as he expertly handled the matching greys stepping out lively in front of his curricle.

'As far as I am concerned, any hour before midday is the crack of dawn,' Lord Gideon Grayson—Gray to his closest friends—assured him dourly as he huddled down on the seat beside him, the high collar of his fashionably cut jacket snug about his ears despite the warmth of this August summer day. 'I barely had time to wake, let alone enjoy my breakfast.'

'Kippers, eggs and toast, accompanied by two pots of strong coffee,' Sebastian said cheerfully.

'All eaten, as I recall, while you perused today's newspaper.'

'My valet was rushed through my ablutions, and…'

Sebastian stopped listening to Gray's complaints at this point. He was too full of anticipation at the prospect of the challenge of seducing Juliet Boyd to allow anything—or anyone—to shake him out of his good temper.

'…and now my closest friend in the world is so bored by my company that after dragging me forcibly from my own bed and home he cannot even be bothered listening to me!' Gray scowled up at him censoriously.

Sebastian gave an unrepentant grin as he glanced down at the other man. 'When you have something interesting to say, Gray, I assure you I will listen.'

'Could you at least try to be a little less cheerful?' his friend muttered sourly. 'I do believe I am feeling a little delicate this morning.'

'A self-inflicted delicacy!' The two men had done the rounds of the drinking and gambling clubs yesterday evening—Sebastian had won, Gray had not—after which his friend had left to spend several hours in the bed of his current mistress, before returning to his home in the not-so-early hours.

'You are in disgustingly good humour this morning, Seb.' Gray gave another wince. 'Have you taken a new mistress to replace Lady Hawtry?'

'Not yet.' Sebastian grinned wolfishly. 'But I intend doing so in the next two weeks.'

'Oh, I say!' Gray's interest quickened. 'I hope you are not intending to try your luck with Dolly Bancroft during your stay at Banford Park? I warn you, next to your brother Lucian and yourself, Bancroft is the best swordsman in England!'

'You may rest easy concerning both my interest in Dolly's bedchamber and Bancroft's prowess with the sword,' Sebastian assured him dryly. 'Dolly and I are no more than friends and never will be.' Especially now that he knew Dolly had been bedded by both his brothers!

Gray arched a dark brow. 'But you admit there *is* a lady involved in our uncharacteristic behaviour in attending a summer house party?'

'Of course,' Sebastian drawled, but he had no intention of sharing his particular interest in bedding the newly widowed Countess of Crestwood.

'Tell me I do not see the parson's mousetrap snapping at your booted heels…' Gray mocked.

Sebastian gave a humourless laugh. 'You most assuredly do not.' He was even more determined to avoid that state after seeing both his brothers succumb over the last year.

'I must say neither of your brothers seems to mind it so much.' Gray's thoughts travelled the same path. 'I am not sure that I should mind, either, if I had one of their wives for my own!'

'In that case, feel free to find your own wife, Gray,' Sebastian jeered. 'But for goodness' sake, do not attempt to find one for me.' His interest in any woman, Juliet Boyd included, did *not* include marriage!

'Yes, Sebastian, she has arrived.' Dolly answered his silent question once the greetings were over and Gray had departed to the library to share a glass of reviving brandy with his host. 'She has asked for tea in her bedchamber, however, and has every intention of staying there until it is time to come down for dinner. But I have given you adjoining bedchambers. The balconies of your rooms are connected also,' she confided warmly.

Sebastian smiled his satisfaction with the arrangement. 'I trust I will be seated next to her at dinner too?'

'Sebastian, I am not sure your interest in the Countess is altogether wise…' Dolly suddenly looked troubled.

'If it were "wise", Dolly, I doubt I should wish to pursue it!' he teased. 'Now, if I have your permission, I believe I would like to retire to my own bedchamber and rest a little before dinner.'

'Rest?' His hostess's brow arched speculatively.

'I assure you I have no intention of intruding upon the privacy of the lady before we have even been formally introduced,' he pointed out.

'That will come later, one assumes?' Dolly teased.

'Hopefully, yes,' Sebastian murmured.

There had been many rumours circulating about the Countess of Crestwood since her husband's sudden death—most of them unpleasant, to say the least. But none of them had even hinted at her ever being involved in a liaison with another man, either before or during her marriage. Or, indeed, since her marriage had ended….

So Sebastian spent the hours before dinner

resting in his bedchamber, all the time aware that the beautiful but elusive Juliet Boyd was in the room adjoining his. All was silent behind the closed lace curtains at the windows, however, and the French doors into her bedchamber from the balcony remained firmly shut against the warmth of the day.

But she *had* accepted the invitation, as Dolly had said she would. And Juliet could not remain in her bedchamber for the whole of her stay here….

Juliet had never felt so nervous as she stood hesitantly in the cavernous hallway of Banford Park, delaying her entrance into the drawing room, where the other guests of the Countess and Earl of Banford could be heard chattering and laughing together as they gathered before dinner.

Dolly Bancroft had been very welcoming upon Juliet's arrival that afternoon. William Bancroft had been equally charming.

No, it was not her host and hostess's lack of welcome that Juliet feared, but the reactions of their other guests, once they realised that Juliet Boyd, Countess of Crestwood, was amongst their number. For Dolly's sake, Juliet sincerely hoped that none of those guests decided to depart once they realised they were to share their stay here with the 'Black Widow', as Juliet was all too aware she had been cruelly labelled after her husband's death.

She should not have agreed to come here, Juliet told herself, for what had to be the hundredth time since accepting the invitation. Much as she might have wanted to give Helena a little treat after their long period of enforced mourning, Juliet knew she should not have allowed herself to be persuaded into believing that these two weeks at Banford Park was the means by which to do it.

Perhaps she would have felt differently if she had been able to have the fiercely protective Helena at her side. Instead Helena had done as she had said she would, and accompanied Juliet as her maid—a role her cousin seemed to be enjoying immensely. She had cheerfully left Juliet's bedchamber a few minutes ago, after first dressing her hair and helping her into her gown, to go upstairs and gossip with the other maids.

'Will you allow me the honour of escorting you into the drawing room, Lady Boyd?'

Juliet turned sharply, relaxing slightly when

she saw that it was her host who stood solicitously beside her, proffering his arm. A tall and handsome man in his fifties, who now looked down at her with shrewd hazel eyes, the Earl reminded Juliet very much of her father.

'I was just admiring this portrait.' Juliet glanced up at the painting upon the wall which she had, in truth, only just noticed.

'My great-grandfather—the seventh Earl of Banford.' The Earl nodded. 'A singularly ugly man, was he not?' he drawled disparagingly.

Juliet could not help the chuckle that escaped her lips; the seventh Earl had indeed been a very unattractive man!

'Shall we…?' His great-grandson, the tenth earl, offered her his arm a second time.

'Thank you,' Juliet accepted shyly, and placed her gloved hand on top of that arm.

She had chosen to wear a fashionably high-waisted gown of dark grey silk this evening, with only the barest hint of Brussels lace at her bosom and around the edges of the short puffed sleeves. A row of pearls was entwined amongst her dark curls, her only other jewellery matching ear-bobs and the plain gold wedding band on her left hand.

Juliet would have liked to remove even this symbol of Edward's ownership of her, but knew that would only add to the speculation that had followed so quickly after Edward's death and still remained rife.

Although she very much doubted that the wearing of her wedding band or the demure style of the grey silk gown would make the slightest difference to the gossip that was sure to ensue the moment her presence here was known!

'My wife always maintains that it is best to do exactly that which pleases oneself. On the premise, I believe, that it is impossible to please all people all the time,' the Earl confided.

Juliet turned to give him a startled glance. 'It has been my experience that it is impossible to please any of the ton any of the time!' Juliet murmured, some of the tension easing from her slender shoulders. 'Did your wife also suggest that it might be beneficial if you were to wait out here in the hallway this evening in order that you might gallantly offer to escort me into the drawing room?'

The Earl gave a inclination of his head. 'I do believe she may have mentioned some such thing, yes.'

Juliet gave a husky laugh. 'You are too kind, My Lord.'

'On the contrary, my dear, I consider myself deeply honoured,' he replied. 'Now, let us go into the drawing room and set the tongues a wagging, hmm?' He encouraged her almost as gleefully as his wife might have done.

It seemed to Juliet as if all eyes suddenly turned in the direction of the doorway as she entered the room on the arm of the Earl of Banford, the conversation faltering. Then Dolly swiftly filled that silence by engaging in conversation with the handsome and fashionably attired young man standing beside her.

A young man who stared boldly at Juliet, with unfathomable whisky-coloured eyes....

Sebastian was barely aware of Dolly's conversation as, along with all others present, he stared across the room as the Countess of Crestwood entered on the arm of their host.

She was incredibly beautiful—even more so than when Sebastian had last seen her, at some ball or other a couple of years ago, and his interest in her had first been piqued.

He became aware of the finer details about her. Such as the rich darkness of her hair and the entwined string of pearls. The smoothness of her brow. The thick lashes that edged eyes of the deepest green. Her small, perfect nose. The pouting bow of her sensuously full lips. The proud and slightly challenging uplift of her little pointed chin.

Her breasts were as full as ever, and they spilled creamily against pale grey lace, but her waist and hips appeared more willowy than when he had last seen her across that crowded ballroom, and the skin at the swell of her breasts, throat and arms was as translucently pale as the pearls in her hair.

'I advise that you close your mouth, Sebastian—before the drool threatens to spoil the perfection of your cravat!' Dolly whispered beside him in soft mockery, bringing a dark scowl to Sebastian's face as he realised Dolly had a point. He had been staring intently at Lady Boyd for several minutes.

Had anyone else but Dolly noticed his marked interest? he wondered, disgusted with himself. A quick glance at his fellow guests assured him that their interest was as engaged on the lady as his own had been.

'It is time for us to go into dinner,' Dolly informed him as she received a nod from her butler, where he stood discreetly in the doorway. 'Bancroft will be escorting his mother, the Dowager Countess, of course. Might I suggest, as the two of you are sitting together, that you offer your own arm to the Countess of Crestwood?'

Having been staring so intently at Juliet Boyd, Sebastian now found himself momentarily disconcerted by Dolly's suggestion. But only momentarily. Was he not the rich and eligible Lord Sebastian St Claire, brother of a Duke? Moreover, at the age of seven and twenty, had he not been considered by all the female members of the ton— debutantes and matrons alike—as the foremost catch of the Season, since both of his brothers had proved themselves unavailable by taking a wife?

More importantly, meeting Juliet was the only reason he had come here—so what was he waiting for…?

Despite the Earl of Banford's presence at her side, Juliet's appearance in the drawing room had been as dramatic as she had feared it might.

Following that initial stunned silence a muted conversation had been resumed by the female guests, at least, as they gossiped in whispers behind their spread fans. The male guests had been less quick to hide their surprise at her appearance here, and for the main part had just continued to openly stare at her.

One man in particular…

An arrogantly handsome man, dressed in the height of fashion in tailored black evening clothes, a grey waistcoat and snowy white linen. The same man with whom Dolly Bancroft had endeavoured to make conversation when Juliet first entered the drawing room.

The very same man who had made absolutely no effort to disguise his inattentiveness to that conversation as he'd continued to stare at Juliet with narrowed, enigmatic eyes. Rather beautiful long-lashed eyes, the colour of the mellow whisky her father had once favoured, Juliet couldn't help noticing admiringly.

She had expected the frosty disdain of the ton this evening. Had been prepared for that reaction. To find herself being regarded so familiarly by a man she did not even know, and who was obviously nothing more than a fashionable rake, did not sit well with her. It did not sit well at all!

Juliet's already ruffled calm deserted her totally as she saw Dolly take a firm hold of the man's arm and push him slightly in her direction. Was her intention to have him cross the room and offer to escort Juliet into dinner? An intention, for all the previous familiarity of the man's gaze, that he surely could not welcome!

Juliet snapped her fan open in front of her before she turned her back on the pair to engage the Earl in conversation. 'It seems that we have succeeded in creating something of a stir amongst your other guests despite your efforts, My Lord,' she bit out tartly. The humiliation of having a man forced to escort her into dinner burned beneath the surface of her emotions.

No matter how kindly meant Dolly Bancroft's invitation had been, Juliet knew she should not have allowed herself to be persuaded into coming here! She should not have exposed herself to—

'Would you care to introduce me, My Lord?'

Juliet felt a quiver down the length of her spine at the first sound of the man's smoothly cultured voice. That quiver turned to a shiver as she turned to find that Dolly's rakishly handsome companion had acceded to her urgings and was now standing in front of Juliet, looking down the length of his arrogant nose at her, the expression in those whisky-coloured eyes hidden behind narrowed lids....

Only Juliet did not need to see the expression in those beautiful eyes to know that this man felt the same contempt towards her as every other person here. Nor did she care to guess what leverage Dolly had exerted to persuade this man into doing her bidding....

Until this moment Juliet had believed Dolly to be totally devoted to the Earl of Banford, but it would have taken more than a simple request from their hostess to persuade this young rake into committing possible social ruination by showing a preference for the notorious Countess of Crestwood. It led Juliet to wonder, with inner distaste, if this young man were possibly the Countess of Banford's current lover...

'Lady Boyd, may I present Lord Sebastian St Claire?' the Earl said, doing as requested and dutifully making the introductions. 'Lord St Claire—Lady Juliet Boyd, Countess of Crestwood.'

Sebastian knew by the gleam of interest in the Earl's eyes as he made the introductions that Dolly must have confided to her husband Sebastian's intentions towards the Countess. His mouth tightened in displeasure at the breach of confidence even as he gave her an abrupt bow. 'My Lady.'

'My Lord.' The Countess made a graceful curtsey, but made no effort to extend to him her gloved hand.

Sebastian scowled at the omission. 'Will you grant me the honour of escorting you into dinner, Lady Boyd?'

'"Honour", My Lord?' She raised dark, mocking brows.

He inclined his head. 'I would consider it so, yes.'

Her laughter was light and derisive. 'Then you are singular in your preference, My Lord.'

Damn it—this first conversation with Juliet Boyd was not going at all as Sebastian had hoped it might!

In his imaginings she had been as instantly taken with Sebastian as he already was with her. To such an extent that he had envisaged them talking alone together. Walking alone together.

Sitting alone together. Most definitely being alone when they made love together…!

A muscle flickered in Sebastian's tightly clenched jaw as he imagined first removing the pearls from her hair, before releasing the glossy curls so that they tumbled down the length of her slender spine. Next he would remove her gown, turning her so that he might unfasten—slowly— the row of tiny buttons from her nape down to her bottom, lingering, after releasing each button, to kiss the smoothness of the silky skin he had just exposed. When the last button had been unfastened he would then allow the gown to fall about her ankles, leaving her wearing only her chemise and stockings, with the fullness of her breasts pouting temptingly beneath the thin material, her nipples a dark delight that Sebastian would taste and possess until he'd had his fill…

'It would appear we are the last to go into dinner, Lord St Claire,' Juliet prompted sharply. He seemed lost in thought. Perhaps contemplating that social ruination, if the pained expression on his face was any indication!

He drew his thoughts back to his surroundings with an obvious effort. 'I apologise for my preoccupation, Lady Boyd,' he murmured huskily as he extended his arm to her.

'Do not give it another thought, Lord St Claire,' Juliet assured him as she placed her gloved hand lightly upon his sleeve. She was aware of the muscled strength beneath her fingertips. 'After all, it is not every day that you are asked to act as escort to the notorious Black Widow!' she added waspishly.

'I— *What* did you call yourself?' he exclaimed.

Her smile was completely lacking in humour. 'I assure you I am well aware of the unflattering names I have acquired since…since the death of my husband,' she told him. 'Do not fear—you will have done your duty to our hostess once I am seated. I will not be in the least offended if you then ignore me for the rest of the evening.' Rather, she would prefer it!

Juliet now recognised Lord Sebastian St Claire as being the youngest brother of the aristocratic Duke of Stourbridge. A young lord, moreover, who had long been considered by the ton to be one of their most eligible—and elusive—bachelors. As such, his presence here was attracting as much attention as her own, making their belated entrance to the dining room together all the more sensational.

A puzzled frown marked his brow. 'Why should you imagine I might wish to ignore you?'

Juliet smiled slightly. 'To save yourself from further awkwardness, perhaps…?'

For the first time Sebastian considered that perhaps it had *not* been kind on Dolly's part— or indeed his own!—to invite Juliet Boyd to Banford Park for these two weeks. That after all the talk and speculation this past year and a half, concerning her husband's unexpected death, this woman would obviously be uncomfortable at making her first public appearance in some time.

Just as she was obviously aware of the unkind things that had been said about her following Crestwood's death—cruel and malicious gossip, for the most part, which, even if it were true, could not have been at all pleasant for the lady to hear….

He fleetingly touched the hand that rested on his arm. 'I assure you I feel no awkwardness whatsoever at being seen in your company, Lady Boyd.'

Her glance was scathing now. 'And I am just as sure, as the Duke of Stourbridge's youngest brother, you would consider it impolite to admit to such an emotion even if you did.'

'On the contrary, My Lady,' Sebastian countered. 'If you know anything of the St Claire family at all, then you must know that we prefer—in fact, go out of our way—*not* to bow to the dictates of Society.'

Yes, Juliet had heard that the St Claires were something of a law unto themselves. Even the head of that illustrious family, the aristocratic Duke of Stourbridge.

After years of being considered the biggest catch any marriage-minded mama could make for her daughter, the Duke had caused something of a sensation almost a year ago by choosing to woo and marry a young woman the ton had had no previous knowledge of.

Juliet moved to sit in the chair Lord St Claire drew back for her. 'Be assured, My Lord, in this circumstance you are in the company of one guaranteed to help you succeed in doing exactly that!'

She had been so busy settling herself into her seat that for a moment she had not realised he had taken the chair beside her.

'Oh, dear,' she said now, as she looked up and

found herself between the Earl of Banford, seated at the head of the table, and Lord St Claire to her right. 'Have you succeeded in inciting Lady Bancroft's ire in some way, Lord St Claire?' she asked.

He raised brows the same unusual teak and gold colour as his hair, laughter gleaming in those whisky-coloured eyes. 'On the contrary. Lady Bancroft—Dolly—and I have always been the best of friends.'

Juliet continued to look at him for several long seconds. 'Indeed,' she finally murmured enigmatically, before turning away to indicate, she hoped, a complete lack of interest in the subject.

Sebastian would have liked to pursue the conversation further, to know the reason for that enigmatic glance, but he was prevented from doing so as his first course was served to him—by which time Lord Bancroft had drawn the Countess into conversation, giving Sebastian no further opportunity to talk, but every chance to study Juliet Boyd from between narrowed lids.

For all that she must know she was still attracting more attention from their fellow guests than was polite, the Countess of Crestwood stoically ignored that interest as she continued to converse and smile graciously with their host between sips of her soup.

Did she have any idea, Sebastian wondered, how enticing her mouth was, with its top lip slightly fuller than the bottom? How seductive the deep green of her eyes? How the translucent paleness of her skin begged to be touched?

Sebastian longed to feel the slender coolness of her hands upon his own heated flesh....

To Juliet's dismay, her discomfort had only increased once she was seated at the dinner table, and she felt her every move being avidly watched by her fellow guests. No doubt with the intention of gossip and comments later. Nor was she as unaware of the man seated on her right as she would have wished to be!

Lord Sebastian St Claire was without a doubt one of the most handsome men she had ever seen. A few years younger than her, of course. With that dark, unusual-coloured hair and the mellow flirtation of those whisky-coloured eyes. A sensual mouth that could either smile with derisive humour or curl back in contempt. A square and firm jaw that spoke of a determination of character that was only to be expected from the brother of the arrogant Duke of Stourbridge.

More disturbing, perhaps, his black evening clothes had been tailored perfectly to display the width of his shoulders, his tapered waist, the strength of his muscled thighs and his long, long legs.

Juliet had been out for barely one Season before her husband had offered for her, but even so she could appreciate that Lord St Claire was that most dangerous of men—a rake and a libertine. A man, she felt sure, who felt absolutely no qualms in availing himself of a woman's charms. All women, of any age. Whilst remaining free of any emotional entanglement himself.

After years in a miserable marriage, Juliet could only envy such an emotionally carefree existence as Sebastian St Claire's.

Envy, but never emulate.

She was aware that many widowed ladies her age took advantage of their freedom from the encumbrance of a husband and marriage to indulge in affairs that gave them either satisfaction in the bedchamber or the heart. After being the wife of Lord Edward Boyd, a cold and merciless man, Juliet had no desire for either!

'...care to go boating with me on the lake tomorrow, My Lady?'

Her eyes were wide as she turned to St Claire. 'I beg your pardon?'

He smiled in satisfaction at her obvious surprise. 'I enquired if you would care to go boating on the lake here with me tomorrow?'

Exactly what Juliet thought he had said!

Chapter Two

'Or perhaps,' Sebastian amended smoothly as he saw the way the Countess's eyes had widened incredulously at his suggestion, 'you would prefer it if we were simply to stroll in the gardens?'

Those green eyes narrowed now, and the tension in her body was almost palpable. 'I have no idea what incentive Dolly has offered you in exchange for your being pleasant to me, Lord St Claire,' she hissed beneath her breath, so that neither their host—or the other guests should overhear, 'but I assure you most strongly that *I* do not appreciate such attentions!'

Sebastian was so taken aback by the accusation in her tone that for a moment he could make no reply. She actually believed that he and Dolly were lovers!

His own gaze narrowed to steely slits, his jaw rigid in his displeasure. 'And *I* assure *you*, Lady Boyd, that you are mistaken in your assumption concerning my *friendship* with Dolly.'

She adamantly refused to back down from his disapproval. 'Mistaken or not, your—your forced attentions to me are most unwelcome.'

No, this evening was not proceeding at all as Sebastian had hoped it would!

Neither was he accustomed to having his temper roused in this way. The St Claire family always maintained control over their emotions, whether it be boredom, amusement or anger. Not so for Sebastian, it appeared, when it came to Lady Juliet Boyd.

Sebastian suddenly realised what she'd said, and removed the tension from his body and the anger from his gaze. '*Forced* attentions?' he repeated quietly.

'Of course they are forced,' she said scornfully. 'Do you imagine I did not see the look of distaste on your face earlier when I entered the drawing room?'

Distaste? Sebastian remembered being dazzled by her exceptional beauty. But distaste? Never!

He shook his head. 'I believe you are mistaken, My Lady.'

'I do not think so,' she maintained stubbornly.

'You are calling me a liar?' His voice was dangerously soft.

'I am merely stating what I saw,' she retorted.

'What you *think* you saw,' he corrected firmly. 'Am I to infer from these remarks that you would prefer *not* to stroll in the gardens with me tomorrow?' he asked dryly.

The Countess glanced at him quizzically, a frown between those mesmerising green eyes. 'My preference, My Lord, is for you to leave me in peace,' she finally murmured. 'Coming here at all was a serious error of judgement on my part. In fact, I am seriously thinking of making my excuses and leaving in the morning.'

Sebastian had only subjected himself to the tiresomeness of this house party because he was intent on seducing this woman—he certainly had no intention of allowing her to escape so easily!

'Are you not being a little over-hasty, Lady Boyd?' His tone was pleasantly cajoling now. 'I believe Dolly told me that this is your first venture back into Society since your time of mourning came to an end. Is that so?'

After the awkwardness of this evening it was likely to be Juliet's *last* venture into Society, too!

She liked Dolly immensely, and had always found the other woman a complete antidote to the formality of the stuffy rules that so often abounded at any occasion attended by the ton. But if Dolly believed she was doing Juliet a kindness by casting one of her own lovers into Juliet's path, then she was under a serious misapprehension. The attentions of a man such as Sebastian St Claire—a renowned rake and a flirt, and moreover several years her junior—was the last thing Juliet needed to complicate her life. Now or at any other time.

'I do not consider my decision any of your business, My Lord.'

'No?' He quirked mocking brows. 'You do not think it would cause embarrassment for Dolly if you were to leave so soon after your arrival?'

Juliet raised a cool eyebrow of her own. 'On the contrary, My Lord, I believe I will be saving Dolly from further embarrassment by removing myself from her home at the earliest opportunity.'

'So your intention is to run back to the safety of your estate in Shropshire at the first hint of opposition?' Sebastian needled.

Juliet gasped. 'You go too far, sir!'

He appeared completely unruffled by her anger. Instead he leant forward to place his hand on her gloved one as it rested on the tabletop, his lips a mere whisper away from the pearl-adorned lobe of her ear as he whispered, 'My dear Countess, I have not even begun to go too far where you are concerned!'

Juliet felt the colour come into and then as quickly fade from her cheeks as she looked up and saw the flirtatious intent in that whisky-coloured gaze. How *dared* he talk to her in this familiar way?

'You are causing a scene, sir,' she snapped as she deftly extricated her hand from beneath his. 'I believe it might be better, for both our sakes, if you were to refrain from talking to me for the rest of the evening.'

He gave a wicked smile. 'Will that not look a little strange, when we have seemed to be getting along so well together?'

'*Seemed* is the correct word, sir,' Juliet assured

him frostily. 'This conversation is now at an end.' She moved slightly in her seat, so that her shoulder was firmly turned against him, and began to converse with her host about the expectations of the weather for the forthcoming week.

She had never before met a man such as Sebastian St Claire. A man so forthright in his manner. A man who refused to listen to or accept the word no.

Juliet had always accompanied Edward to London in spring for the Season, attending such parties and balls with him as he had deemed necessary, and giving a ball herself towards the end of the Season, to which all suitable members of the ton had been invited. Lord Sebastian St Claire had *not* been amongst her guests.

St Claire's eldest brother, the haughty Duke of Stourbridge, had several times been invited to dine privately with them, and Juliet could see a certain resemblance between the two brothers in colouring, and in that inborn air of arrogance. But young rakes such as Sebastian St Claire had not entered into Edward's lofty circle of acquaintances, nor consequently, Juliet's own.

Even as she continued to talk to the Earl of

Banford, their conversation soon including his mother, the Dowager Countess, Juliet found her attention wandering as she wondered what Edward would have made of the young Lord St Claire.

He would not have approved of him.

No, he was too young. Too irresponsible. Too rakish. Too everything that Edward had disapproved of.

Suddenly that realisation was enough for Juliet to want to make a friend of St Claire, in spite of her own reservations!

The candle was still alight in Juliet Boyd's bedchamber when Sebastian stepped out onto his balcony to enjoy a last cigar before retiring to his bed, but the lace curtains once again made it impossible for him to see the occupant of the room, and whether or not she was already abed.

It had certainly been an interesting evening, if a frustrating one. That frank, almost intimate conversation with the Countess had been enjoyable, but it had been followed by the irritation of having her completely ignore him for the rest of the meal—as she had stated she intended doing. Even more frustrating, she had disappeared completely by the time the gentlemen had rejoined the ladies in the drawing room, after enjoying several glasses of excellent port.

Would she carry out her threat to leave in the morning?

Sebastian had come to realise this evening that in her acceptance of Dolly's invitation, and by placing herself at the very centre of Society, which had judged and condemned her a year and a half ago, Juliet Boyd was being an exceptionally brave woman—but he had not expected her to be quite such a stubborn one, too!

Yet, if anything, that stubbornness—the way the sting of her anger had brought the colour to her cheeks and given her eyes the appearance of glittering emeralds—had only succeeded in deepening Sebastian's interest in her….

Dolly would have to talk to her, somehow persuade her into staying….

The faint click of a door catch warned Sebastian that he would soon cease to be alone. He dropped his cigar and ground it beneath his shoe, then moved back into the shadows mere seconds before the doors of the Countess's bedchamber opened and she stepped out onto her balcony.

Sebastian's breath caught and held in his throat as she moved forward to stand next to the balustrade and look up at the bright starlit sky.

This venture out onto her balcony before retiring had been one of pure impulse, Sebastian had no doubt. She was prepared for bed: her hair—those glorious dark curls that he had earlier imagined cascading over her creamy shoulders and down her back when it was released—actually reached the whole length of her spine to rest against her shapely bottom. It was stunning—so thick and dark, and bathed with silver by the moon shining overhead. She wore a robe of pale green silk over a matching nightgown, but with the moonlight shining down so brightly even the two items together could not disguise the fullness of her unconfined breasts beneath, nor the gentle curve of her waist and temptingly rounded bottom above long and slender legs.

She was desire incarnate.

A goddess…

'Who is there?'

Sebastian had no idea what he had done to give himself away. Drawn in an unconscious breath at the sight of her beauty? Or perhaps made a movement forward towards the temptation she offered so innocently?

Whatever it had been, it had alerted Juliet Boyd to his presence, and she turned in the moonlight to look at the exact spot where Sebastian stood so silently, watching her from the shadows of the house behind him.

Knowing further concealment was now ridiculous, Sebastian stepped forward to make her an adroit bow. 'My Lady.'

Juliet gave a gasp, and raised a startled hand to her throat as she easily recognised the man standing so large and formidable on the balcony. 'What are you doing here?' She sounded breathless.

And indeed Juliet *was* breathless! She had already had cause to remark upon this man's audacity once this evening, but even so she had never suspected that he would later attempt to enter her bedchamber uninvited!

She stiffened in outrage. 'How *dare* you presume to invade my balcony in this way, My Lord?'

He gave every appearance of being completely unruffled by her displeasure as he drawled nonchalantly, 'You are mistaken, My Lady.'

Juliet drew herself up indignantly. 'I cannot mistake the evidence of my own eyes, sir!'

He gave a twisted smile. 'That was not the mistake I was referring to.'

She eyed him frowningly. 'What, then?'

He shrugged those broad shoulders, instantly drawing Juliet's attention to the fact that he appeared to have removed his black frock coat and cravat, revealing a silver brocaded waistcoat that was tailored to the flatness of his stomach. His billowing shirt was now unfastened at the throat, revealing a light dusting of dark hair upon his chest.

Juliet quickly averted her gaze from this glimpse of his bared flesh, even as she became aware of her own state of undress. Helena had come to Juliet's bedchamber earlier, to remove the pins from her hair before helping her into her night attire—the pale green silk and lace gown and robe that were all Juliet was wearing now, as she engaged in conversation with the disreputable Sebastian St Claire!

Sebastian could almost see the panic of thoughts rushing through Juliet's head as she gathered her robe about her and prepared herself for flight. 'I merely meant to point out that the door behind me leads into *my* bedchamber, and therefore I am standing upon my own balcony rather than yours.'

She hesitated. 'Your own balcony…?' Her gaze moved to the open doors behind him, before lowering to the space between them, her eyes widening as she obviously saw the low ironwork that separated the two balconies but was concealed amongst the potted plants placed either side of it. Her throat moved convulsively. 'It appears that I owe you an apology, Lord St Claire.'

'Do not be over-hasty with that apology,' Sebastian drawled, before stepping lithely over the ironwork that separated them. 'There. You see. An apology is no longer necessary.' He gave an unrepentant grin as he now stood only inches away from her.

Juliet trembled slightly. Despite being married for so long, she had little experience upon which she might draw in order to deal with this man's outrageous behaviour!

St Claire had stared at her so boldly, so familiarly earlier this evening, when she'd first entered the drawing-room on the Earl's arm. After their introduction he had chosen to bandy words with her, before proceeding to flirt with her during dinner—until Juliet had made a sharp end to it.

Finding herself alone with him now—on the balcony of her bedchamber, the hour late, the moonlight shining overhead, wearing only her night attire—could be considered scandalous!

No, it *was* scandalous, Juliet recognised with a sinking feeling—and it was exactly the sort of behaviour the ton were so avidly seeking in order that they might condemn her all over again.

She put out a shaking hand. 'You must return to your own balcony this instant!' she ordered.

'Must I?'

He was suddenly standing much too close to her. So close that Juliet could smell the freshness of his cologne and the faint aroma of cigars that clung to his clothing. Worse, his eyes, those warm, whisky-coloured eyes, were gleaming down at her in the moonlight as he easily captured and held her gaze.

Nevertheless, she must stand firm against all temptations… 'Yes, you most certainly must!' Juliet averred firmly.

He gave her a considering look. 'Why?'

'Because we cannot be seen here alone together like this!' she gasped.

'That is hardly likely, now, is it, Juliet?' He gave a pointed look at their surroundings, to indicate that no candles glowed in the other bed-chambers to show that any of the other guests had yet retired to their rooms for the night.

No doubt they were all still downstairs in the drawing room, Juliet surmised impatiently, discussing the scandal that the presence of the notorious Countess of Crestwood in their midst represented!

'I have not given permission for you to address me by name.' Her chin rose challengingly. 'And I trust you are aware, *Lord St Claire*, of the reason the ton labelled me the Black Widow?'

Sebastian frowned slightly at the mention of that name once again, discovering that he took serious exception to it. 'For the main part, I choose to ignore malicious gossip.'

The Countess arched dark brows. 'And what if on this occasion it is not merely malicious? What if it is true?'

His gaze became fixed on those clear, unblinking green eyes as she continued to meet his gaze in challenge. 'Is it?' he asked quietly.

She gave a humourless laugh. 'I have no intention of answering such a question!'

'I am glad of it,' he replied simply. 'It really does not signify what I or anyone else believes about your husband's death.'

'*It—does—not signify?*' she repeated incredulously, those green eyes now flashing angrily.

'No,' Sebastian reiterated, and he reached out to lightly clasp the tops of her arms and pull her slowly, purposefully towards him. 'As I have absolutely no interest in becoming your second husband, it is doubtful you will ever have a reason for wanting me dead.'

He was wrong—because Juliet had never felt more capable of inflicting physical retribution upon another person in her life as she did at that moment! 'There you are mistaken, Lord St Claire.' She snapped her indignation as she attempted to pull away from him. 'At this moment I can think of nothing I would enjoy more than to see you consigned to the devil, where you so obviously belong!'

He gave a husky laugh, refusing to release her

despite her struggles. 'You believe my past misdeeds are serious enough to send me to the pits of hell?'

'You do not?' Juliet gave him a scornful glance.

'It is a possibility, I suppose,' he conceded, after appearing to consider the matter closely. 'Drunkenness. Gambling. Debauchery. Hmm, it does seem more than a possibility, does it not…?'

The lowering of his head towards hers slowly blocked out the moonlight overhead, and Juliet became very still as she stared up at him. 'What are you doing?' she breathed unsteadily.

He raised an eyebrow. 'As you seem to believe I am going to the devil anyway, I cannot see that one more indiscretion is going to make the slightest difference to my hellish fate!'

'You—' Juliet had no more chance for protest as Sebastian St Claire's mouth laid claim to hers.

That arrogantly mocking mouth, which never seemed far from a smile. That firm, experienced mouth. It parted Juliet's lips to deepen the kiss even as he pulled her closer against his body, in order to mould her much softer curves to the hard contours of his muscled chest and thighs.

In the whole of her thirty years Juliet had never

known any other man's kisses but Edward's. And they certainly hadn't prepared her for the warm seductiveness of Sebastian St Claire's lips as they parted hers, or for the way the tip of his tongue delicately moved in exploration against them before sweeping into the heat beneath as he deepened and lengthened the kiss.

Was this arousal? Juliet wondered, slightly dazedly.

There was an unaccustomed warmth between her thighs as his mouth continued to plunder and claim hers. Her breasts had firmed, and the nipples tingled achingly where they were pressed so firmly against his brocade waistcoat. His hands caressed the length of her back, the movement causing the tips of her breasts to stroke against his body, and Juliet groaned low in her throat at the sensation that this caused throughout her body.

What was happening to her? Juliet wondered wildly.

She had never experienced any of these sensations on those occasions when Edward had pushed her nightgown up to her chin before he thrust the hard thing between his legs painfully inside her, his member so long and thick that the first time he had taken her Juliet had actually fainted as Edward ripped through the barrier of her innocence.

It had been the same every time Edward had come to her bed—he took her in a cold, silent way—and Juliet had always had to fight to keep the tears from falling, knowing that her tears would only anger Edward into making her suffer even worse degradation.

So Juliet had suffered the pain as Edward had thrust himself between her thighs, eventually giving a grunt and collapsing heavily on top of her, rather than suffer the verbal and physical retribution that would rain down on her should she attempt to refuse him.

Thankfully Edward had not come to her bedchamber quite so often during the last few years of her marriage, but on the occasions when he had done so no amount of pleading on her part had succeeded in softening his demands. She was his wife, he had told her coldly, and as such it was her duty to lie back, open her legs, and give satisfaction to his physical needs—whenever and whatever they might be.

The memory of those miserable nights with Edward was enough to kill any possibility of Juliet ever finding pleasure in any man's arms—even Sebastian St Claire's!—and she wrenched her mouth free of his before pushing him away, her hands held out defensively in front of her as she backed away from him.

Edward was dead, Juliet reminded herself desperately. She was free of him at last. Not just free of him, but of *all* men. Juliet had promised herself after Edward's death that she would never again suffer the torment of belonging to any man.

'Do not come near me again!' she warned harshly. She knew by the raising of his hand that St Claire was about to do exactly that.

Sebastian had meant only to cup the side of Juliet's face, to lay the soft pad of his thumb soothingly against lips slightly swollen from his kisses. But his hand fell back to his side, and his gaze became searching as he saw the wildness glittering in the deep green of her eyes. Like those of a rabbit cornered by a bigger and stronger predator....

Who was responsible for causing this look of desperation in such a lovely and delicate woman?

Chapter Three

Sebastian had no idea quite what he would have said or done next, as a loud knock on the outer door to Juliet's bedchamber preventing him from doing anything.

'Perhaps you should go and answer that,' he advised softly, as Juliet continued to stare up at him rather than respond to the persistence of a second knock.

'Not before I am *sure* you understand it is my wish for you to stay well away from me in future!' Her hands were clenched.

'I understand.' He gave her a terse inclination of his head.

Juliet gave him one last narrow-eyed look before turning sharply on her heel to enter her bedchamber, the softness of her slippers making little noise as she hurried across the room to open the door.

Sebastian stepped back into the shadows. No matter what Juliet might choose to think of him, it had never been his intention to involve her in the sort of scandal that his being found with her on the balcony of her bedchamber was sure to incur.

His brows rose as he saw that her late-night visitor was Dolly Bancroft....

Juliet's legs were still trembling as she quickly opened the door, and her breasts were quickly rising and falling in agitation from her time in Sebastian St Claire's arms—on her balcony, of all places! So disorientated did Juliet feel that she could only stare blankly at Dolly as she stood in the dimly lit hallway, still dressed in her evening finery.

Her hostess looked slightly flustered. 'I am sorry to disturb you, Juliet, but there has been a slight accident.'

Was it Juliet's imagination, or had Dolly Bancroft given a swift glance behind Juliet before speaking? As if she had suspected—no, *expected!*—that Juliet would not be alone in her bedchamber?

Dolly Bancroft was the person responsible, Juliet felt sure, for giving Sebastian St Claire the bedchamber next to hers. With those adjoining balconies!

Still in that spirit of 'kindness', perhaps…?

Her mouth thinned. 'An accident?' she enquired.

'Your maid.' Dolly reluctantly drew her attention from the bedchamber back to Juliet. 'Her name is Helena, I believe?'

Juliet drew in a sharp breath at this mention of her cousin. 'What has happened?' she asked anxiously.

Dolly sighed. 'The silly girl seems to have fallen on the stairs and injured her ankle.'

Was her cousin in pain? How badly was she injured? More importantly, had a doctor been called?

'A footman has carried her up to her room, and one of my other guests—Mr Hallowell—is a physician. He has gone up to examine her even as we speak,' Dolly Bancroft answered Juliet's question before she even had the chance to voice it.

'I must go to her,' Juliet said.

'I am sure there is no need for you to trouble yourself, Juliet.' Dolly frowned at the suggestion. 'Mr Hallowell is perfectly competent, I assure you.'

'Nevertheless, I intend to go and see my— Helena for myself.' Juliet turned to pick up a candle to light her way up the stairs to the servants' quarters. 'Surely it would have been better for you to have sent one of the servants to inform me, rather than abandoning your other guests?'

Dolly pursed her lips and her gaze no longer quite met Juliet's. 'I thought it best, in the circumstances, if I came and informed you myself.'

'Circumstances?' Juliet repeated dryly. 'What might those be, Dolly?'

'I— You—' Dolly Bancroft looked uncharacteristically flustered. 'I simply thought it best,' she repeated briskly.

'Dolly?'

The other woman was suddenly every inch the Countess of Banford as she paused to turn in the hallway and look at Juliet down the length of her pretty nose. 'I really must return downstairs to my other guests now, Juliet.'

'Of course.' Her own manner was just as haughty. 'In that case you and I will speak again in the morning, Lady Bancroft.'

Some of the starch left Dolly's expression. 'Why all this fuss, Juliet?' She gave a conspiratorial smile. 'Surely you must agree that St Claire is devilishly handsome?' She laughed softly. 'And, not only that, he is the lover that all the women of the ton secretly wish to have as their own!'

Juliet drew herself up to her little over five feet. 'Then they are welcome to him!' she announced.

'Most of them would be only too happy if they could get him. Unfortunately they are not the object of Sebastian's current interest.' Dolly gave her a knowing look.

Juliet's gaze faltered a little and her expression became wary. Was Dolly saying that it was she, in particular, whom St Claire desired? That actually, it was *he* who was the instigator of their adjoining bedchambers?

Of course Dolly was not saying that, Juliet instantly chided herself; she and His Lordship had not even been introduced until this evening, and the allocation of the bedchambers for the Bancroft guests would have been made long before that.

'Lord St Claire's interest in me is not particular,' she informed the older woman frostily. 'He is simply an opportunist. A man who sought to use my—my discomfort earlier this evening to his own advantage.' Juliet's eyes flashed as she recalled the way the young lord had invaded her balcony only minutes ago and dared to kiss her.

And he was probably on the balcony still—no doubt listening to every word of this conversation!

'Lord St Claire is a renowned rake. Nothing but a seducer of women!' Juliet added for good measure.

Sebastian was eavesdropping on the conversation between the two ladies with increasing displeasure. But he'd had no other choice than to remain, trapped as he was outside on the balcony of Juliet's bedchamber. Any attempt to step back over the dividing ironwork would clearly display him to Dolly's gaze. Yet this last accusation of Juliet's was almost enough to make him step forward in protest—and in doing so give away his hiding place to the already suspicious Dolly.

Something Juliet would definitely not thank him for!

But the captivating Countess had to know that Sebastian was still outside on her balcony. Just as she must also be aware that he would overhear her every word. No, her every *insult*…

Sebastian had no idea at that moment whether he wished to soundly spank Lady Juliet Boyd's delectable bottom, or just kiss her until she was weak and wanting in his arms! Or whether doing either of those things would bring that trapped look back into her eyes. The same expression Sebastian had seen and questioned a few minutes earlier….

'Sebastian is usually too busy avoiding those avaricious women to rouse himself into seducing any of them,' Dolly continued.

'Then I wish he would stop avoiding them and let himself be caught!' Juliet snapped. '*I* certainly have no interest in knowing Lord St Claire any better than I already do!'

Dolly gave a rueful shrug. 'I fear, Juliet, that you will have to inform Sebastian of that yourself.'

Sebastian knew that she just had….

Juliet, reluctant as yet to go downstairs to breakfast and face any of the other guests, requested that the maid Dolly had sent to help her dress return downstairs once this task had been completed, and bring a tray up to her bedchamber.

She had not slept well, and a single glance in the mirror earlier had shown her that this was all too apparent in the dark shadows beneath her eyes and the pallor of her cheeks. Both those things seemed all the more noticeable once her hair was secured on her crown in loose curls.

Juliet had told herself that her restless night was because of her concern for Helena and her badly twisted ankle, but inwardly Juliet knew her insomnia had been for another reason entirely.

Because of another person entirely.

Lord Sebastian St Claire.

Juliet had half expected that he might still be on her balcony when she'd returned from visiting Helena's room the previous evening. Or, worse, actually awaiting her in her bedchamber. But she had found both her bedchamber and the balcony empty, and a surreptitious glance onto the balcony adjoining hers had shown her that it was also empty, the doors firmly closed, and no lighted candle visible in the bedchamber itself. Indicating that Lord St Claire had either gone to bed or he had rejoined the men downstairs playing cards. Juliet strongly suspected the latter.

One thing she knew for certain: she would not

be able to leave today as she had planned. Helena's ankle was indeed very badly swollen, and Mr Hallowell had advised that she must stay in bed for the day, and perhaps tomorrow, too, to allow for the swelling to go down. More importantly, he'd stated that Helena should not travel any distance for at least the next few days, to aid her recovery. And Juliet could not—would not— depart Banford Park without her.

Another reason for her disturbed and sleepless night.

For if she could not leave Banford Park, then she could not escape seeing St Claire again, either….

'Is there enough tea in that pot for two?' A familiar voice interrupted her unwelcome thoughts.

It seemed that Juliet could not escape the persistence of Sebastian St Claire even in her own bedchamber!

Her eyes were wide with disbelief as she stood up to turn and find him standing in the doorway that opened onto her balcony. 'My bedchamber is *not* a public thoroughfare, sir!'

'I should hope not.' He grinned unrepentantly as he stepped fully into the room.

Juliet supposed she should be grateful that he was at least more suitably dressed this morning, in a fitted superfine coat of dark green, with a paler green waistcoat neatly buttoned beneath, a white cravat meticulously tied at his throat, and black Hessians worn over buff-coloured pantaloons. But that was all she could be grateful for.

'I meant, My Lord, that I do not recall giving you leave to just enter my bedchamber whenever you please!' Her eyes flashed her indignation at the liberty he had just taken.

'Not yet,' he acknowledged ruefully. 'I live in the hope that you will soon do so.'

Juliet watched somewhat incredulously as he bent to pick up her own teacup and sip the cooling liquid from the very same spot she had, only seconds ago, those beautiful whisky-coloured eyes deliberately meeting hers over the china cup's delicate rim.

He was still trying to seduce her, Juliet recognised with an uncomfortable fluttering sensation in her chest.

Sebastian St Claire really was too handsome for his own good. Or for any woman's good, either—including her own.

* * *

This would not do. It really would not do!

Sebastian recognised the signs of Juliet's impending temper. The glitter of her eyes. The bright spots of colour that appeared in her cheeks. The tilting of her stubborn chin. The tightening of her determined jaw.

He placed the cup unhurriedly back in its saucer. 'The other female guests are intending to stroll down to the village to look at the Norman church.' His derisive expression showed exactly what he thought of that plan. 'I thought perhaps you might prefer to go on a carriage ride with me?'

If anything, her jaw clenched even harder, until he could almost hear her teeth grinding together. 'Then you were mistaken!'

'You are looking pale this morning, my dear Juliet,' Sebastian observed soothingly. 'Hopefully a little fresh air will bring some of the colour back into your cheeks.'

She drew herself up to her full diminutive height. '*Lord St Claire—*'

'Yes…?' His expression was innocently enquiring.

This man was incorrigible, Juliet decided in

total frustration. Absolutely impossible! 'I have *no* wish to go on a carriage ride—or indeed anything else—with you!'

He raised dark brows. 'You would rather that we spend the morning together here instead?'

Juliet blinked. By 'here' did he mean in her *bedchamber*? Or was he merely referring to Banford Park?

Whatever his meaning, Juliet was not agreeable to either suggestion. 'I have no desire to spend the morning in your company *at all*, My Lord.'

'Then it is your intention to depart today, as planned?'

'You must know that it is not.' She snapped her impatience, sure that he could not have helped overhearing her conversation with Dolly Bancroft the evening before. She'd certainly intended that he hear the remarks she'd meant for *him*!

'Must I?'

'My Lord—'

'Could you not call me Sebastian when we are alone? I assure you I already think of you as simply Juliet,' he murmured huskily.

'I repeat, I have *not* given you permission— What are you doing?' Juliet gasped as he took a step that brought him within touching distance, her eyes widening in alarm as she stared up at him.

Sebastian scowled as he once again saw that look of wariness in her face. The same emotion he had recognised in her yesterday evening. An emotion that had kept him awake for some time after he had retired to bed.

He knew that Juliet's husband had been a much admired and respected member of the House, and an invaluable advisor to the War Cabinet during England's years of war against Napoleon. He also knew the Earl of Crestwood had been a casual acquaintance of his eldest brother, Hawk. There had never, to Sebastian's knowledge, been even a whisper of scandal attached to the Earl's name.

Until after his death.

Even then it had been his wife's name that had been whispered by the closed ranks of the ton.

But if not Edward Boyd, then who could have put that look of fear into Juliet's eyes? Whoever or whatever it had been, Sebastian had no intention of adding to it—but he couldn't give up his pursuit of her now. 'Juliet, would you please do me the honour of accompanying me on a carriage ride this morning?' He gave her an encouraging smile.

Juliet was momentarily disconcerted by the sweetness of his smile. 'It is no more acceptable for the two of us to be alone in a carriage than it is for us to be alone here,' she declared.

'It is acceptable to me, Juliet,' he assured her. 'And to you, too, I hope?'

This man disturbed her. Disturbed, as well as confused her.

Two very good reasons why she should not allow herself to be persuaded by the beguiling boyishness of his smile! 'I think not, Lord St Claire.' She used his title deliberately.

Those whisky-coloured eyes looked directly into hers. 'You have such an intense interest in Norman churches?'

'I am not interested in them in the least,' she admitted. 'And you do not appear to have any interest in your own good name,' she added waspishly. 'To pay marked attention to me once is to risk your reputation,' she explained at his raised dark brows. 'To do so twice may mean you lose it completely!'

His mouth quirked. 'I believe I am the only one who needs be concerned with that unlikely occurrence.'

'My Lord, you have far more to lose by this association than I—'

'Juliet, will you please stop arguing and just say yes to my suggestion of a carriage ride?' he interrupted.

Juliet was torn. On the one hand it would be nice to get away from the curious and censorious gaze of the other guests at Banford Park. But accepting St Claire's invitation would surely only expose them both to further speculation and gossip.

It would also put her in the position of being completely alone with him in his carriage….

'You have hesitated long enough, Juliet.' Sebastian decided to take matters into his own hands. 'I will collect my hat and gloves and meet you downstairs no longer than ten minutes hence.' He strode purposefully towards the door.

'Sebastian!'

A satisfied smile curved his lips at her use of his given name and he turned slowly to look at her.

She closed her eyes briefly. 'Could you…? Would it be to much to ask that you return to your own room in the same way that you arrived?' She frowned. 'It would not do for someone to see you leaving my bedchamber at this hour,' she explained ruefully.

Sebastian chuckled softly as he inclined his dark head in acknowledgement of her point. 'Ten minutes, Juliet. Or I will be forced to come looking for you.'

It was impossible for her to miss the threat behind his words. Just as it had been ultimately impossible for her to resist the beguiling nature of his smile. A smile that could charm the birds out of the trees if he so wished. A smile that had certainly charmed Juliet into behaving less than sensibly…

'…the Black Widow—'

'I wish you would not call her by that disgusting name!' Sebastian exclaimed as he and Gray stood talking together in the cavernous entrance hall of Banford Park whilst Sebastian waited for Juliet to join him. 'Address her as either Lady Boyd or the Countess of Crestwood.'

Gray grimaced. 'I noticed your marked interest yesterday evening, and was merely enquiring as to whether her presence here could possibly be the reason for our attendance at this house party?'

'Perhaps,' Sebastian said coolly. 'You have some objection to make?' he added challengingly.

'I would not dare to, old chap,' Gray retorted. 'You may like to give the impression that you live a life of idle pleasure, but I am well aware of how often you spar in the ring, and the many hours a week you spend honing your skill with the sword! If it's any consolation, Seb, I am in complete sympathy with your interest in the widow. I had forgotten how beautiful she was until I saw her again yesterday evening.'

Sebastian appreciated this observation even less than he had his friend's earlier remarks. 'I hope it is not your intention to practise your own charm upon her, Gray?'

Gray opened wide, innocent eyes. 'I make a point of never incurring the displeasure of a man who can fight and handle a sword better than I!'

The tension in Sebastian's shoulders relaxed slightly as he finally saw the teasing humour in the other man's gaze. 'Tell me, Gray, what do you know of Edward Boyd?'

'The husband?' His friend gave a shrug. 'Would your brother Hawk not be the best man to ask such a question?'

'Unfortunately, Hawk is not here.' Sebastian's eldest brother might give the impression that he was too aristocratically top-lofty to even notice lesser beings than himself—which included just about everyone!—but that indifference was a façade; Hawk's intelligence was formidable, and if he chose he could be the most astute of men. Certainly Hawk's opinion of Edward Boyd would be worth hearing.

'Most people seem to have held Crestwood in high esteem,' Gray observed with a slight frown. 'He was a hero at Trafalgar, don't you know?'

Of course Sebastian knew of the Earl of Crestwood's war record. He might have been still at school when the famous sea battle had occurred, but as a fifteen-year-old youth he had of course been very interested in it, and had read about the heroes of that battle.

His interest in the Earl's wife had come much later, when he had happened to see Juliet during a ball at which he'd been forced by Hawk into acting as escort to their young sister Arabella during her first Season.

Tiny, almost ethereal, the Countess had nevertheless possessed a presence, an otherworldly beauty, that had instantly captured Sebastian's interest.

He realised now that perhaps he should have paid more attention to Crestwood that night as he'd stood so arrogantly at Juliet's side. That he should have observed more closely the relationship that existed between the married couple….

'Our host is probably the chap you need to speak to if you want to know more about Crestwood,' Gray suggested.

'Bancroft?'

Gray nodded. 'Both members of the House of Lords. Both were advisers to the War Cabinet during the war against Napoleon. Bancroft is sure to know something of the other man.'

'Never mind that for now, Gray…' Sebastian's interest was swiftly distracted as he spotted Juliet, moving gracefully down the wide staircase to where he stood waiting.

A silk beribboned bonnet of the same peach colour as her high-waisted gown covered the darkness of Juliet's curls, and she carried a lacy parasol to keep the worst of the sun's rays from burning the pale delicacy of her complexion.

Everything about Juliet Boyd was delicate,

Sebastian acknowledged with a sudden frown. From the top of her dark curls down to her tiny slippered feet.

Juliet's gaze became wary as she looked up and saw the fierce expression on Sebastian's face as she joined him. 'Am I interrupting…?' She voiced her uncertainty.

'Not in the least, Lady Boyd,' Sebastian's companion assured her warmly. It was a fashionably dressed dark-haired, grey-eyed gentleman that Juliet vaguely recalled as being seated some way down the dinner table from her yesterday evening. 'Lord Gideon Grayson,' he introduced himself smoothly as he gave a courtly bow.

Juliet curtseyed, at the same time raising her hand. 'I am pleased to meet you, Lord—'

'If it's all the same to you, Gray, the Countess and I are in something of a hurry,' Sebastian cut in, before the other man could take her hand. Instead he placed that gloved hand on his own arm and held it there by placing his hand firmly on top of it. 'Enjoy your morning, Gray,' he added mockingly.

With her fingers firmly tucked in the crook of his arm, Juliet had little choice but to follow as

Sebastian strode arrogantly across the hallway and out through the front door to where one of the grooms stood waiting beside a gleaming black curricle drawn by two matching greys.

Juliet did not need to be told that the vehicle belonged to Sebastian St Claire; the rakish style of the carriage matched its owner perfectly!

'Were you not a little rude to Lord Grayson just now?' Juliet ventured, once Sebastian had aided her ascent into the carriage before dismissing the groom to step in beside her and take up the reins.

'Was I?' he said evasively, his expression unreadable beneath the brim of his hat as he flicked the greys into an elegant trot.

Juliet fell silent as she pretended an interest in the countryside that surrounded Banford Park. Pretended, because after that scene in the hall her thoughts were all inward!

She knew she should be used to the cuts and snubs of the ton after being the subject of them so recently. And she was. It was just that after his earlier contempt for such behaviour she had expected more of Sebastian St Claire. The fact that he had not even wanted to introduce her to a man who was obviously his friend showed Juliet how naïve had been that expectation.

No doubt it was all well and good for St Claire to accost her on the privacy of her balcony or in her bedchamber. To whisk her away from curious eyes in his curricle. But to have him actually introduce her to one of his friends was obviously too much to ask.

For all Juliet knew she could be the subject of some sort of wager between St Claire and his friends. It was common practice, she believed, for gentlemen to make such wagers at their London clubs. In this case perhaps the first man to bed the Black Widow was to become the winner of this wager.

'Juliet…?'

Her eyes flashed with anger. 'I have changed my mind, My Lord,' she snapped, her back rigid. 'I wish for you to take me back to Banford Park immediately!'

Sebastian glanced down at her searchingly. Whatever thoughts had been going through her head the last few minutes they had not been pleasant ones—as the anger in those deep green eyes testified.

He shook his head. 'Not until you tell me what I have done to upset you.'

'I am not upset,' she denied.

'No?' Sebastian rasped, patently not amused.

She drew in a ragged breath. 'Would you please turn your curricle around and return me to Banford Park?'

'No.'

'No…?' she echoed uncertainly.

They were some distance from Banford Park now, but instead of continuing on the road as he had intended, Sebastian turned the greys down a rutted track, entering a grove of trees before pulling his horses to a halt.

Before Juliet could so much as voice a word of protest he had jumped lithely down from the curricle to come round and offer her his hand, so that she might join him on the ground.

She made no effort to do so, but instead raised her chin in challenge. 'I should warn you, Lord St Claire, that I have no intention of allowing you to seduce me!'

Sebastian found himself grinning at the fierceness of her expression. 'I assure you, my dear, that my preference is for the comfort of a bed, or perhaps even a well-upholstered sofa, when my thoughts turn to seduction!'

She blinked her surprise. 'Then why have you brought me here?'

'To take a stroll in the sunshine, perhaps? To breathe in the fresh, clean air? To appreciate the beauty that surrounds us?'

It *was* a pretty spot, Juliet acknowledged frowningly, with the dappled sun shining through the trees overhead upon wild flowers in bloom in pinks and yellows and purples.

Except Sebastian had been looking at Juliet and not the flowers or the trees when he'd made that last remark....

Warmth coloured her cheeks as he continued to look at her with unconcealed admiration. 'I can as easily appreciate all of those things from my balcony at Banford Park.'

The humour left his gaze. 'I believe we can talk more privately here, Juliet.'

Juliet didn't care for the sudden and probing intensity of that whisky-coloured gaze. 'Concerning what subject, sir?'

'If you join me I will tell you.' He held out his hand for a second time.

Juliet continued to eye him warily, at the same time impatiently dismissing her feelings of alarm. She was a woman of thirty years. Had been married and widowed. She ran the house, and the smaller estate she had moved to after Edward's death, with a competency that surprised even her. So why should a man younger than herself, whose reputation was that of a rake and an incorrigible flirt, give her reason to feel in the least uncertain of herself?

He should not!

'You really are behaving most childishly, My Lord,' she told him frostily, but she moved to place her gloved hand on his so that she might descend from the curricle.

Sebastian's face hardened as he ignored that hand and instead reached up to place both his hands about her waist, before lifting her aloft and swinging her out of the carriage.

For several seconds, as he lifted her, Juliet found their gazes on a level, and her body was perilously close to Sebastian's as she stared into the golden depths of his eyes and saw—

'I insist that you put me down *at once*, Lord St Claire,' she instructed him breathlessly.

'And if I choose not to do so?' His expression became one of amusement as he looked pointedly at the precariousness of her position as he held her aloft, several feet from the ground.

Her eyes flashed deeply green. 'You have been warned, My Lord!'

His amusement deepened. 'One kiss, Juliet,' he murmured throatily. 'One kiss and perhaps I will consider your request— Ow!' He yelped as Juliet's booted foot made painful contact with his knee, and he quickly lowered her to the ground before bending to grasp his injured joint. 'That was not kind, Juliet.' He scowled up at her.

She looked unrepentant. 'My only regret is that it was not many inches higher!'

Surprisingly, Sebastian found his amusement returning. 'I am thankful that it was not! You— Where are you going?' he demanded as she turned to begin walking away from him down the rutted track. 'Juliet…?' He began to hobble after her.

She spun sharply round. 'It is my intention to walk back to Banford Park if *you* will not return me there.'

'That really is not necessary—'

'I consider it very necessary, Lord St Claire,' she

scorned. 'Against my better judgement I allowed myself to be persuaded into taking a carriage ride with you. My reserve has been completely borne out by your ungentlemanly behaviour towards me just now.' She put up her parasol against the sun's rays and turned and resumed her walk in the direction of Banford Park.

'Juliet?' Sebastian could only stand and watch in frustration as she ignored him to continue her walk. Her face might be hidden by her raised parasol, but the ramrod-straightness of her back was more than enough to tell him of her anger.

Chapter Four

Juliet's temper had not abated in the slightest by the time she returned to Banford Park, some twenty minutes or so later. So it was perhaps fortunate that it was the Earl of Banford and not his Countess who chanced to greet her as she stepped inside the house; Juliet had not had the chance as yet to finish last night's conversation with Dolly Bancroft!

The Earl eyed her quizzically. 'You look slightly…flushed, Lady Boyd. Perhaps you would care to join me in my study for some morning refreshment?'

'I fear I am not good company at the moment, My Lord.' Juliet was feeling hot and bothered from her walk, and still flustered and out of sorts from this latest debacle with Sebastian St Claire.

He gave her an understanding smile. 'Has my wife been causing mischief again?'

'Oh, no— Well… Yes, actually,' Juliet acknowledged flatly when she saw the Earl's patent disbelief at her initial denial. 'But it is not all Dolly's fault,' she allowed fairly. 'I am sure Lord St Claire can be very persuasive when he chooses.' She was not altogether sure how much she could say to the Earl concerning her suspicions about his wife's friendship with St Claire.

'And have *you* found him to be so?' her host asked gently.

'Not in the least!' Juliet assured him vehemently.

Too vehemently? Perhaps. But after this morning Juliet intended being more on her guard than ever where Sebastian St Claire was concerned.

'Perhaps Lord St Claire has deceived Lady Bancroft into believing him to be more agreeable than he is?' she suggested tactfully.

'Do not look so concerned, my dear Lady Boyd.' William Bancroft said softly. 'I assure you that any friendship between my wife and St Claire has always been of a purely platonic nature.' He looked serious. 'I think that perhaps you should be made aware that, although he has certainly earned his reputation with the ladies, St Claire does not choose to "persuade" as often as the gossips care to imply that he does....'

Juliet felt the colour warm her cheeks. 'I must warn you, My Lord, that I really cannot even *think* of joining you for refreshment if you intend to continue discussing Lord St Claire with me.'

'As you wish, my dear.' The Earl stepped forward to place a hand lightly beneath her elbow. 'Tea for two, Groves,' he instructed the butler lightly, before guiding Juliet down the hallway to his study.

Much to Sebastian's chagrin, for once in his life he was completely at a loss to know what to do next where a woman was concerned.

He had allowed his desire for Juliet, when holding her aloft in his arms this morning, to overrule his awareness of that guardedness he sensed inside her, and had subsequently paid the price for that miscalculation when she'd walked off and left him. There had been no opportunity to see or speak to her since then.

Consequently, he sat broodingly at the dinner

table that evening, watching Juliet down its length as she conversed easily and charmingly with Gray, sitting on one side of her, and the elderly and courtly Duke of Sussex on the other.

Sebastian's censorious glance towards his hostess for this arrangement was met by a pointed glance in her husband's direction, telling him that the Earl was the one responsible for the distance between Juliet and himself at the dinner table.

That Juliet had somehow succeeded in charming the Earl of Banford came as no surprise to Sebastian. Nor the fact that Gray and the Duke of Sussex seemed equally as enchanted by her company. What man could look at her—dressed this evening in a deep green silk gown, her hair an abundance of ebony curls, several of those curls temptingly loose against the long length of her creamy throat—and not be charmed?

Certainly not Sebastian. He found his hooded gaze shifting often in her direction as she chatted softly with her dining companions—whilst his own meal seemed to progress with excruciating slowness, and culminated in his imbibing far too much wine and not eating enough food.

If this continued he would be foxed before the meal even came to its painful end!

Even as Juliet responded to the polite dinner conversation of Lord Gideon Grayson, she was aware of St Claire's dark and brooding gaze fixed upon her whenever she chanced to glance up.

'Do not be too hard on him, Lady Boyd,' Lord Grayson drawled, after one such irritated glance. 'I assure you Sebastian is not usually so marked in his attentions,' he added dryly as Juliet looked at him enquiringly.

She frowned her annoyance. 'You are the second gentleman today to leap to his defence, sir!'

Gideon gave a rueful shrug. 'Sebastian is a capital fellow.'

'So I am informed,' she said, obviously unimpressed.

'But you still doubt it?'

Of course Juliet doubted it; so far in their acquaintance St Claire had tried—and failed—to seduce her at every opportunity that presented itself!

Lord Grayson raised his brows at her censorious expression. 'Has it not occurred to you that perhaps you should be thanking Sebastian rather than cutting him so cruelly?'

Her eyes widened. 'Thanking him for what, pray?'

'Has your time here not been a little easier today? Your fellow guests a little less...cool in their manner towards you?' he asked.

Juliet thought of the picnic lunch she had enjoyed earlier today—a picnic lunch that her tormentor had been noticeably absent from! Surprisingly, several of the ladies had included her in their conversation as their party sat in the shade of one of the oaks beside the river that ran through the extensive grounds of Banford Park.

'I am sure you must be aware that Sebastian is considered something of a setter of fashion,' Lord Grayson continued lightly. 'If he has decided it is time to welcome you back into Society, then you may be assured the rest of the ton will quickly follow his example.'

'And I suppose you are telling me that Lord St Claire was demonstrating that "welcome" earlier today, when he did not even have the good manners to introduce us properly?' Juliet pointed out.

Lord Grayson looked at her for several seconds

before answering. 'No, I cannot claim Sebastian had your own comfort in mind at that time...'

'Then—'

Lord Grayson looked rueful. 'I believe I have already said too much.' He lifted his wineglass and silently toasted her, before sipping some of the ruby-red liquid and turning to engage the young lady seated on his other side in conversation.

The Duke of Sussex took advantage of the younger man's distraction to begin conversing with Juliet on the deplorable state of the country since the war against Napoleon had come to an end. Something the Duke seemed to assume Juliet had some interest in—possibly because of her husband's involvement with the War Cabinet in the years before his death. Whatever the elderly man's reasoning, his comments did not require any input from Juliet except for an occasional polite nod or smile. Giving Juliet ample time in which to ponder Lord Grayson's last remarks to her.

The fact that he was a close friend of the irritating St Claire indicated to Juliet that his judgement lacked impartiality; as far as Juliet was concerned the arrogant and ridiculously self-assured Lord St Claire was the very *last* man in need of her gratitude or understanding—or indeed anyone else's!

Certainly Juliet felt no such softening of her regard as she watched him approach her after dinner, when the gentlemen rejoined the ladies in the drawing room. Juliet was not sure, but it seemed to her, by the reckless glitter in that whisky-coloured gaze and the slight flush to his cheeks, that His Lordship had imbibed far too much wine and port this evening to allow for even his usual questionable caution.

Indeed, that concern was borne out by the way he took a firm hold of her arm the moment he reached her side and urged, 'Walk out onto the terrace with me, Juliet.'

'I believe you would find it more beneficial to your current mood if you were to retire to your bedchamber, My Lord,' she insisted in low icy tones, but her outward demeanour was one of smiling graciousness as she sensed they were once again the subject of curious eyes.

He arched dark brows. 'Was that a proposition, Lady Boyd…?'

Juliet drew her breath in sharply. 'You must

know it was not!' She gave him a warning glance from beneath lowered dark lashes.

'One can but live in hope,' he drawled, with a noticeable lack of concern.

The serene smile Juliet bestowed upon him was not matched by the angry glitter in her eyes. 'Release me at once, sir, and cease this licentious behaviour!' she hissed.

Sebastian frowned down at her. Juliet truly believed him to be foxed?

Admittedly Sebastian had been imbibing rather too freely during dinner, but he had put an end to that the moment he'd realised he felt a strong desire to stand up and walk the length of the room before grasping Gray by the throat and squeezing the life out of him—just because he, and not Sebastian, was the one sitting beside Juliet, and the recipient of one of her rare and beautiful smiles.

Strangling the life out of one of his best friends had not seemed to him to be a rational idea!

Sebastian felt no qualms, however, at the thought of using the fact that Juliet believed him to be foxed if it gave him the slightest advantage…

'Only if you will agree to help me to my bedchamber…?'

She looked disconcerted by the suggestion. 'You know that is not possible.'

He shrugged. 'Then I will remain here and endeavour to dazzle you with my wit and charm.'

'I assure you at this moment you do not possess either wit *or* charm!'

Sebastian grinned unabashedly at her vehemence. 'Implying that I might when I am *not* foxed…?'

'Implying that—' Juliet broke off to eye him in utter frustration. 'I really think it advisable if you retire to your room now, My Lord—before you do or say something you might later regret.'

'And what might that be?' He raised dark brows. 'Kissing your hand, perhaps?' He raised her gloved fingers towards his lips, but instead of the courtly kiss she was expecting, at the last moment Sebastian turned her hand and kissed the delicacy of her wrist, his fingers tightening about hers as she gasped and tried to pull sharply away. 'No, I feel no regret,' he murmured, after considering for a moment. 'Perhaps if I were to take you fully into my arms and—'

'I have reconsidered, Lord St Claire,' she cut him off in alarm. 'If you wish it I will see that you are safely delivered to the privacy of your bedchamber!'

He gave a seductive smile. 'Oh, I most certainly wish it, my dear Juliet.'

'Just remain here—endeavour to try not to get into any more mischief while I am gone!—and I will make your excuses to Lord and Lady Bancroft.'

'And your own, dear Juliet,' Sebastian advised softly.

Her mouth tightened. 'I will be but a few minutes.'

Could it really be so easy? Sebastian wondered, watching as Juliet gracefully crossed the room to talk quietly with their host and hostess. Of course she did believe him to be more than slightly the worse for drink, and so perhaps incapable of attempting her seduction once they were alone... A completely erroneous assumption—as the rapid hardening of Sebastian's thighs just at the thought of making love to Juliet testified only too well!

Not that he would seduce her before he had apologised for his behaviour this morning, of course. One should not even attempt to make love to a woman who was as displeased as Juliet still appeared to be.

Sebastian's gaze narrowed with displeasure as he watched his host stroll the length of the room to his side, whilst Juliet remained in conversation with Dolly Bancroft.

The Earl raised mocking brows. 'Lady Boyd seems to feel you may be indisposed, St Claire?'

'Lady Boyd is—' He broke off, his mouth tightening in frustration at the neat way Juliet had outmanoeuvred him.

'A very beautiful but equally mysterious young lady,' Lord Bancroft finished for him, not even attempting to hide his amusement at the other man's predicament.

Sebastian's gaze focused on his host. 'Mysterious…?'

The older man gave him an enigmatic smile. 'There are certain inconsistencies to the Countess that I find…questionable, shall we say?'

Sebastian's unhappiness with this conversation increased. 'Is it not impolite of you to discuss one of your guests in this way?'

'Do not attempt to tell me how to behave in my own home, St Claire!' The usual good humour had left Lord Bancroft's eyes, and his gaze had become steely. 'Considering your own continued interest in the Countess, you and I perhaps need to talk further,' he stated. 'Would ten o'clock in my study tomorrow morning suit you?'

Sebastian looked irritated. 'What is this all about, Bancroft?'

'Not here, St Claire.' The cordial smile returned to his host's lips, and the tension left his shoulders as he once again looked his usual amiable self. 'Dolly is about to propose a game of charades. I suggest you join us,' Lord Bancroft said lightly, before leaving to return to his wife's side.

Sebastian, as any man who valued his reputation as a gentleman of fashion, would as soon take a walk to the gallows as engage in a game of charades. Besides, he was too disturbed by Bancroft's strange behaviour just now to concentrate on such inanity.

Juliet, Sebastian noted, also remained as a spectator to the game rather than a participant. She had moved to stand near one of the sets of French doors that had been opened out onto the terrace to allow the warm evening air into the drawing room, completely ignoring Sebastian's existence as she gave every appearance of enjoying the fun as their fellow guests made complete cakes of themselves.

So intent was Juliet's attention on the party game that she did not even notice when Sebastian slipped out of the matching set of doors further down the drawing room and made his way silently across the terrace to where Juliet stood, chuckling at Gray's antics as she leant against one of the velvet drapes.

Totally oblivious of Sebastian standing directly behind her....

This second evening at Banford Park had definitely been easier to bear than the first, Juliet decided. She was enjoying watching the game of charades—not taking part, but certainly not feeling excluded, either.

Because, as Lord Grayson claimed, St Claire had set the example he wished his peers to follow by making her socially acceptable once more?

Grateful as she was for a slight melting of the frost that had previously been shown to her, it was not quite within Juliet to allow that the outrageous Lord St Claire and his marked attentions towards her were indeed responsible for that change. Even if they were, he need not have been so persistent in his interest—especially as she had given him every indication that she wished him to cease all such attentions. Besides, there had been no one else but themselves present when he'd intruded onto her balcony yesterday evening. Or when he'd invaded the privacy of her bedchamber this morning.

Juliet became very still as she felt something touch the exposed nape of her neck. A fly, perhaps? Or possibly a bee…

'Do not turn around, Juliet,' Sebastian St Claire urged huskily, just as she would have done so.

Juliet stiffened. St Claire was standing directly behind her, in the shadow of the curtained doorway. Juliet's wide-eyed glance about the room showed that none of the other guests seemed in the least aware of his presence.

He was standing so close to her that Juliet could feel the heat of his body through the thin material of her gown. As she had yesterday evening, Juliet also smelled the sharp tang of male cologne and the cigar he must have smoked earlier with his port.

The fact that he was standing so close to her implied that the feather-light touch she had felt against her nape had very likely been St Claire's fingertips against her bare flesh…!

She flicked her fan open, bringing it up in front of her mouth so that their conversation would not be visible to the other guests. 'What do you think you are *doing*?' she whispered fiercely.

'Something I have been longing to do since Dolly interrupted us yesterday evening,' came St Claire's unapologetic reply. 'Did you know that your skin is as soft as velvet?' Once again those fingertips caressed the length of her nape.

Juliet was instantly aware of that quivering sensation once more as those fingers ran the length of her spine. Just as she had the previous evening, Juliet wondered whether it could be pleasure she was feeling. Certainly no one else had ever made her feel such a warmth and tingling in her body before. It was not an unpleasant feeling, and nor was she repulsed as she had always been whenever Edward had touched her.

On the contrary, that warm and tingling sensation was now spreading across her shoulders and down into her breasts…

'Has anyone ever likened your hair to the colour and texture of sable?' he murmured, and she couldn't suppress a tiny shiver as the warmth of his breath moved the curls at her nape.

It was strangely disturbing to have him standing behind her like this and for no one else in the drawing room to be aware of it. Again, this was not an unpleasant feeling—more of a deliciously wicked one that Juliet could enjoy without feeling any regret or embarrassment.

'Does your skin taste as good as it feels, I wonder…?' he whispered.

Juliet gasped, and her back arched involuntarily as she felt the softness of his chiselled lips against her nape, those quivers down her body increasing in urgency as she felt the gentle rasp of his tongue against the bareness of her flesh.

'Mmm, it tastes even better than it feels,' he murmured appreciatively as he alternately kissed and licked a heated path down the length of her spine. That path came to a halt as he reached the top of her gown. 'May I…?' he asked huskily.

Juliet was too hot, too confused by the strange clamouring of emotions she was feeling, to immediately comprehend his meaning. By the time she *did* understand what he was asking Sebastian had already unfastened most of the buttons down the back of her gown!

'I ask that you do not turn around, Juliet,' Sebastian reiterated as she once again made an attempt to do so, placing his hands firmly upon her shoulders to accompany this reminder as he held her in place. 'I wish for you to remain exactly as you are so that I might…explore.'

Juliet's gaze moved wildly about the drawing room, but no one was paying her—or consequently him, where he stood hidden by the drapes—any attention. They remained engrossed in their party game.

Having Sebastian touch her in this way was so sinfully wicked that Juliet could not possibly allow him to continue. Could she…? Yet with her gown unbuttoned down her back did she really have any choice but to remain standing exactly as she was?

Did she even *want* a choice?

Juliet could not deny that she felt a curiosity. A wanting. An aching to know if the sensations she was feeling really were pleasure.

Juliet gasped again as she felt the heat of Sebastian's hands about her waist. Only the thin material of her silk chemise separated those hands from her bare flesh. That gasp became a tiny moan as his hands shifted beneath the loose material of her high-waisted gown to move caressingly upwards to just below the pertness of her breasts.

'Shh, sweet…' Sebastian murmured soothingly.

How could Juliet possibly remain silent when those hands touched her so intimately? When she could feel her nipples become engorged in anticipation of caresses yet to come?

She felt a warm flooding between her thighs as Sebastian continued to touch her just beneath her breasts. A hot dampness in her most secret place. A clenching spasm deep inside her as Sebastian's hands trailed a slow path from her breasts down to her waist and then back again.

'You must stop, Sebastian!' she protested agonisingly from behind her fan. Her knees seemed in danger of buckling beneath her.

His only reply was to tighten his hands about her waist as he held her more firmly in place and his lips explored the bareness of her shoulder, licking, gently sucking.

Juliet was in no doubt now—this *was* pleasure!

Unimaginable, indescribable pleasure.

It was a sensation unlike any Juliet had ever known before.

A sensation she wanted to continue….

Sebastian knew that he should stop. That he *must* stop soon or risk exposing them both to a scandal that the ton would never forgive or forget.

But finally being able to kiss Juliet, to touch her, to feel her pleasure in his caresses, to hear her little panting breaths and feel the response of her body, was feeding his own desire, so making it impossible for Sebastian to do anything other than continue the wild, illicit caresses.

Her skin smelt of spring flowers and tasted like silken honey as he continued to explore its smoothness with his lips, feeling the arch of Juliet's back as he ran his tongue down the ridges of her spine. Her bottom was pressed against him, and the hardness of his throbbing, aching arousal fitted perfectly against her.

That Juliet was completely naked beneath her chemise Sebastian had no doubt, and he allowed one of his hands to glide lower down over her stomach, to cup her between her parted legs. He was able to feel her dampness through the thin material that was the only barrier to his questing fingers.

A barrier Sebastian pushed impatiently aside, skilfully drawing the material of her chemise up to her waist.

Growling low in his throat, he was finally able to touch, to explore the soft and downy thatch where the hard bud of her arousal was hidden.

She was swollen.

So swollen.

And so responsive as Sebastian lightly stroked, above and below, never quite touching that engorged nubbin as his fingers became wet and slick.

'Please…!' Juliet's groan was so low and aching that Sebastian felt a leaping response between his own thighs. 'I want—Sebastian—I need—'

Sebastian knew what she wanted, what she needed, what she craved.

What he craved, too.

But not here.

How could either of them enjoy complete pleasure when they were standing here so publicly?

When anyone in the room might turn at any moment and see them together?

Juliet's slippered feet no longer touched the floor as Sebastian placed a strong arm about her waist, and she felt herself being lifted, carried backwards out of the room and into the dark shadows of the terrace before he lowered her to turn her in his arms. His mouth claimed hers hungrily.

The new, craving sensations in Juliet's body caused her to return the hunger of that kiss as she silently pleaded, begged for an end to the tormenting, unbearable ache between her thighs.

Her lips parted to the hard invasion of Sebastian's tongue, and those moist, rhythmic caresses once again pushed her to the brink of— Of what…?

Juliet didn't know.

But she wanted to know.

She *needed* to know!

'…was most enjoyable. But I am so warm after all the excitement that I simply must go outside and take some air.'

Juliet barely had time to register that she and Sebastian were about to have their privacy interrupted before he wrenched his mouth from hers to place silencing fingertips against her lips. He swiftly manoeuvred her backwards, even further into the shadows.

Only just in time, too, as the elderly Duchess and Duke of Sussex strolled out onto the terrace before crossing to stand at the balustrade.

Juliet looked up in the gloom at Sebastian face, to find the darkness of his gaze glittering down at her.

In laughter, or in triumph?

Chapter Five

'Personally, I fail to see what is so funny in the two of us nearly being found together in such a compromising situation.' Juliet stood in the middle of her bedchamber, frowning her consternation as Sebastian, having refastened her gown for her, stood before her, clutching his sides with laughter. 'Lord St Claire, you must desist!' She glared at him reprovingly when her previous admonition had no effect.

His laughter finally ceased, although his eyes continued to gleam with merriment as he looked at her, and a grin still curved those sculptured lips. 'I apologise. I simply found myself imagining how the Duke's jowls would wobble and the Duchess's mouth gape open like that of a fish if they had happened to turn and see us as we made good our escape!'

'That is most unkind, My Lord.' Although Juliet could not deny that their flight from the terrace *had* been in the nature of an escape.

The Duke and Duchess of Sussex had stood at the balustrade for several minutes, talking softly together on the success of the evening, before the Duchess had linked her arm with her husband's and the two had begun to walk down the terrace.

Thankfully in the other direction from where Juliet and Sebastian had still been hiding in the shadows.

An occurrence which had caused Sebastian to take a firm clasp of Juliet's hand before pulling her down the steps into the garden, to stride around to the side of the house.

And all that time Juliet had clutched at the front of her unbuttoned gown in an effort to stop it sliding completely from her body, her mood one of horror as she imagined what a pretty sight she would look, with her gown about her ankles and wearing no more than her chemise and her stockings!

Luckily that had not happened, and the two of them had been able to find access to the house through one of the servant doors. They had then proceeded to sneak through the house and up the back staircase to Juliet's bedchamber. Much like two thieves in the night!

Juliet knew she had never behaved in such an undignified manner in the whole of her thirty years. And as for finding the situation *amusing*, as Sebastian St Claire so obviously did…!

'Can you not imagine it, my dear Juliet?' he prompted with an irrepressible smile. 'The Duke's jowls a-wobbling and the Duchess opening and shutting her mouth like a fish!' He went off into another bout of laughter.

Juliet could imagine it—she would just rather not. What had happened this evening—especially her own behaviour—was no laughing matter. 'Do you ever take anything seriously, My Lord?' she murmured critically.

He sobered immediately. 'Of course I do. Family. Honour. Loyalty to friends.'

Family. Honour. Loyalty to friends. They were indeed fine sentiments.

They did not signify where Juliet was concerned, however. She was neither friend nor family to Sebastian St Claire. As for honour— Juliet's own honour was in shreds!

'I think it better if you leave now.' She spoke softly, avoiding so much as looking at him as she rearranged her perfume bottles on the dressing table. 'This evening was—'

'I trust you are not going to say regrettable?' Sebastian cut in sternly.

Regrettable? Of *course* Juliet regretted it! Her only consolation was that it had not been the complete success Sebastian had hoped for. 'I was about to express my doubts that this evening's little adventure would be enough to win the wager for you!' she said scornfully.

'What wager?' He frowned down at her.

'Oh, come, My Lord.' Juliet gave a disdainful grimace. 'It is common knowledge that young gentlemen such as yourself enjoy certain wagers at their clubs. Escapades like curricle races to Brighton at midnight? Or the seduction of a certain woman…?'

Sebastian winced at the accusation. It was true that many such wagers took place in private—at least he had thought it was in private!—at the gentlemen's clubs. It was also true that a year or so ago Sebastian *had* entered into such a wager himself, concerning another Countess. Although he very much doubted that was the wager Juliet referred to…

'To my knowledge there is no such wager in existence where you are concerned,' he denied. 'And what do you mean by a man such as I…?' he grated.

Juliet gave him a pitying look. 'You are nothing but a rake, sir. A scoundrel. Indeed, a privileged fop, who meanders his way through life, imbibing too much alcohol, seducing women and laughing at anything or anyone who does not share those excesses!'

As set-downs went, this was certainly the harshest that Sebastian had ever received. In fact, it was the first of its kind that he had ever received!

He was a St Claire. The youngest brother of the Duke of Stourbridge. As such, he was untouchable—both in word and deed.

Except Juliet Boyd's opinion of him had touched him in a way he did not care to dwell upon. Perhaps because he suspected that essentially she had only spoken the truth…? He *had*

122 *The Rogue's Disgraced Lady*

made such wagers as those she had accused him. He *was* also a rake, and often behaved the scoundrel. And, as his two older brothers were so fond of telling him, his profligate lifestyle left much to be desired.

But he was the youngest son of a Duke, damn it, and had been left his own estate in Berkshire and a veritable fortune to support it and himself on the death of his parents more than eleven years ago. More wealth than even Sebastian could run through in a dozen lifetimes.

What choices did a third son have but the church—for which he had no inclination!—or to live the life of a profligate?

Sebastian's intention, his interest in Juliet Boyd, had been no more than the light-hearted seduction of a woman who had so far proved elusive to all men but her husband. He had certainly not expected to have his very lifestyle brought into question by that lady.

He gave a stiff bow. 'Once again, let me assure you that I know of no such wager where you are concerned, Lady Boyd. I apologise if I have offended you with my unwanted attentions. I assure you that it will not happen again.' He turned abruptly to cross the room and open the door before stepping out into the hallway.

Juliet felt as if her chest were being squeezed, making breathing difficult and speech impossible, as she watched him leave her bedchamber. The grimness of his countenance had erased all evidence of his usual handsome good humour, making him instead every inch the aristocrat he was.

Juliet remained standing in the middle of the bedchamber as the door closed behind him with a loud click of finality. At which time Juliet ceased even trying to maintain her dignity and instead collapsed weakly onto the bed, her shoulders shaking uncontrollably as tears fell hotly down her cheeks.

It really did not signify whether or not a wager concerning her seduction did or did not exist when her own behaviour this evening had been so shocking. Scandalous, even. The sort of behaviour that only a woman of loose morals could possibly have enjoyed. Women of breeding, of decency, did not—*should* not—feel physical pleasure in the way that she had earlier, when Sebastian had caressed and touched her in such an intimate way.

* * *

'It would appear, Sebastian, that you have been scowling at my other guests in such a way as to cause them to completely lose their appetites!'

The darkness of Sebastian's scowl did not lessen in the slightest as he turned to look at Dolly as she entered the dining room to sit down beside him at the breakfast table. A deserted breakfast table apart from the two of them, he now noticed. Although he seemed to recall there *had* been several other people present when he'd entered the room ten minutes or so ago...

He grimaced. 'I doubt it will hurt some of them to miss a meal or two.'

'True,' Dolly acknowledged with an amused laugh.

Sebastian gave up even the pretence of eating his own breakfast and leant back in his chair. 'Dolly, I am thinking of taking my leave later this morning—'

'You cannot!' Dolly looked shocked at the suggestion. 'I really cannot allow you to even think of doing such a thing, Sebastian,' she continued lightly. 'You will quite put out the even number of my guests. Besides, we are to have a ball tomorrow evening, and I am sure you would not want to deny the daughters of the local gentry the opportunity to see and perhaps dance with the eligible Lord Sebastian St Claire!'

Sebastian did not return her teasing smile. 'I am sure they would be all the better for being denied it!'

'What is wrong, Sebastian?' Dolly looked at him in genuine concern as he stared down grimly into his teacup. 'You do not seem at all your usual cheerful self this morning.' She gave him an encouraging smile.

'You mean, my usual privileged and foppish self? Given to excesses and licentious behaviour?' Sebastian didn't attempt to hide his displeasure concerning Juliet's opinion of his character.

Dolly looked taken aback. 'What on earth do you mean, Sebastian?'

He grimaced in self-disgust. 'The description is entirely fitting—do you not agree, Dolly?'

Sebastian had indulged in much deliberation over the last twelve hours. Since Juliet had told him exactly what sort of man she believed him to be. The sort of man he undoubtedly was, Sebastian had realised during those hours of reflection.

'Of course it is not—' Dolly broke off to consider him closely. 'Who has said such things—surely not Juliet?' she exclaimed. 'Have the two of you argued?'

Sebastian gave a hard, humourless laugh. 'I do not believe it can be called an argument when I merely listened as she told me exactly what sort of man she believes me to be.' His expression darkened. 'It did not paint a pretty picture.'

'No, I would not think it did, if it was the one you have just told to me,' Dolly conceded. 'What she thinks of you bothers you that much?' she asked shrewdly.

Sebastian's scowl turned blacker than ever. 'Only in as much as it appears to be true!'

Dolly shrugged. 'Easy enough to change if you wish it, surely?'

He snorted. 'And how would you suggest I go about doing *that*? Hawk is the Duke. Lucian is a war hero. And I very much doubt the church would suit me, or I it! No, it appears I'm stuck with being the profligate rake.'

'I believe Bancroft mentioned he is in need of

another gamekeeper... No, perhaps not,' she said hastily, as Sebastian's gaze became steely at her levity.

Sebastian took advantage of Dolly's introduction of the Earl into the conversation. 'Bancroft expressed a wish to talk to me this morning. Do you have any idea what it can be about?'

Dolly shook her head. 'I am sure Bancroft will tell you that himself shortly.'

'In other words you have no intention of discussing it with me even if you do know?' Sebastian guessed wryly.

'I would rather not,' Dolly admitted. 'What did you do to Juliet to make her say such hurtful things to you? Dare I ask what had happened shortly before this...exchange?'

Sebastian shifted uncomfortably. 'No, Dolly, you may not.'

He had no intention of telling Dolly—or anyone else, for that matter—what had transpired between himself and Juliet prior to the verbal tongue-lashing he had received from her that had resulted in his present foul mood. He might be all of the things Lady Juliet Boyd had accused him of, but he was also a gentleman, and a gentleman did not discuss with a third party his relationship with a lady. Or the lack of it!

'However, I do not believe I am being indiscreet by confiding that she is of the opinion that my marked interest in her is due entirely to a wager amongst the gentlemen at my club.'

Dolly raised an eyebrow. 'Such wagers do exist, do they not?'

'To my knowledge, none that concern the Countess!' Sebastian glowered fiercely.

'Did you inform Juliet of that?'

'I did.' He gave a humourless smile at the memory. 'She chose not to believe me.'

'Hmm.' Dolly nodded thoughtfully. 'You know, Sebastian, I am not at all convinced that life can have been particularly pleasant when spent with a man of such high moral reputation as Admiral Lord Edward Boyd...'

'You think perhaps he was not so perfect in his private life?' It was something that Sebastian was also beginning to suspect....

'I offer it merely as an explanation for Juliet's condemnation of your own licentious behaviour,' his hostess said airily.

Sebastian's gaze narrowed. 'Dolly, I do not suppose that you and Boyd ever—'

'No, we most certainly did not!' She laughed huskily. 'My dear, he was far too much the paragon to form an alliance with one such as I. And I am sure his sort of perfection must have been very tiresome to live with on a daily basis.'

Sebastian made an impatient movement. 'Surely you are not suggesting that tiresomeness was enough to merit his being pushed down the stairs to his death?'

Dolly grimaced. 'I am merely saying that Juliet might be forgiven if she *did* want to be rid of such a man. I believe that if Bancroft should ever become so pompous and self-important I might consider taking such action myself!'

Sebastian gave a throaty chuckle. 'If every dissatisfied wife in Society were to follow Juliet Boyd's example as a way of ridding herself of a disagreeable husband then I believe there would be only widows left—'

Sebastian broke off abruptly as he heard a shocked gasp behind him, turning sharply to see the edge of disappearing silken skirts as the eavesdropper on his conversation with Dolly made good her escape.

He stood up abruptly. 'Dolly, please tell me that was not she!' he groaned. But he knew by the consternation on his hostess's face that it had indeed been the Countess of Crestwood who had overheard their damning conversation....

Once dressed, Juliet had gone upstairs to check on Helena, who was thankfully much improved yet still in considerable discomfort, before proceeding down to the breakfast room. Her intention had been to seek out Sebastian and offer him an apology for some of the things she had said to him the previous evening. She had come to realise, through the long hours of a sleepless night, that it was herself she was angry with, not him.

She had heard the murmur of conversation as she'd approached the breakfast room, coming to a halt in the hallway when she heard Edward's name mentioned. She'd regretted that hesitation almost instantly, as she hadn't been able to help but overhear the rest of the conversation.

Sebastian St Claire believed her as guilty of

Edward's death as surely as did every other member of the ton!

Hateful, *hateful* man. And to think it had been her intention to apologise to him this morning for her insulting remarks to him the previous evening! How much more hurtful had been his own comments just now than anything she had said to him.

'Juliet!'

She glanced back over her shoulder to see Sebastian pursuing her down the hallway, his expression grim as his much longer strides brought him ever closer, making a nonsense of Juliet's attempt to avoid him.

She came to a sudden halt in the hallway and turned to face him. 'Do you have more accusations you wish to make, Lord St Claire? Possibly to my face this time?' she challenged scathingly. 'Do you not think that overhearing you accuse me of killing my husband is enough insult for one morning?' Her hands were shaking so badly that she had to clasp them tightly behind her back.

Sebastian frowned. 'I do not believe myself guilty of having done that.'

'No?' Juliet's chin was raised in challenge, her

eyes sparkling angrily. Anger was by far a better emotion than the tears that threatened but which she absolutely refused to shed.

'No,' he maintained harshly, those whisky-coloured eyes dark and stormy. 'I accept it was wrong of Dolly and I to repeat the—the speculation that has abounded since your husband's sudden death. But at no time did either of us claim to be expressing our own views on the subject.'

Juliet eyed him in a seething fury. 'Perhaps you would care to do so now?'

No, Sebastian did not believe that he would. Juliet's mood was such that anything he said to her now, especially concerning his opinion of the circumstances of her husband's death, was sure to be misconstrued by her. 'Perhaps the speculation would not be so rife if you ceased to maintain your own silence on the subject...'

'What would you like me to say, Lord St Claire?' she scorned. 'That it was *I* the servants believe they heard arguing with Edward only minutes before he fell to his death? That I hated my husband so much, wanted rid of him so much, I deliberately and wilfully pushed him down the stairs in the hopes that he would break his neck?'

No, Sebastian had no desire to hear Juliet say those things. He did not want to even think of this beautiful and delicate woman behaving in such a cold and calculating way. Nor to imagine what desperation she'd felt—what Edward Boyd's behaviour towards her could possibly have been— to have driven her to such lengths in order to be rid of him….

A nerve pulsed in his tightly clenched jaw. 'Are you telling me that is what happened?'

'Oh, no, My Lord.' Her laugh was hard and humourless. 'It is not for me to tell you anything. You must decide for yourself what you believe to be the truth.'

His mouth tightened. 'Is that not difficult to do when you steadfastly refuse to defend yourself?'

She gave him a pitying look. 'I am certainly not so naïve as to even attempt to proclaim my innocence to one who has so obviously already decided upon my guilt.'

Sebastian made an impatient move. 'Then you presume too much, madam.'

'Do I?' Juliet Boyd snapped. 'All evidence is to the contrary, My Lord.'

Sebastian had never experienced such frustration with another human being as he felt at that moment towards Juliet Boyd. Could she not see that her words and actions, her continued refusal to defend herself, only damned her as being the murderess the ton believed her to be? To others, if not to him.

Her eyes, those beautiful green eyes, viewed him coldly. 'Are you not relieved, My Lord, that I did not take your attentions to me more seriously?'

'My *attentions*, as you call them, were never intended to be taken seriously,' he bit out curtly.

'Of course they were not.' She gave him a disdainful glance. 'Everyone knows that Lord Sebastian St Claire does not take anything in life seriously!'

Once again she meant to insult him. And once again Sebastian realised he had no defence against those insults....

Dolly claimed that if he felt so inclined Sebastian had the means and the ability to change his way of life. That, third son or not, he did not *have* to live the life of idleness and pleasure he had so far enjoyed.

Until the last twelve hours Sebastian had never had reason to even question that life! Nor did he thank Juliet for being the reason he was questioning it now….

'If you will excuse me, Lady Boyd, I have a prior engagement.' He gave a less than elegant bow. 'Please accept my apologies for any insult, real or imagined, that you may have felt during the conversation you overheard earlier. I do assure you that no insult was intended by either Lady Bancroft or myself.' He turned sharply on his heel and took his leave.

Tears burnt Juliet's eyes as she watched him go. She knew that Sebastian St Claire's lighthearted pursuit of her was finally at an end. That she had rended his interest in her asunder with her criticism of him and the way he lived his life.

Chapter Six

'You are here, too, Gray?' Sebastian did not even try to hide his surprise upon finding his friend already seated in the Earl of Banford's study when he duly presented himself there at the assigned hour of ten o'clock.

Nor did Sebastian attempt to conceal his irritation as he refused to take the seat the Earl offered, facing him across the width of his leather-topped desk; Sebastian had suffered through enough such interviews over the years with his brother Hawk, to know better than to meekly sit and accept the set-down he believed was coming. A set-down he deeply resented.

'I am perfectly comfortable standing, thank you,' he assured the older man, and he moved to stand with his back towards the window, hands clasped behind his back, the width of his shoulders blocking out most of the sunlight.

The Earl nodded. 'My wife tells me that you and Lady Boyd have argued…?'

'What the—?' Sebastian's scowl deepened as he stiffened resentfully. He had believed his earlier conversation with Dolly to be of a private nature, known only to the two of them. And in part to Juliet Boyd herself, of course… 'Dolly had no right to relate any of that conversation to you,' he said, outraged.

'I am afraid that she did.' The Earl's expression was sympathetic, but at the same time determined. 'You see, it is not in our interest that you argue with Lady Boyd.'

'"Our interest"?' Sebastian's brow darkened ominously as he looked at the earl and Gray. 'Would someone kindly tell me what on earth is going on?'

'Calm down, old chap,' Gray advised him.

'No, I do not believe I will,' Sebastian grated.

'At least hear what Bancroft has to say before you threaten to call him out,' Gray soothed.

The Earl rose to his feet, as if he too found the confinement of being seated irksome. 'Have you not wondered why it was, when two weeks ago you made your request to my wife that she invite the Countess here to stay, she had already done so?'

'Why should I?' Sebastian shrugged. 'The two ladies were friends once, were they not?'

'Perhaps,' the Earl acknowledged cautiously. 'But I am afraid in this instance that friendship did not signify. My wife issued the invitation to Lady Boyd at my behest.'

'You have lost me, I am afraid.' Sebastian's morning so far had not been in the least conducive to holding on to his temper, and the Earl's enigmatic conversation now was only succeeding in increasing his annoyance.

'I am sure you are aware of the...rumours surrounding the Earl of Crestwood's death?'

'Not you, too!' Sebastian strode forcefully, impatiently, into the middle of the book-lined room. 'You—' he looked pointedly at the Earl of Banford '—gave every indication that you'd befriended the Countess yesterday evening. And you—' his eyes glittered dangerously as he turned his attention on Gray '—flirt with the lady every time the two of you meet. Am I now to believe that you *both* think her capable of killing her own husband?'

'That is the whole point of this conversation, Sebastian.' Once again it was Gray who answered softly. 'The simple answer is we do not *know* what the lady is capable of.'

'Boyd has been dead these past eighteen months,' Sebastian said coldly. 'If by some chance Juliet did do away with him—' his gaze narrowed '—then I am sure she was justified.' That look of wariness, almost of apprehension, he had on several occasions seen in Juliet's eyes, certainly seemed to indicate that someone—and who else could it be but Crestwood?—had given her good reason to fear.

'Ah.'

'Hmm.'

Sebastian easily noted the glance that passed between the other two men in accompaniment to their unhelpful replies.

He could not ignore the uneasy feeling that was starting to settle in the pit of his stomach. The Earl claimed Dolly had invited Juliet here at *his* behest. And Gray, Sebastian now recalled, had made only a nominal complaint at being dragged along to a summer house party he would normally have refused to attend. Gray had also been the one chosen to sit next to Juliet at dinner yesterday evening in Sebastian's stead. Now he discovered that Gray and the Earl of Banford were far better acquainted than he had previously thought....

'Very well.' He seated himself in one of the winged armchairs beside the unlit fireplace before looking at the other the two men with grim determination. 'One or both of you had better tell me exactly what is going on, or you will leave me with no choice but to go to the Countess of Crestwood and inform her of this conversation.'

'You know, Grayson, I do believe you and Dolly may have been correct in your opinion of St Claire's intellect,' the Earl commented with approval.

'Seb's a capital chap,' the younger man answered blithely.

'Seb is fast becoming a blazingly angry one!' he warned them harshly.

'Very well.' The Earl looked him straight in the eye. 'I am happy to talk frankly, but before doing so I will require your word as a gentleman that once this conversation is over you will not discuss its details with a third party.'

Sebastian knew without the other man saying so that in this case the 'third party' he referred to was the Countess of Crestwood….

Up till now Sebastian had always found Dolly's husband to be an affable and charming man. A man it was difficult not to like, but with no more to him than that.

These last few minutes of conversation showed there was much more to the Earl of Banford, and to his own friend Gray, than Sebastian had previously realised…and he didn't like knowing that at all.

'…and so you see you have totally misjudged poor St Claire, I am afraid, dear Juliet,' Dolly admonished gently as the two women sat together in her private parlour.

Juliet had been reluctant to accept Dolly's invitation to join her here when the other woman had come upon her still standing in the hallway after Sebastian had so abruptly taken his leave. After all, Dolly had been just as guilty of discussing her as Sebastian had! To now hear that he had actually been *dismissing* the idea of Juliet being guilty of any involvement in Edward's death, rather than accusing her, made her feel more than a little foolish.

For now it appeared she owed Sebastian not one apology but two!

'After all the gossip and speculation this last year and a half, it is a subject about which I am naturally a little sensitive,' Juliet acknowledged stiffly.

'But of course, my dear.' Dolly gave her hand an understanding pat. 'I can be a sympathetic ear if you ever feel the need to talk privately….'

How Juliet longed to tell someone about her years as Edward's wife. Longed to tell of those nights when he had come to her bed and taken her with cold indifference to the pain he was inflicting. Of his cruelty in the early months of their marriage, when she'd still thought it worth pleading for his gentleness and understanding. Pleas she had ceased to make after that single occasion when Edward had shown her just how much *more* pain and humiliation he could inflict when thwarted.

Oh, yes, Juliet longed to tell someone of those things, but knew that she never would….

'I thank you for the offer, Dolly.' She smiled, to take any offence from her refusal. 'But for the moment I would much rather discuss how I am to go about apologising to Lord St Claire for this latest misunderstanding.'

If Dolly was disappointed in Juliet's determination not to talk about the past, then she gave no indication of it as she instead laughed huskily. 'Oh, my dear, you must not be so eager to concede that you were in the wrong. Men are fond of believing themselves in the right of it, you know, and to eat a little humble pie on occasion does them no harm whatsoever.'

Despite her earlier tension, Juliet found herself laughing at Dolly's nonsense. 'But in this case Lord St Claire *was* in the right of it…'

'I did not say you have to punish him for ever, my dear.' Dolly gave her a conspiratorial smile. 'Just long enough for him to feel the cold chill of your displeasure. The ball I am giving tomorrow evening should be time enough to allow yourself to forgive him.'

Juliet raised dark brows. 'So I *am* to forgive him, then?'

'Of course.' Dolly gave a gracious inclination of her head. 'I have found with Bancroft that it is by far the best way. By the time I have finished forgiving him he is usually so befuddled he has quite forgotten that he was not actually to blame for our fall-out, and is just grateful that we are...friends again!'

Juliet felt colour warm her cheeks as she realised what sort of friendship the other woman was alluding to. 'You quite misunderstand my relationship with Lord St Claire—'

'It is still early days yet, Juliet,' Dolly pointed out.

She shook her head. 'I assure you I have no intention of ever becoming that sort of friend with Sebastian St Claire.'

Or any other man....

Sebastian's expression remained outwardly calm as the Earl talked. Which was not to say that he was not disturbed by the older man's conversation—only he had no intention of revealing his own thoughts at Bancroft's talk of agents of the Crown and treachery.

Bancroft, it appeared, had for some years been involved in such a network of agents, of which Gray—a man Sebastian had known since childhood—appeared to be a member! Dolly, too, if Sebastian understood the Earl correctly; all those years Dolly had been the mistress of one member of the aristocracy or another she had been reporting information back to Bancroft!

'So it appears Crestwood was either responsible himself for passing along privileged information, or it was someone else close to him in whom he confided,' Bancroft finished gravely.

Sebastian realised he had been guilty of allowing his thoughts to wander. But, hell, what man would *not* when confronted with such a fantastic tale? 'Let me see if I understand this clearly. You are saying that Crestwood, or someone close to him, for years passed along privileged information to the French? That such information was used to forestall several English efforts to defeat Bonaparte, and also to aid the Corsican's escape from Elba two years ago?'

'I am saying exactly that,' the Earl confirmed.

Sebastian's brother Lucian had resigned his commission in the army when Bonaparte had finally surrendered, but he had returned to duty the following year, along with his fellow officers, in order to participate in the battle at Waterloo, following Napoleon's escape from Elba. Lucian had returned from that last battle a hard and embittered man, and most of his friends had not returned at all....

Sebastian raised an eyebrow. 'You also believe that this "someone close" to the earl was his wife? That if the heroic Crestwood did not do it, then it must therefore have been Juliet who was the traitor?'

Gray frowned. 'Crestwood was a hero and a gentleman, Seb. But he was not a man who had close friends as you and I do. In effect, there *was* no other person close to him except his countess. Now Crestwood is conveniently dead, and so unable to deny or admit these allegations.'

Sebastian stood up restlessly. 'You are claiming that Lady Boyd deliberately pushed Crestwood down the stairs to his death in order to cover up her duplicity?'

His friend nodded. 'It is reasonable to suppose that Crestwood finally discovered his wife's treachery, and that when he confronted her with it, she pushed him down the stairs to stop him from making her conduct public.'

'Is it not a simpler explanation that the man was foxed?'

'The man did not drink strong liquor of any kind.'

'Then perhaps he fell.'

'He stood the deck of his own ship for over twenty years—are you seriously expecting us, or anyone else, to believe that he lost his balance at the top of his own staircase?' Gray calmed with effort. 'Besides, several of the servants heard the sounds of an argument only minutes before the Earl's fall.'

Sebastian gave a disdainful snort. 'Servants have been known to say anything if they believe it might earn them a guinea or two!'

'No such bribery was offered,' the Earl assured him.

Still Sebastian could not countenance the idea that Juliet was guilty of deliberately murdering her husband, let alone of treason. Although the sacrifice Lucian and his friends had made during the war said he had to hear Bancroft out... 'The man was such a prig that he had no real friends, and such a paragon that he did not drink alcohol. Therefore it *must* be his wife who is the one guilty of treason? Of pushing Crestwood to his death so that he could not reveal her perfidy?' Sebastian shook his head. 'That seems to be rather a leap to have made on so little evidence, gentlemen.'

'There is more, St Claire.' The Earl's tone immediately drew Sebastian's attention. 'Lady Boyd's aunt, the sister of her mother, lived in France with her French husband—Pierre Jourdan. As a child, Juliet Chatterton spent many summers in France, with this aunt and uncle and her young female cousin.'

'Does that mean that *every* English man or woman who has connections with the French, however tenuous, is suspect? My own valet is French. Does that make me guilty of treason, too?'

'You are not taking this at all as I had hoped, St Claire.' The Earl looked most unhappy with Sebastian's response.

Possibly because Sebastian would much rather not think of Juliet in the role Bancroft and Gray had chosen to thrust her into!

She was full of defensive bristles, yes. But what woman would not be when she had come to Banford Park knowing she was entering the lions' den? That all of Society believed her as guilty of killing her husband as Bancroft and Gray so obviously did? But Sebastian had seen that air of vulnerability and fear that Juliet was normally at such pains to disguise.

Until now Sebastian had assumed that fear to have somehow been caused by Crestwood's treatment of her during their marriage, but logically it *could* likewise be apprehension at the thought of discovery…

Two weeks ago he had told Dolly that he did not care one way or the other whether or not Juliet had killed her husband, but his loyalty for Lucian said he should take Bancroft's suggestion of treason much more seriously.

'The Countess's young cousin arrived in England six years ago, after her parents were killed during a raid by French soldiers on their manor home,' Bancroft continued remorselessly. 'The girl was held prisoner by the French for a week before managing to escape and flee to England. We can only guess at what she must have suffered at the soldiers' hands.'

'Would those events not mean that Juliet Boyd has every reason to hate the French rather than aid them?' Sebastian pounced on this inconsistency in their argument.

'Alternatively, she may have been responsible

for betraying her relatives to the French because she knew of their sympathies towards the English,' Bancroft pointed out.

Sebastian felt a coldness slither down the length of his spine at the thought of the beautiful Juliet betraying her family and husband—his brother Lucian and his fellow soldiers, too—in the way Bancroft described. It could not be true. Could it?

'There is something else, St Claire,' the Earl added.

'Go on,' he rasped.

'Two weeks ago a missive to a known French agent was intercepted by one of my own agents. It read simply, "Active again. J."'

Active again. J.

And the missive had been sent two weeks ago.

The exact time Dolly had issued her invitation to Juliet to attend this summer house party....

'I have always believed, my dear Juliet, that if a woman decides to take a lover then she should at least ensure he is an accomplished one,' Dolly Bancroft advised archly.

Juliet's cheeks burned at the thought of the intimacies she had already allowed Sebastian St Claire. Intimacies Juliet had shared with no other man….

She shook her head. 'I assure you I have no intention of taking a lover.'

'Why would you not?' The other woman looked scandalised. 'You have been widowed these last eighteen months, Juliet; do not tell me you do not miss the pleasure of having a virile man in your bed?'

How could Juliet miss something she had never known? Something she had only begun to guess at since Sebastian had touched and caressed her…?

Would this burning in her cheeks ever stop? 'I am not sure this is a—an altogether fitting conversation, Dolly.'

'I am sure it is not!' Her hostess laughed naughtily. 'But men, I am sure, discuss such things at their clubs all the time, so why should the ladies not do the same when alone together? I can claim with all honesty that Bancroft is a wonderful lover. Was Crestwood the same?'

'Dolly!' Juliet gasped weakly.

The other woman's gaze was shrewdly searching. 'I see by your reaction that he was not.' She gave a disgusted shake of her head. 'How disappointing for you. I am of the opinion that being proficient in the art of lovemaking is as important for a man to learn as running an estate or riding a horse.'

Juliet really was unused to such frank and intimate conversation. 'Crestwood ran his estate with precision, and he could ride a horse, as well as any man.'

'Then it was only as a lover that he failed to please?' Dolly nodded knowingly. 'One only has to look at St Claire to know how wonderful he would be as a lover. The width of his shoulders. His muscled chest and the flatness of his stomach. As for the pleasure promised by his powerful hips and thighs... My dear, I am sure he is virile enough to keep even the most demanding of women happy in his bed!'

All this talk of pleasure and virile men, and most especially of Sebastian St Claire's bed, was only increasing Juliet's discomfort. But in a way that made her breasts swell beneath her gown and their tips harden as she once again felt that strange warmth between her thighs she had known when Sebastian had touched and caressed her so intimately the evening before….

Sebastian's mouth thinned. 'I agree the truth needs to be established. But,' he added firmly, 'I refuse to condemn Lady Boyd on what amounts to superficial evidence.'

William Bancroft gave an inclination of his head. 'I am pleased to hear it.'

Sebastian's gaze narrowed suspiciously. 'You are?'

'But of course.' The older man resumed his seat behind the leather-topped desk. 'That is the very reason we are having this conversation.'

'Explain yourself, if you please.'

'Seb—'

'Do not concern yourself, Grayson,' the Earl interjected. 'St Claire is quite right to advise caution. To accuse someone of treason is a serious business. And while Lady Boyd—this French agent—remained inactive, indeed there was no need for haste. The fact that she—or he— is now back amongst us, prepared to take up their treasonous role once more, has changed things somewhat. I should, of course, have had this conversation with you some weeks ago, St Claire, when you first spoke to my wife concerning your interest in the Countess of Crestwood. I delayed doing so only because I felt it best to wait and see if the lady returned your interest.'

'She does not.'

'Oh, we believe that she does.' The earl smiled knowingly.

'Then you believe wrongly.' Sebastian glared coldly at the older man. 'Lady Boyd has strongly resisted all my advances.'

'She is naturally cautious, I admit.' The older man nodded. 'But I have known the lady for some years, dined with her and Crestwood on a number of occasions, and as such I have had ample time in which to study her. She is a woman of reticence. Of reserve. So much so that she is polite to all but allows none close to her. You have managed to breach that reserve on several occasions in the last few days, I believe…?'

'Damn it, I refuse to discuss a lady in this way!'

'You do not need to do so, St Claire. Dolly is talking with Lady Boyd even as we speak. I have no doubt that she will ably ascertain whether or not the lady has developed a…*tendre* for you.'

'You go too far, sir!' Sebastian could never remember feeling so angry with anyone before.

'I go as far as I need!' the Earl assured him evenly. 'If Lady Boyd is guilty of all we suspect, then I consider my actions as necessary as a soldier's in battle when confronted with the enemy.'

'*If* she is guilty!' Sebastian repeated pointedly. 'Until you have positive proof of that I, for one, will not condemn the lady.'

'I was hoping that you might feel that way….'

He eyed the older man suspiciously, even as a nerve pulsed in his tightly clenched jaw. 'Exactly what are you suggesting…?'

William Bancroft eyed him speculatively. 'Why, that you find some way to go about either proving or disproving the lady's innocence, of course.'

'*Some way?* What way do you have in mind, exactly?' Sebastian wanted to know.

The other man shrugged. 'A man and a woman are apt to discuss many things once the bedding is over.'

Sebastian stared at the other man as if he had gone completely insane. Bancroft *must* be insane if he really thought that Sebastian could play

Juliet so false. Was this Dolly's idea of what Sebastian should do in order to change his life from one of idleness and pleasure?

Family. Honour. Loyalty to friends…

Those were the things Sebastian had last night informed Juliet Boyd he took seriously. To behave in the way William Bancroft described—to bed Juliet, make love to her, with the sole intention of discovering her innocence or guilt in treason and murder—would be to behave completely without honour.

But if the Countess of Crestwood really *was* as guilty as Bancroft seemed to think, then did not Sebastian also owe it to Lucian, to all his brother's friends, so many of whom had fallen at Waterloo, to apprehend someone who might have been instrumental in aiding Bonaparte's escape from Elba and so precipitated that bloody battle?

Which left loyalty to friends…

The Earl gave a weary sigh. 'I am well aware of what we ask of you, St Claire, and appreciate that you will need some time to think on it.'

'Why do you not merely question the lady and be done with it?' Sebastian, despite that loyalty he felt towards Lucian, was still loath to agree to such a nefarious and ungentlemanly plan.

'As I have already explained, while Agent J was inactive there was no haste to do anything but keep a silent watch. Now that Agent J *is* active again we stand a chance of locating and ultimately arresting a whole network of French agents. Besides, at this moment in time we do not have enough evidence to either question the Countess in connection with treason and murder or indeed clear her name of all such charges.'

He was asking Sebastian to find and then produce that evidence….

His gaze narrowed on the two men. 'And if I had not succeeded in finding favour with the Countess? Who was to take my place in her bed then? You, Gray?' He looked accusingly at the other man, knowing by the way Gray moved uncomfortably in his chair that his surmise was a correct one. 'You are both mad, I think!'

'Your own brother returned from Waterloo, Seb. Mine did not.' Gray's face was pale and tense.

Sebastian's fingers involuntarily clenched into purposeful bunches of five. What would Hawk do in such a situation? What would Lucian do if offered the chance of avenging some of the friends he'd lost at Waterloo?

'And if I refuse?' He eyed the Earl warily.

'Then be assured I will take your place, Seb,' Gray told him bluntly. 'I feel no reservation, no hesitation in attempting to woo and win the Countess's confidence. I will bed her, too, if it will give us the answers we require.'

Gray to flatter and charm Juliet? *Gray* to seduce her? To bed her? Never!

'I feel no hesitation, either, in giving you both my answer,' Sebastian said stiffly.

Gray sat forward anxiously. 'Seb, I ask that you do not act in haste—'

'You no longer have any part in this conversation, Gray,' he told his friend. 'The two of us will talk together at some later date about the role you have played in this farce.' A later date when Sebastian was not so angry he felt like striking Gray rather than talking to him, his steely tone warned! He turned back to Lord Bancroft. 'I will endeavour to engage the Countess's interest further,' he accepted, feeling utter distaste for such deceit. 'But only on the understanding that I do this for Juliet Boyd's own sake, and not your own,' he added firmly. 'When I have assured you of her innocence, I will then expect you to apologise both to her and to me.'

If Sebastian succeeded in assuring these two men of Juliet's innocence....

Chapter Seven

'You look perfectly lovely this evening, Juliet.' Helena beamed at her approvingly as Juliet stood in front of the cheval mirror, studying her reflection.

Her cousin, restless from being confined to her room for two days now, had this evening insisted that she was recovered sufficiently from her fall to come downstairs and help Juliet prepare for dinner. Juliet knew she should have insisted that Helena rest her ankle further, but she had nevertheless appreciated her cousin's help in dressing and arranging her hair. She wanted to look her best this evening.

Following her candid conversation earlier today with Dolly Bancroft, she had decided to give Sebastian St Claire the opportunity in which to make his apologies to her, at least. The rest of Dolly's advice she was less sure about!

Unfortunately there had been no opportunity to see or speak with Lord St Claire after talking to Dolly. He had gone out riding late this morning, and had not returned until much later in the afternoon. So this evening would be the first available opportunity Juliet would have to see him again. And for him to see her.

Dolly had advised that Juliet take Sebastian as her lover. The question was, did Juliet *wish* to take a lover? Not if, as she had always thought, all men were as brutish as Crestwood had been! Dolly's description of her own relationship with William Bancroft seemed to imply that they were not, but still Juliet felt uneasy—

She was getting far ahead of herself!

After their two fallings out there was absolutely no reason to presume that Sebastian still wished to become her lover….

Sebastian paid little attention to his fellow guests as they gathered in the drawing room before dinner, his mood not improved since that morning, despite riding for an hour across the countryside in order that he might pay an unexpected call upon Lucian and his bride of less than one month at their own Hampshire estate.

The recently married couple had welcomed him most warmly; it had been Sebastian's own distraction that had prevented him from enjoying the visit. Within a few minutes of his arrival Sebastian had known that he should not have gone there. Lucian was so obviously happy with his bride, and Sebastian's word to Bancroft prevented him from discussing with his brother any of the conversation of this morning in any case.

There was no one, it seemed—not Lucian, not Gray, not Dolly—with whom Sebastian could talk about the web of intrigue in which he now found himself entangled.

The fact that Juliet Boyd looked breathtaking and innocently lovely as she entered the drawing room at that moment did not improve Sebastian's temper. To such an extent that he realised he was actually scowling across the room at her as she fell into conversation with the Duchess of Essex.

Juliet's gown this evening was of cream satin and lace that complemented perfectly the pearly translucence of her skin, its low neckline revealing the full swell of her breasts. The darkness of her hair was arranged artfully in tiny curls about the beauty of her face and nape, the green of her eyes made all the deeper by a fringe of thick dark lashes and her mouth a full and sensuous pout.

Sebastian stiffened as she turned and seemed deliberately to meet his gaze, leaving him with no other choice but to make an abrupt bow of acknowledgement before turning immediately away again, his hands clenching tightly at his sides.

This was going to be so much harder than he had imagined if he could not even bring himself to relax when Juliet was only in the same room as himself. How on earth would he get close enough to her to ascertain her innocence if he did not get a firmer grip on his emotions? After all, he was ultimately doing this with the intention of proving her innocence to those who seemed all too ready to believe in her guilt.

'Good evening, Lord St Claire.'

For the first time in their acquaintance Juliet Boyd had approached *him*! Yesterday Sebastian would have rejoiced in that fact. Today he could not rid himself of the weight of duplicity pressing down upon him so heavily.

'Can it be that you are still angry with me, My Lord...?'

Juliet felt nervous, and not a little foolish, as she attempted to flirt with Sebastian. She had watched other women do it for years, of course, but it was a different matter entirely to behave in such a fashion herself. There had been little occasion for her to do so during her one and only Season, and Edward would have dealt with her most severely if he had so much as suspected her of flirtation during their marriage.

But if she and Lord St Claire did not talk to each other, how was he to be persuaded into making his apologies to her?

He looked so very handsome this evening, too, in a tailored black superfine, snowy white linen beneath a waistcoat of the palest silver, white pantaloons fitted quite shamefully to the long muscled length of his hips and thighs, and polished black Hessians.

Ordinarily Juliet knew she would not have noticed how perfectly a man's clothes were tailored to him. That she did so now where

Sebastian was concerned was due, she had no doubt, to the candidness of Dolly Bancroft's conversation that morning.

Juliet felt warm just looking at him as she recalled that conversation. She was totally aware of the width of his shoulders and muscled chest. The flatness of his stomach. The promised power of his thighs…

Oh, dear Lord!

Juliet flicked her fan open and wafted it up and down in front of her face in an effort to cool her burning cheeks.

His gaze was narrowed as he looked down at her. 'I believe it is *you* who were angry with *me*, ma'am,' he pointed out rather curtly.

Juliet tried to remember how, over the years, she had seen other women behave in the presence of such an attractive man as he.

A glance from beneath lowered lashes, perhaps?

No, that had only made him scowl all the more!

A mysterious little smile that hinted at invitation?

No, that had only made him narrow his gaze on her questioningly!

Perhaps she should just be herself, after all? Sebastian had seemed to find that attractive enough yesterday evening, when he'd made love to her so illicitly.

Juliet snapped her fan closed and gave up every pretence of flirtation. 'We both know I have good reason to be angry with you, Lord St Claire.'

'Then I wonder you have troubled yourself to seek me out,' he retorted.

Her smile was brittle. 'I did not "seek you out", as you call it, Lord St Claire. I was merely passing this way in order to talk to Lord Grayson, and it would have been rude of me not to have acknowledged you at least. If you will excuse me…? My Lord!' she exclaimed sharply as Sebastian reached out and grasped her wrist, so that she could not escape without drawing attention to the two of them. 'You are hurting my wrist, sir!' Her eyes flashed up at him warningly.

Sebastian would have liked to do more than hurt Juliet Boyd's wrist—he wanted to wring her damned neck! First she threw him completely off balance by approaching him. Then she seemed almost to have been flirting with him, before transforming into her usual waspish self. This woman was such a tangle of contradictions she had Sebastian tied up in knots!

He gave a hard smile. 'Take my advice, Juliet, and stay well away from Lord Grayson.'

'I *beg* your pardon?'

She looked so outraged. So indignant. So hurt... Yes, this woman was a mass of contradictions that promised to drive Sebastian quietly out of his mind!

His grip on her wrist gentled and he pulled her slowly towards him, watching as her eyes opened wider and wider as he pulled her ever closer. Until she stood so near to him their bodies almost touched. Until he could see the quick rise and fall of her breasts. The trembling of her slightly parted lips. Feel the softness of her breath against his throat.

God, he wanted to crush Juliet's lips beneath his own. Just as he longed to rip the gown from her body before making love to her until she screamed out in pleasure. Until she screamed out her innocence!

The image of making love to her formed so vividly in his mind that Sebastian felt his thighs hardening. Throbbing. Aching...

His jaw clenched. 'You are playing a dangerous game, my lady!'

Juliet blinked her confusion. 'Game, My Lord? I have no idea what—'

'I am sorry to interrupt, but it is time to go into dinner.'

Juliet turned blankly to look at Dolly Bancroft, where she stood beside them, smiling. The Duke of Essex stood to one side, waiting to escort their hostess in to dinner, but otherwise the drawing room had emptied of the other twenty or so guests.

Leaving Sebastian once again to escort Juliet into dinner….

Something she was sure neither of them desired after this latest heated exchange.

Far from feeling remorse at the wrong he had done her this morning, Sebastian seemed almost angry with her. Coldly, remorselessly so. And Juliet had seen far too much coldness and remorselessness during her marriage to Crestwood to tolerate any more of it.

'How kind of you to wait for me, Your Grace.' She stepped away from Sebastian to place her hand upon the Duke of Essex's arm, thereby allowing him to escort her into dinner. The Duke was far too much the gentleman to point out that she had taken Dolly Bancroft's place.

Sebastian's eyes blazed deeply golden as he turned from watching Juliet's departure on the arm of the Duke of Essex. 'Do not!' he grated, as Dolly Bancroft would have spoken as he offered her his arm. He had no intention of discussing her husband's conversation of this morning with her. Or indeed anything else!

'Did I not initially try to persuade you from your interest in Juliet?' Dolly nevertheless attempted.

'*Before* you saw that my interest could be to your husband's advantage?' Sebastian scorned. 'Perhaps one day I may be able to forgive you for this, Dolly—but it is certainly not going to be today!'

'Life cannot always be a game, Sebastian.' She sounded wistful.

Sebastian looked down at her bleakly. 'When all of this is over I think it best if you and I do not meet again for some time.'

The hurt she felt was reflected in the deep blue of her eyes, but the inclination of her head was as gracious as always. 'As you wish.'

What Sebastian wished was that he had never seen Juliet Boyd. Never desired to bed her. Never come to Banford Park in pursuit of her. More than anything else he wished he could just leave here today, now, and forget he had ever been told of the suspicions harboured against her.

But Sebastian's sense of fair play, his honour, his loyalty, said that he could do none of those things. That, no matter how Juliet might one day despise him for his actions, he owed it to her to see that she was given every opportunity to prove herself innocent of Bancroft's accusations.

Or not…

'Are you feeling unwell, Juliet…?' Helena hovered behind her as she sat in front of the mirror. Juliet had dismissed her cousin once she had helped her out of her gown, wishing to be alone when she removed the pins from her hair, but Helena's glance at her reflection showed Juliet's face to be exceedingly pale, the green of her eyes the only colour, and there was a frown of tension upon her brow.

Altogether it had not been a successful evening. Yet another unpleasant exchange with Sebastian St Claire had occurred. Followed by a lengthy dinner when Juliet had found herself seated between two gentlemen who wished only to converse on fox hunting and their hounds. She had then been persuaded into partnering Lord Grayson in a game of whist, all the time aware of Sebastian as he sat at the next table, partner to the beautiful Lady Butler. Juliet's distraction at the other woman's obviously flirtatious manner had been such that she and Grayson had lost miserably. Juliet had been relieved when she could at last excuse herself and retire to her bedchamber.

The greatest disappointment, of course, had been the way Sebastian had seemed too preoccupied to notice her. For the first time in her life Juliet had deliberately set out to see if she could attract the attention of a certain man, and the man had shown her nothing but indifference!

'I have a slight headache, that is all,' she assured her cousin ruefully. 'But I am perfectly capable of taking down my own hair. It would please me if you would go back upstairs and rest your ankle.' She smiled encouragingly, knowing that she wished only to be alone to lick the wounds to her pride.

She maintained that smile until Helena turned and left the bedchamber, only relaxing into dejection once she knew herself to be completely alone.

What Juliet would have really liked to do was go out onto her balcony and breathe in some of the warm summer air. But she was loath to do so after the last time she had done just that. It would be too humiliating if by chance Sebastian happened to find her there once again. If he were to assume that she was deliberately trying to attract his attention.

Not that it was particularly likely; if Sebastian had already retired to any bedchamber then it was probably Lady Butler's!

Sebastian was sprawled atop the bedcovers in a state of disarray, drinking brandy copiously, when he heard the first scream.

It had not been easy to turn down Lady Butler's obvious invitation to retire with her to her bedchamber, without causing offence, but somehow Sebastian had managed it. As he had also managed to procure a decanter of brandy and a glass from a footman, before mounting the staircase two steps at a time and then striding to his bedchamber to close the door firmly behind him.

Watching Gray's solicitations to Juliet Boyd for two hours had induced a need in Sebastian not to see or speak to anyone else this evening. He had thrown open the doors out onto his balcony before undressing down to his pantaloons, his intention to lie down upon his bed and get roaring drunk before hopefully falling into an unconscious stupor.

The fear and desperation he heard in Juliet's scream wiped all thought of sleep from Sebastian's mind, and he slammed his glass down on the bedside table before jumping to his bare feet.

It did not even occur to him to use the door out into the hallway. He rushed out onto his balcony to vault over the top of the ridiculous barrier before throwing open the door to Juliet's room, fearful of what or who he might find there.

The bedchamber was lit by a single candle placed on the dressing table, its reflection in the mirror behind adding more light to the room.

The bedchamber showed only one occupant. Juliet.

She lay alone in the centre of the bed, her fingers tightly clutching the bedclothes to her chest as she tossed and turned her head on the pillow.

Her eyes were firmly closed.

Sebastian stood very still beside the bed as he

looked down at her. That Juliet was still sleeping, probably completely unaware that she had cried out, was obvious.

Her hair was a midnight curtain on the pillow beneath her. Her shoulders were bare, except for the thin straps of a white silk nightgown, and the revealed swell of her breasts was full and creamy.

Sebastian felt the fierceness of his expression soften as he took in how beautiful she looked. How fragile. How utterly—

'No!' Juliet suddenly cried out again, her eyes still closed but her features contorted. 'Do not! Please do not!' She sat up abruptly in the bed, her eyes wide and fearful as she stared straight ahead. 'Please!' she groaned achingly once again, before burying her face in her hands and beginning to sob.

Her distress was unbearable. Certainly more than Sebastian could bear anyway!

He quickly sat down on the side of the bed to reach out and draw her into his arms. 'You are safe, Juliet,' he assured her fiercely. 'There is no one here who shall harm you.' His arms tightened about her and he held her cradled against his chest.

* * *

Juliet froze as she became aware of bare flesh beneath her cheek.

Arms like steel bands were about her, holding her so tightly she could not break free.

Crestwood!

He was here. In her bedchamber. And if he was here it could mean only one thing!

She could not bear it. Not again. Never again could she lie unmoving, silent, while he—

No, Crestwood was *not* here!

He could not be here.

Crestwood was dead….

Then who was holding her so tightly?

The skin Juliet felt beneath her breast was smooth and deeply muscled, rather than pale and lined, with no sign of that flabbiness of flesh she had become used to in a man thirty years her senior, and the softness of hair that covered this chest and stomach was dark rather than coarsely grey.

Juliet raised her gaze almost fearfully to the firmness of jaw, and above chiselled lips, a long aquiline nose, high cheekbones, eyes the colour of honey, and dark hair shot through with gold in rumpled disarray onto the broadness of those wide shoulders.

'Lord St Claire!' she gasped in recognition, even as she attempted to pull away from him. His arms tightened to prevent her. 'You must release me, My Lord!' She breathed unevenly.

'Why must I?' His voice sounded dark and mesmerising in the silence of the bedchamber.

'Because—because—you should not be here, Sebastian,' Juliet whispered shakily. 'Why did you come?' She pulled back slightly to look into the brooding darkness of his face.

Such a handsome face. So sinfully, magnificently handsome…

Sebastian's breath caught in his throat as he looked into the deep green of Juliet's eyes. 'You do not remember, do you?'

Her throat moved convulsively as she swallowed. 'Remember what, My Lord?'

'You called me Sebastian just now,' he reminded her huskily. 'And I am here because you cried out loudly in your sleep and I heard you.' His eyes narrowed as he saw the sudden wariness in her expression before her gaze dropped away from his. 'Who did this to you,

Juliet? Who has hurt you enough that you are plagued by nightmares that make you cry out even in sleep?'

Her face had been pale before, but now it grew even paler. 'I do not know what you mean, My Lord—'

'Do not lie to me, Juliet,' he warned harshly, his hands grasping the tops of her arms as she would have pulled away from him. 'Did Crestwood do this to you? Did he frighten you in some way? Is that why you—?' He broke off, his jaw tight.

She raised startled eyes. 'Why I what, Sebastian?'

She was so beautiful, so utterly desirable as Sebastian held her soft lushness in his arms, that he did not want to think of anything else—to see or feel anything but Juliet. At this moment she was all that mattered.

Juliet knew Sebastian was going to kiss her the moment she saw the hunger in his gaze as it dropped to the softness of her lips. Knew it. And craved it…

She had no memory of calling out in her sleep or of what she had said. But she could imagine what it might have been. She had been dreaming of Crestwood. Of how so often he had hurt her. How there had never been anyone there, ever, to stop him from hurting her.

Not so tonight. Tonight Sebastian St Claire was here. In her bedchamber. Not Lady Butler's, as Juliet had imagined. And Juliet *wanted* him to hold her. To kiss her. To caress her. To block out and destroy for ever all those painful memories of Crestwood that so tormented and disturbed her.

'Juliet…?' St Claire groaned as she raised her lips willingly to his.

Such a strong and sensuous mouth as it claimed hers. His shoulders were hard and muscled beneath Juliet's fingers as she clung to him. He felt so firm and smooth, and the muscles rippled beneath the warmth of his skin. Those muscles told her that no one would get past him, that if she wished it he would protect her.

Even from a ghost…

Her eyes closed and her lips parted willingly beneath the gentle sweep of his tongue. That tongue flicked lightly over her inner lip and the small ridge of her teeth before exploring further as it moved teasingly against hers.

Sebastian felt the leap of his body and the hardening of his thighs as Juliet's tongue began a sensuous duel with his. Moving enticingly forward, before retreating, tempting him deeper still. Her warm curves pressed against him were driving him wild with desire, and he could hold back no longer as he thrust fully inside her mouth, to possess her with his tongue.

It was not enough. It would never be enough with this particular woman. Sebastian wanted all of her. Wanted every part of her to be his!

Even as his mouth continued to claim hers, he slipped the thin ribbon straps from her shoulders and down her arms, moving slightly to let the material fall down to her waist before he pulled her back against him, crushing her bared breasts against his chest. Such softness. Such warm, tempting softness. A softness Sebastian had so longed to touch, to kiss.

He moved one of his hands to cup beneath one of those gentle slopes, testing the weight of her breast against his palm, able to feel if not see the pout of her nipple. Knowing even as he ran the pad of his thumb against that pouting softness and felt it harden that he had to have it in his mouth so that he might pleasure her with his tongue.

Juliet felt bereft when Sebastian pulled his mouth from hers to look down at her with eyes of dark honey-gold that seemed to be asking her a question.

'Do not stop, Sebastian,' she pleaded huskily. 'Please, do not stop!'

Whatever question had been in his eyes, she appeared to have answered it, and his gaze continued to hold hers as he lowered his head to place his caressing lips against the gentle curve between her neck and shoulder. Those lips were feather light as they moved lower. And then lower still.

Juliet gasped, her nails digging into his shoulders as she realised his destination. 'Sebastian…?'

'Let me, Juliet.' He raised his head to take one of her hands in his and kiss the palm, before placing it down on the bed beside her and then doing the same with its twin. 'I promise I will not hurt you.' His eyes looked intently into hers. 'I will never hurt you. Do you believe me?'

She moistened her lips with the tip of her tongue, her eyes wide and apprehensive as she reached to clutch and pull the material of her nightgown up over the bareness of her breasts. 'What—what are you going to do?'

'Nothing you will not enjoy, I promise.' He made no effort to touch her, to use physical coercion of any kind. 'Do you trust me not to hurt you, Juliet?'

Did she trust him? If she said no would he stop now? If she said no at some later point would he still stop?

Sebastian could read the thoughts racing through Juliet's mind. Could read them—and wanted to do physical harm to the man who had caused such apprehension inside her. Sebastian was convinced now that it had to have been Crestwood. Even Bancroft, suspicious and accusing, had agreed there had been no other man in Juliet's life this last twelve years but her husband.

Damn Bancroft! Now was not the time to think of either the man or any of the things he had said to Sebastian this morning.

His hands moved up to gently frame either side of Juliet's face.

'Tonight is for you, Juliet. Only for you.'

Much as it might kill him, Sebastian meant to

give this woman pleasure—as much pleasure as she could take—whilst taking nothing for himself but the knowledge of that pleasure. Whatever will-power it took, whatever he suffered later, Sebastian was determined to replace that look of fear on Juliet's face, in the dark green depths of her eyes, with one of joy.

'Juliet…?' he prompted gruffly.

Juliet remained unmoving, not even breathing as she looked at him. Her gaze was seeking. Probing. Searching, no doubt, for any sign in his expression that said he lied. Sebastian's gaze remained fixed and steady on hers.

'Yes,' she finally breathed. 'Yes, Sebastian, I will trust you.' She allowed the material of her nightgown to fall softly down to her waist.

Chapter Eight

Sebastian moved back slightly, so that he might drink his fill of her. The candle-light added a glow to skin as smooth and white as unmarked snow, and the long length of her ebony hair cascaded silkily over her shoulders, down the length of her slender back and waist.

Her breasts were perfect. Not too large and not too small, but a perfect pouting swell, the nipples a deep rose-pink, the tips full and still aroused from his earlier caresses.

'Do not be afraid, Juliet, I am only going to kiss your breasts,' he assured her gently, when he saw the tension in her face and the sudden rigidity of her shoulders.

Juliet swallowed hard, not sure what he meant—until he lay across her thighs and she felt the warmth of his lips and mouth close about the tip of her breast. She gasped slightly as heat coursed through her body the moment she felt the rasp of his tongue against the sensitive nipple.

Her back curved instinctively as she arched into that caress, her eyes wide as she looked down at him. His eyelids were closed as he drew her more fully into his mouth, the slight drawing sending strange, pleasurable sensations through her body to centre between her thighs.

Juliet's arms moved up—one to curve about Sebastian's shoulders, the other to cradle the back of his head, her fingers entwining in the silky thickness of his hair as she held him to her.

His hand moved to cup and hold her other breast, the pad of his thumb moving caressingly across its tip. Juliet watched as the nipple swelled and hardened beneath his ministrations.

Until now her body had always been a mystery to her, something that Crestwood had taken whenever he pleased but which Juliet had tried not to even acknowledge existed in between those times. She had believed that her breasts were only there to suckle the child she had never had, but now, as her body trembled and warmed, as a low groan escaped her throat, she became aware of how sensuous, how pleasurable it was to have a man touch her in this way.

She made a protesting movement when Sebastian released that hardened tip, that movement turning to a moan of pleasure as he turned the attentions of his mouth and tongue to her other breast.

Juliet had no idea what was happening to her as the warmth increased between her thighs and she felt herself swelling there, aching as Sebastian continued to kiss and stroke her breasts, teeth gently biting as he rolled her other nipple between thumb and finger, squeezing slightly, never painfully, just enough to increase the intensity of her pleasure.

He was such a big man, so strong and muscled, and yet he made love to her with a gentleness that totally belied that strength. That gentleness encouraged Juliet to start touching him tentatively in return.

Sebastian groaned low in his throat as he felt Juliet's hands moving, caressing, as she sought out the muscled contours of his back and chest. His thighs, already hard with arousal, tightened and throbbed as he drew her deeper into his mouth, laving that hardened tip even as he increased the pressure of his caresses on its twin.

She fell back against the pillows and Sebastian followed, only relinquishing her breast to kiss the flatness of her stomach, the erotic dip of her navel. Juliet gasped, but didn't protest as Sebastian dipped his tongue into that hollow, filling it as he longed to fill all of her.

Her nightgown was still draped across her hips and thighs, hindering any further exploration. 'May I?' he asked, and he moved up on his knees to look at her, taking the silent blinking of her eyes as a yes before he pulled back the bedclothes. Slowly he peeled her gown down over her hips and thighs, revealing the triangle of black curls between her legs. 'No.' Sebastian stilled her hand as she would have covered herself. 'You are very beautiful, Juliet. All of you,' he assured her huskily, as he bent to place a kiss on those silky curls. She smelled deliciously of spring flowers and woman.

Juliet was too shocked to speak, to protest any further as Sebastian threw her gown onto the floor beside the bed, leaving her completely uncovered. She kept her gaze fixed on his face rather than look down at her own nakedness.

His hair fell silkily onto his shoulders, his chest and the flatness of his stomach as naked as Juliet now was. His eyes were dark as he looked down at her, his gaze moving slowly, caressingly across her breasts to the gentle curve of her own stomach, and then lower still, that gaze becoming hungry as it stilled on the darkness of the curls between her thighs.

Juliet felt very hot there, strangely damp, was sure that her curls were wet, too. She moved as if to stop him as he gently parted her legs. 'No—'

'Yes, Juliet,' Sebastian encouraged throatily, and he moved to kneel between her parted legs, holding her gaze with his as one of his hands moved to cup between her thighs just as he had the night before. Except tonight two of his fingers parted her silky curls to touch her more intimately.

Juliet's eyes widened as those two fingers squeezed slightly together, trapping something there and causing a fresh rush of heated wetness between her legs. 'What—?' she gasped.

'It is the centre of your pleasure, Juliet,' Sebastian reassured her, his gaze holding hers captive as his fingers began to stroke her. First softly and then gradually more firmly.

Again and again those fingers stroked, until Juliet felt so hot, such a burning ache, she wasn't sure if she wanted him to stop or continue. Her fingers dug into the mattress beside her as the pressure inside her built and grew to such a degree that she felt she might explode within.

'I am going to kiss you now,' Sebastian murmured.

But instead of moving upwards Sebastian moved down, towards her parted thighs. His fingers released her and his lips took their place, drawing her place of pleasure into his mouth as he rasped his tongue rhythmically against her.

Juliet had never known such intimacy existed. Part of her wanted to protest, but another part of her was eager to know this intimacy. And every other one too....

Again and again Sebastian stroked his tongue across the hard button nestled between Juliet's curls. Then he moved his fingers back to continue that caress and went lower still, his tongue lightly tracing her swollen folds before plunging moistly inside her.

The instinctive arching of her hips allowed him to plunge deeper still, in the same rhythm as his fingers continued to caress that hard button above. The dampness between her thighs increased, flooding her, and Sebastian sensed she was poised on the edge of release.

His mouth returned to that pulsing bud even as his fingers circled her swollen sheath, feeling her contract about his fingers as they entered her one slow inch at a time.

Juliet could feel the pleasure building, growing inside her. A hot ache she could not describe would soon break free and leave her shattered and broken in its wake.

'Sebastian—I cannot! I—' Her protest died in her throat as he moved up to claim her mouth fiercely with his, even as his fingers continued to move into and then out of her, his thumb caressing that tiny nub above with the same slow and sensuous rhythm.

His tongue plunged into her mouth at the same time as his fingers claimed her below, this dual assault on her senses driving her into a frenzy of need as her hips moved up to meet those thrusts.

The release, when it came, was like nothing

Juliet had ever dreamed of—beginning between her thighs in a hot burst, before spreading outwards to claim every part of her as she inwardly convulsed in a continuous outpouring of unimagined pleasure until she finally lay spent beneath him.

No one had ever told Juliet—she had never dreamt—would never have guessed… She had never known that such pleasure as this existed!

It was beyond description. Beyond anything she could have imagined.

Sebastian broke the kiss as he gently slid his fingers from inside her, cradling Juliet in his arms, resting his head against her temple as her body continued to quiver and spasm in little aftershocks of pleasure.

Her release had been so beautiful, so complete, that the unfulfilled ache of Sebastian's own body did not signify. All that mattered at this moment was Juliet. He wanted only to give her pleasure, to feel her pleasure. His own arousal was unimportant.

Finally she stirred slightly in his arms. 'You did not— You have not—'

'Neither will I.' Sebastian moved up on his

elbow to look down searchingly into her flushed and beautiful face. 'Have you never known that pleasure before?'

The blush in her cheeks deepened. 'Never,' she breathed huskily.

What sort of man had Crestwood been? Sebastian wondered angrily. What sort of man could even *look* at Juliet and not want to give her pleasure time and time again?

'Have you never discovered these pleasures for yourself, Juliet?' he asked, with caution for her obvious shyness with intimacy. 'Are you not familiar with your own body?' he added as she looked confused.

'I have arms, legs—and—other parts of my body, like any other woman.' She still looked puzzled.

'But when bathing or dressing have you never…explored your own body? Touched your intimate places? Learnt of the pleasure they might give you?' Sebastian persisted.

Juliet looked shocked by the suggestion. 'Of course I have not!'

Sebastian gave a slight shake of his head. Juliet was thirty years old, had been married for over ten of those years; it was unbelievable to think that he was the first to ever give her pleasure.

'Give me your hand…' He held his own hand out to her, palm upwards.

'Why?' She eyed him suspiciously.

'Please?'

She moved her hand up reluctantly and placed it in his, gasping as she realised his intent when he took it and guided it down between her thighs. 'Sebastian…!'

'I only want to show you, Juliet, nothing more,' he encouraged huskily as she would have wrenched her hand away. 'Just feel. Touch…'

Juliet had never done anything so shameless. Had never even thought of—

She was not just damp between her legs, but wet. So very wet. The folds of her sheath still felt swollen and sensitive. It was such a strange…

She gave a start as Sebastian guided her fingers to that nub hidden amongst her curls. It felt hard still, and the caress of her fingers caused another quake of pleasure inside her.

She looked up at him in wonder. 'Are my breasts still as sensitive too…?'

'Feel,' he said gruffly, once again leaning on

his elbow as Juliet raised her hands to cup her breasts, before running a fingertip lightly across one nipple.

Again her thighs contracted hotly. 'I had no idea…' she gasped.

Sebastian smiled wickedly. 'Tonight is for you, Juliet. Only for you.'

Her hands fell back to her sides, her eyes deep, dark pools of green as she stared back at him. 'I still do not understand why you have not taken your own pleasure.'

His smile was gentle as he smoothed a dark curl from the dampness of her brow. 'The only thing I require tonight is pleasuring you,' he assured her.

Juliet really did not understand. What she had just felt, experienced when Sebastian made love to her, was unlike anything she could ever have imagined. But she knew well enough a man's need for release. And Sebastian had not attained the release that was all Crestwood, it seemed, had ever wanted or taken from her.

Juliet could see by the long length of arousal so clearly outlined beneath Sebastian's pantaloons that he wanted to take that from her, too.

She swallowed hard. 'I do not mind if you wish to—to take your own release now.'

A frown darkened his brow. 'Is that what Crestwood did to you? Took his own pleasure while giving you nothing in return?'

Her gaze slid away from his. 'Is that not what all men do?'

'Did I?' he pointed out.

She moistened dry lips. 'No, but—I know that you want to.' She glanced down at that telling bulge in his pantaloons, before looking up at him with a quick frown.

Sebastian shook his head. 'What I want and what I do are two entirely different things. I told you, Juliet, tonight is for you.' He reached down to pull the bedcovers up and over the two of them. 'Sleep now,' he murmured. 'And when you wake I intend giving you pleasure all over again.'

'A woman can—can do that twice in one night?' she gasped.

He smiled at her surprise. 'If the man knows what he is doing, as many times as she wants or needs.'

'Is that not a little unfair, when a man can only do it the once?'

She really was an innocent, Sebastian realised with dawning wonder. 'Some men can find release several times in one night,' he revealed.

Her eyes widened. 'Can you?'

'With the right woman, yes.' He stroked light fingers down one of her burning cheeks. 'I suspect that with you I might manage to make love all night long without becoming tired or satiated.'

'And yet just now you did not?'

The ache in Sebastian's thighs was becoming more painful by the second with all this talk of his own release. 'Do you know how to give a man pleasure in the way I did you?'

She moistened dry lips. 'There is a—a way to do that?'

Once again Sebastian decided that if Crestwood were alive then he would have no choice but to kill him!

Not that Crestwood was unique in his complete disregard for his wife's pleasure during lovemaking. There would not be as many married women of the ton ready to take a lover if their husbands were satisfying them in their marriage bed!

But Sebastian's father, the late Duke of Stourbridge, had been at great pains to impress upon all three of his sons that when a man took a woman to bed, be she liaison or wife, she was deserving of receiving *all* of his attention—to her pleasure, as well as his own. A man did not selfishly take his pleasure without giving it in return.

Juliet's innocence concerning intimacy, her lack of knowledge of lovemaking, were entirely due, Sebastian now realised, to the fact that her husband had been one of those selfish men who simply took his own pleasure from the woman spread beneath him—from Juliet!—whilst withholding that same pleasure from her.

Yet, at the same time as he wanted to kill Crestwood, Sebastian also knew that he wanted to thank him—for in effect Crestwood's lack of care and attention to Juliet's needs made Sebastian her first real lover. The thought of introducing her, initiating her, into all the pleasures to be had between a man and a woman, was more erotic than anything Sebastian had ever known.

'There is a way.' He nodded. 'But not tonight, Juliet. Tonight, and all of tomorrow too, are only for you.'

'We cannot just spend the day in my bedchamber, Sebastian!' She looked scandalised at the thought.

'Then we shall have to see how inventive we can be at finding other places and opportunities for your pleasure, shall we not?' Sebastian settled down on the pillows and gathered Juliet to his side, so that she rested her head upon his shoulder, before he turned to blow out the candle.

'No!' Juliet cried sharply as she realised his intent. 'I prefer to always leave one candle alight in my bedchamber,' she explained shakily, when Sebastian looked a question at her.

'Why?'

Why? Because Crestwood had always blown out the candle as soon as he entered her bed-chamber with the intention of taking his pleasure! Because in the dark she had not seen, only felt, what he was doing to her! Because at night even now, in the dark of her bedchamber, she would still lie waiting, dreading Crestwood's climbing into her bed and painfully taking her…

'The moon is bright tonight, Juliet. Will that not suffice?' Sebastian asked.

'I wish the candle to remain alight,' she repeated stubbornly, avoiding that searching whisky-coloured gaze as he continued to look down at her.

'Juliet, would you care to talk about—?'

'No!' Again she spoke sharply, trembling slightly just at the thought of reliving any of her marriage after experiencing something so wonderful as Sebastian's lovemaking. 'I wish to sleep now, Sebastian. Only to sleep.' She closed her eyes, effectively shutting him out.

Sebastian lay awake long after he knew by the even tenor of her breathing that Juliet was asleep.

She was a woman of almost one and thirty, and must have known of all the gossip and speculation she would have to face in agreeing to come here to Banford Park. Yet she had met that controversy with all the grace and confidence of the countess she undoubtedly was. But here, in the privacy of her bedchamber, she became the young and naïve eighteen-year-old girl she must have been when Crestwood had married her, twelve years ago.

There were many more ways, Sebastian realised, for a man to abuse a woman than with his fists....

'You wish us to go boating on the lake?' Juliet was wide-eyed as she repeated Sebastian's suggestion as to what they might do for the rest of the morning. The rest of the morning because it was now almost noon…

Juliet had been slightly disorientated when she'd awoken early that morning to find Sebastian St Claire in bed beside her. Even more disconcerting had been the memory of waking in the night and finding herself once more aroused by the feel Sebastian's lips and hands upon her body as he made love to her for a second time. As she found pleasure and release for a second time!

Sebastian had not apologised to her for his conversation with Dolly, after all, but last night he had done so much more for her than that. Last night, for the very first time, Juliet had known and appreciated fully what it was to be a woman. To enjoy intimacy with a man.

Sebastian had been lying on his stomach beside her, still sleeping, when she'd awoken later, and Juliet had indulged herself for a few minutes by just looking at him. That dark hair shot through with gold had been tousled on the pillow, lashes of the same colour resting against high cheekbones. His was a strong face rather than hard, his features chiselled but not unrelenting, the mocking curve of his mouth softened in sleep. The bareness of his shoulders were firm and muscled, his back long and sensual, almost begging to be touched. A temptation Juliet had not been able to resist as she ran her fingertips lightly over that golden flesh.

Yesterday, after talking with Dolly Bancroft, Juliet had wondered how it would feel to take a lover. Now she knew. It was truly wonderful. Liberating, in fact. As Juliet had quickly discovered when her caresses had become bolder still.

Sebastian's lids had risen over eyes the colour of warm honey, and the smile he'd given her had been slow and seductive. 'Again…?'

'Again…' Juliet had groaned happily, past all pretence where Sebastian was concerned; he knew her body far better than she did, so how could she possibly feel any lingering shyness with him?

They had spent another enjoyable hour in bed together before Juliet had reminded Sebastian that her maid would be arriving shortly to bring her breakfast and then help her to dress. Muttering about only having to undress her again once he returned, Sebastian had kissed her briefly on the lips before climbing smilingly out of bed and crossing the room, to depart out onto the balcony to his own bedchamber.

Only just in time as Helena had entered, after the briefest of knocks, with Juliet's breakfast tray. Obviously her cousin had not for a moment expected that Juliet might not be alone in her bedchamber!

Spending the night in bed with Sebastian St Claire, having been introduced by him to the wonders of sensual pleasure, becoming his lover, was not something Juliet felt able to confide in her cousin as yet. It was something to be savoured inside herself for now. A secret for Juliet alone to enjoy.

Just as she had enjoyed Sebastian's return to her bedchamber only minutes after Helena had departed, when, as he had said he would, Sebastian had proceeded to undress her once again, before undressing himself!

Now, an hour later, Sebastian was suggesting they escape from the company of the other guests by going for that row on the lake he had proposed once before.

Sebastian nodded. 'The house is being readied for the ball this evening. I cannot abide all the fuss and bother that precedes such events,' he admitted ruefully as he continued pulling his black Hessians on over black pantaloons. He was already wearing his pale blue waistcoat over snowy white linen and a perfectly tied cravat. His dark blue superfine was lying across the bedroom chair, where he had thrown it an hour or so ago, after returning to the bedchamber to climb back into bed with Juliet.

He had very much enjoyed making love to Juliet these last twelve hours, and had found pleasure in that look of surprise that entered her eyes, and her little gasps, as her release claimed her. As if she still did not quite believe what was happening to her.

Juliet laughed softly as she restyled her hair in front of the mirror. 'All men are the same, it seems.'

Sebastian straightened swiftly. 'I sincerely hope you no longer believe that to be true.'

Juliet glanced at his reflection in the mirror, her face paling slightly as she looked away from the intensity of his gaze. 'I meant only in regard to fuss and bother, of course.'

'Of course.' Sebastian inclined his head as he stood up to cross the room and stand behind her.

Juliet was looking very lovely, in a rose-pink gown that perfectly complemented the darkness of her hair and the pearly lustre of her skin. There was also an added glow about her this morning: her eyes were deeply green, there was a blush to her cheeks, and her lips were slightly swollen from the intensity of the numerous kisses they had shared.

'I meant no offence, Sebastian.' Her gaze was slightly anxious as she looked up at him in the mirror.

'I am not about to beat you even if you did,' he snapped, as he easily guessed the reason for her anxiety. 'Not all men are like your husband, Juliet!' he rasped.

She stiffened, that becoming blush quickly fading from her cheeks. 'I do not recall ever saying that my husband beat me!'

Sebastian met her gaze challengingly. 'Did he?'

She turned away. 'It is far too lovely a morning to discuss Crestwood.'

'You never wish to discuss him, Juliet. Why is that?'

She stood up abruptly to move away from him,

her back towards him as she collected her gloves. 'My husband has nothing to do with our own… liaison.'

'Liaison?' Sebastian repeated harshly. 'Is that what I am to you?'

'Of course.' She was once again the proud and slightly distant Countess of Crestwood—rather than Juliet, the woman Sebastian had made love to so thoroughly the night before and then again this morning. 'What else could we ever be to each other?' she added with cool dismissal. 'No doubt we will enjoy each other's company for the time we are here. Then you will return to your life and I will return to mine.'

Sebastian looked at her searchingly for several long seconds, knowing by the firm set of Juliet's mouth and slightly raised chin that she would not be moved on the subject of Crestwood.

Damn the man, anyway, for not appreciating such a woman as Juliet when he'd had her!

Sebastian gave a rueful shake of his head. 'I do believe you are trying to bring about an argument between us, Juliet,' he chided.

'You are entitled to your opinion,' she accepted haughtily.

Once again Sebastian felt the inclination to put Juliet over his knee and spank her—but in such a way that she would enjoy the punishment. No doubt Juliet would be as surprised by that as she had been by all their lovemaking!

'I am ready to leave, if you are?' In truth, Juliet did not at all wish to argue with Sebastian. She much preferred it when he was making love to her.

He straightened to give her a courtly bow. 'I am completely at your service, ma'am.' The teasing glitter in those whisky-coloured eyes told her which service he referred to.

Juliet felt the colour warm her cheeks. 'You are incorrigible, Sebastian!'

'So I have oft been told!' He chuckled softly, before opening the door for Juliet to precede him from the bedchamber.

Juliet kept her gaze lowered as she swept past him and out into the hallway, relieved that there was no one about to see the two of them leaving her bedchamber together.

Sebastian's words had reminded her all too forcibly that he was considered a charming libertine by the rest of the ton. The ladies in particular.

The recollection confirmed Juliet's claim earlier

that their own relationship was nothing more than a diversion for Sebastian St Claire in a long career of such diversions. It would be extremely foolish on her part to allow herself to feel any more towards him than a curiosity to learn more of the physical pleasure he had already shown her.

Extremely foolish…

Chapter Nine

'There you are, St Claire!'

Sebastian stiffened as he and Juliet reached the bottom of the wide staircase to turn and see their host approaching them from the direction of his study.

'And Lady Boyd, also.' William Bancroft beamed at Juliet warmly as she rose from her curtsey. 'I hope you do not mind if I take Lord St Claire from you for a few minutes, my dear? There is something of import I wish to discuss with him. And I do believe my wife has been looking for you.'

Sebastian refused to release his hold upon Juliet's elbow when he felt her attempt to move away. Instead he kept his steely gaze fixed on the Earl as he answered the other man. 'Can it not wait until later, Bancroft? I was about to show Lady Boyd the delights of boating on the lake.'

Lord Bancroft met the challenge of Sebastian's gaze. 'A pastime not to be rushed, to be sure. Perhaps, as it is so close to luncheon, *you* could wait until later?'

Sebastian's mouth tightened. 'I—'

'But of course we can wait,' Juliet assured the older man, very much aware of Sebastian's tension as he stood so close beside her. 'Lady Bancroft is looking for me, you said…?'

The Earl smiled easily. 'Something to do with the flowers for this evening, I believe.'

'Of course.' Juliet smiled warmly. 'We can easily arrange our outing for another time, Lord St Claire.' She lowered her own gaze as saw Sebastian's eyes blaze with displeasure as she extricated herself from his grasp. 'I will leave you two gentlemen to talk.' She excused herself, before moving away with the intention of going in search of their hostess.

Perhaps this interruption to spending yet more time alone with Sebastian was for the best, Juliet consoled herself as she made her way to the ballroom. Last night had been a revelation to her, but nevertheless it would not do to become dependent upon such intimacy.

It would not do at all….

'I am in no mood for your schemes and manipulations this morning, Bancroft.' Sebastian made no effort to keep the distaste from his tone as he closely watched Juliet's departure from his side. She had taken the cancellation of their outing far too easily for his liking.

The older man dropped his pose of congenial host. 'No schemes or manipulations this time, St Claire, but facts,' he announced curtly.

'Facts!' Sebastian exclaimed as he gave the other man his full attention. 'What do you have this time, Bancroft? A novel printed in French has been found in Juliet's bedroom, and you believe it may be her code book? That is how it works, is it not? Code books? Secret messages? Or perhaps you have discovered something else you believe brands her as guilty of the crimes you related to me yesterday—?'

'If you will calm down, St Claire, and come with me to my study, then I will show you what we have found.' The earl cut across his tirade.

'We?'

'Lord Grayson is awaiting us in my study.'

Sebastian fixed the other man with a steely glare. 'Did I not tell you both to leave this to me? Was that not our agreement?'

Bancroft shrugged. 'Events have overtaken us, I am afraid.'

As he had the day before, Sebastian felt that cold shiver of apprehension down the length of his spine. He had made love to Juliet last night, not once but many times, and the predominant emotion he had sensed in her was vulnerability. There had been wonder at the pleasures he had introduced her to, but also vulnerability at allowing him so close to her, especially in a physical way. She was innocent of the accusations against her. He was sure of it.

So what did Bancroft have on Juliet that made a nonsense of Sebastian's own estimation of her character?

'You are very quiet this afternoon, My Lord.' Juliet eyed Sebastian teasingly as he sat opposite her, capably handling the oars of the small boat they had commandeered for their delayed row on the huge lake in the gardens of Banford Park. 'Perhaps you would rather we had not come boating, after all?'

He frowned darkly. 'Was I not the one to seek you out after luncheon and suggest we resume our plans?'

Yes, he had. But Sebastian's mood since they had strolled outside and procured one of the row-boats had been taciturn, to say the least. 'Did Lord Bancroft have bad news to relate this morning?' she enquired.

Some would call it that, Sebastian acknowledged grimly. Bancroft and Gray did, at least. Sebastian chose to remain unconvinced.

Apparently the papers on top of Bancroft's desk were not in the same order in which he had left them. And the contents of the drawers, the other man believed, had been gone through. The top drawer, although it showed no signs of having been broken into, was nevertheless unlocked, and Bancroft swore that he always locked that particular drawer whenever he left his study.

Someone—and Bancroft and Gray obviously believed it to be Juliet—had rifled through the papers on and in the Earl's desk some time since the three of them had talked together there yesterday morning, which was the last time Bancroft had been in his study.

Sebastian was more inclined to believe the Earl had simply forgotten to lock the drawer, and that one of the maids had disturbed the papers whilst dusting.

He had certainly left the Earl, and Gray, in no doubt that *he* would need a lot more evidence than that with which to accuse Juliet!

Sebastian forced himself to relax now as he smiled across at her. 'It was merely a trivial estate matter he wished to discuss with me,' he dismissed easily.

Juliet looked so beautiful this afternoon. She was still wearing the high-waisted and short-sleeved rose-coloured gown that suited her dark hair so perfectly. She also wore white gloves, and tilted a rose-coloured parasol above her head, to keep the heat of the sun's rays from burning the pale magnolia of her skin. The revealing swell of her breasts above the low neckline of her gown was enough to make Sebastian's thighs harden in arousal.

'Shall we go onto the island, do you think?' he suggested gruffly.

Juliet felt her cheeks warm as she heard that huskiness in Sebastian's tone. Avoiding looking at the seductive honey of his eyes, she instead turned to look at the island in the middle of the lake. It was rather a large island, with a grove of tall fir trees at its centre. A grove of fir trees that would no doubt shield them from all but the most curious of eyes. A grove of fir trees into which, whilst it was perfectly proper for them to be boating on the lake together, it would be considered totally improper for them to be seen disappearing!

'The ladies are all writing letters or gossiping together in the drawing room this afternoon, and the gentlemen have decided to ride into the village,' Sebastian remarked softly.

Juliet's cheeks felt decidedly hot as she realised he had read her thoughts. 'In that case, I believe I might like to explore the island…'

'It is not the island that I wish you to explore, Juliet,' he murmured as he rowed in the direction of the island's mooring.

She gave him a look of rebuke. 'You should not tease me, Sebastian.'

'But you look so lovely when you blush!' He moved to tie the small boat to the moorings, before climbing out onto the small wooden quay and turning to hold out his hand to her.

Juliet was well aware of what she was agreeing to if she took the hand Sebastian offered and went with him into the privacy of the trees. She was both aware and elated at the thought of yet more pleasure as Sebastian kissed and caressed her. In fact, her body had begun to tingle just at the thought of the pleasures he had already shown her.

'Nevertheless…' She reached up and placed her hand in his before standing. 'It is still unkind of you to mock me in this way.'

'I would never do that, Juliet,' Sebastian assured her seriously, and he placed her gloved hand firmly in the crook of his arm before turning to march towards the woods.

'Are you in hurry, My Lord?' Juliet gasped, as she almost had to run to keep pace with his much longer strides.

Sebastian arched dark brows as he slowed his pace. 'Now it is you who is mocking me, My Lady.'

'I would never do that, Sebastian,' she said teasingly, repeating his own remark.

Sebastian returned her smile and determinedly shook off the last remaining feelings of distaste from his conversation before luncheon with Bancroft and Gray. It was a beautiful day. The sun was shining down upon them warmly. The birds were singing gaily in the trees above. And he had Juliet at his side. Juliet, whose beautiful lushness was begging to be made love to.

It was only when they reached the privacy of the grove of fir trees that Sebastian realised he had come ill prepared for what he now had in mind. Ideally he should have thought to bring a blanket with him, that he could spread upon the ground before laying a naked Juliet down upon it. But no one had ever accused him of being slow when it came to improvisation!

He began to shrug out of his perfectly tailored jacket. His valet would no doubt have a fit when Sebastian returned it to him later today, covered in grass stains, but Laurent's sensibilities were the least of Sebastian's concerns at the moment.

'It will be ruined.' Juliet hesitated about accepting Sebastian's invitation to sit down as he spread the jacket on the grass at her feet.

Sebastian lowered himself elegantly onto the garment before holding his hand up to her invitingly. 'We will only talk, if that is what you would prefer…' he offered, when she still hesitated to join him.

Juliet had no idea what she wanted to do. Well…she *did* know—it was only that even the idea of it now seemed perfectly shameless out here in broad daylight!

Not that she was in the least shy of Sebastian seeing her nakedness any more. After the intimacies they'd already shared how could she possibly be? It was just that it seemed so much more scandalous here in the sunshine, where anyone might chance upon them.

Oh, Juliet knew that the majority of the other house guests were engaged in the activities Sebastian had already described, but what if one or several of them decided that boating on the lake seemed a good idea, too? There would be the most horrendous scandal if she and Sebastian were caught in such a compromising position.

And the Black Widow feared the idea of yet more scandal, did she?

'What shall we talk about?' she asked, as she took Sebastian's hand before lowering herself gracefully down beside him. Shameless. She had become shameless in the matter of hours that had passed since Sebastian had come to her bed-chamber the night before.

He shrugged broad shoulders beneath the full sleeves of his white shirt. 'Your childhood, perhaps? Was it happy?'

'Very.' She gave a wistful sigh as she arranged the skirt of her gown decorously about her legs. 'My parents were everything that is good and kind.'

'Mine also.' He nodded. 'I was sixteen when they both died in a carriage accident,' he added, which surprised even himself. He never talked to anyone of the loss he had felt when his beloved parents had died.

'My own parents had also both died by the time I was eighteen.'

Sebastian at once looked concerned. 'I had not realised…' He reached out to clasp both her tightly clenched hands in his. 'You still miss them?'

'Always. You?'

'Always,' Sebastian echoed sincerely. Not that Hawk had not been a capital guardian to him, and Lucian a fine example for any fellow to emulate—and his young sister Arabella was someone for them all to love and spoil. But his parents' marriage had been a love-match. The sort of love that had encompassed all four of their children, too, once they were born. The only consolation any of those four children had had after the accident, almost twelve years ago, had been that their twenty-five-year marriage had been a happy one to the very end.

Sebastian rarely spoke of their deaths to anyone. Of how, at the tender age of sixteen, their loss had devastated him. That he had now revealed as much to Juliet was more than a little unsettling for a man who preferred that people see him only as a charming libertine.

'Your marriage was less happy than your childhood?' he probed delicately.

Juliet instantly stiffened. 'I would rather not speak of that.'

'Was Crestwood such a monster, then?' Sebastian pressed.

'I have said I will not speak of it.' Her eyes were dark at she looked up at him reproachfully.

'No, you said you would not speak of your marriage, not of Crestwood.' Sebastian realised he was angry. So much so that he was deliberately baiting Juliet. Hurting her. And he had no idea why.

Because Juliet's gentleness, her own loss, had encouraged him to speak of his parents, perhaps?

No, the more likely cause was Bancroft's renewed accusations of her this morning!

'The two are irrevocably connected,' Juliet answered him woodenly.

'You did not love Crestwood?'

'I did not love him,' she admitted.

'Perhaps you even hated him?'

Her eyes glittered brightly green. 'Hate is a destructive emotion for the person who feels it.'

Which did not answer Sebastian's question! 'Juliet, I already know from your surprised response to our lovemaking last night and this morning that your marriage was not a happy one—'

'Sebastian, if you continue with this present conversation then you will leave me with no choice but to ask you to return me to the house forthwith!'

Juliet's tension was a palpable thing.

Damn Bancroft. Damn Gray. Damn Dolly, too. To hell with all of them for their distrust of a woman who seemed, to Sebastian, to have already suffered enough unhappiness in her life.

'I apologise, Juliet.' He spoke stiffly. 'I had no right to probe into the privacy of your marriage.'

Now Juliet was the one to feel guilt. Against everything she had hitherto believed, Sebastian had become her lover. As such, it was only natural that he should feel curiosity about her marriage to Crestwood. Especially as she had demonstrated only too clearly her complete in-experience of the type of lovemaking Sebastian had already shown her!

She drew in a deep breath. 'It is I who should apologise, Sebastian. If anyone has the right to ask these things then it must be you. It is only—my marriage was an arranged one. My parents believed, I am sure, that they were making a good choice for me. After all, Crestwood was an earl. A war hero and an admiral.' She gave a weary sigh. 'He was also thirty years my senior. Set in his ways. His beliefs.'

The first two had not been an insurmountable hindrance to their marriage being a happy one. The third, however—his belief that a wife was but another chattel, to be used as Crestwood wished—most certainly had!

Sebastian reached out gently to touch the pale curve of her cheek. 'One of those beliefs being that he did not approve of a woman enjoying the marriage bed?' As so many men of their class did not, Sebastian acknowledged ruefully; a mistress was for pleasure, a wife to provide necessary heirs. Which was the reason so many of the female married members of the ton took a lover for themselves once an heir had been secured.

Juliet's eyes widened. 'This is not a fitting conversation—nor a—a comfortable one, Sebastian!'

No, it was not, Sebastian realised. Neither was it conducive to the seduction which he had intended this afternoon!

'Of course you are perfectly correct, my dear Juliet,' he drawled, and he lay back upon his coat to look up at her. 'Discussing a woman's husband while intending to make love to her yourself is definitely bad form!' He pulled her gently down to lie beside him, before turning on his side so that he could look down into her face. The sun shone down on the dark ebony of her curls, adding a sparkle to her deep green eyes and a golden hue to the paleness of her cheeks. 'You really are the most beautiful women that I ever beheld,' he murmured appreciatively.

Her perfect bow of a mouth curved into a wistful smile. 'You have no further need to spout flowery compliments in order to win me over, Sebastian, when I am so obviously already won.'

'Are you?' he murmured throatily. 'Are you really won, Juliet? Or do I need to make greater efforts in order to capture you completely?'

He was suddenly very close. So close that Juliet could feel the lean length of his warm body pressed against her side. Feel the warmth of his breath against her cheek. See the darker brown flecks in the honey-gold of his eyes as he gazed down at her so heatedly.

She moistened suddenly dry lips. 'Greater efforts, My Lord?' she echoed uncertainly.

'There is more, Juliet,' he revealed. 'So very,

very much more,' he promised, as he lowered his head and his lips claimed hers.

Juliet's lips parted automatically beneath Sebastian's to deepen the kiss, even as her arms moved up to allow her fingers to become entangled in the dark thickness of his hair. She returned his kiss hungrily, fiercely. As if even a few hours of abstinence from their lovemaking had been too long.

It *had* been too long. Far, far too long without the feel of Sebastian's lips and hands upon her body. Sensations no longer denied her as Sebastian quickly unbuttoned her gown to peel it from her and throw it carelessly to one side before turning back to her. His eyes darkened as he gazed down at the full orbs of her breasts, so clearly visible to him through the sheer material of her chemise.

Juliet watched him as he cupped, encircled both those breasts with his hands, before lowering his head to flick the moist tip of his tongue across the already aroused nipples. Not just her nipples were aroused, Juliet acknowledged with a groan, as Sebastian moved one of his hands to stroke his fingers over that hardened nub between her thighs.

Sebastian was constantly overwhelmed, stunned by how Juliet responded so easily, so totally without inhibition, to his every slightest touch. He had never known another woman as responsive as Juliet. Never had a woman opened to him so readily that he could already feel how wet she was beneath those dark curls.

'Sebastian…'

She was shaking beneath him, trembling like an aspen at his ministrations…

'Sebastian…'

His eyes were dark and slightly unfocused as he raised his head at her second, more insistent calling of his name. 'Yes, Juliet?'

Her smile was almost shy. 'You said you would show me today how I might…touch *you*…?'

Sebastian's heart stopped beating as he sat up to look down at her. Only to resume pounding again seconds later, but quicker, more erratically than it had been before, as the full import of her words took flight in his mind.

Juliet looked the siren as she gazed steadily up at him with those cat-like green eyes. Several of her curls had fallen down wantonly onto the bareness of her shoulders. The dampened material of her chemise clung to the twin orbs of her breasts, and the nipples were revealed perfectly as they jutted forward temptingly. Even as the darkness of Sebastian's gaze returned to the flushed beauty of Juliet's face the tiny tip of her pink tongue flicked moistly across those full and sensuous lips that she was now suggesting she pleasure him with.

A siren.

And a temptress.

Did Sebastian have enough control at this moment to tutor her in the delicate art of pleasuring him? Could he hold long enough, if she were to touch him so intimately, not to give in and release like a callow boy at the first touch of her lips, and in doing so probably frighten her half to death?

No—those were not the questions he should be asking himself! The question was, could Sebastian live for another moment *without* the feel of those lips and tongue around his increasingly aroused flesh?

No, he could not!

'May I?' Juliet prompted softly as she reached for the buttons on his pantaloons.

'Yes.' Sebastian's voice was as strained as the pulsating hardness that stretched the material tautly across his thighs as he lay back upon his jacket.

'You will be…patient with my lack of finesse?' she murmured as she slowly unfastened those eight buttons with fingers that shook slightly.

In truth, it was Juliet's innocence about such intimacy, her naïveté concerning all physical pleasure, that increased Sebastian's own arousal and made his thighs throb so painfully.

His gaze became riveted on her face as she slowly folded back the material at his waist to expose him fully to her wide-eyed gaze. He groaned achingly as she once again flicked her tongue across her bottom lip, his hands clenching at his sides as he imagined how it would feel to have that hot, wet rasp moving across his heated flesh.

He dropped his head weakly back on his jacket as he felt Juliet's fingers run inquisitively over the ever increasing tautness of his flesh. If he should look down and see those tiny fingers touching him, caressing him, then Sebastian knew he really would be unable to prevent himself from climaxing. So instead he lay back, to stare up at the blue of the sky as he gritted his teeth and suffered the torture of her caressing hands.

Dear God, he needed to— He wanted to— He had to—

'Hallooo, on the island!'

Juliet drew back in shock as the calling voice acted on her in the same chilling way as having a bucket of cold water thrown over her would have done.

Despite what Sebastian had said earlier, concerning their fellow guests being busy with their own pursuits, someone was approaching the island!

Someone who at any moment was going to catch Sebastian and Juliet in a very compromising position indeed....

Chapter Ten

'What the hell do you want, Gray?' Sebastian glared at the other man as the two of them stood together on the island's small wooden quay, where Gray's boat was now also tied.

Sebastian was still without his jacket, but he had at least straightened and refastened his clothing before leaving the grove of trees, in order that he might confront the other man whilst giving Juliet the necessary time to adjust her own appearance. The evidence of Sebastian's arousal, still straining against his pantaloons as proof of their interrupted activity, was another matter entirely, however!

Grayson frowned darkly. 'To save you from making a catastrophic error in judgement, perhaps?' he clipped disapprovingly.

'Explain yourself,' Sebastian barked.

'Your own and the Countess's non-appearance most of this morning has already been cause for speculation by several of the other guests.' Gray grimaced. 'The fact that the two of you disappeared together immediately after lunch has also been remarked upon.'

'So?'

The other man sighed. 'Seb, you are only supposed to charm the truth out of the woman—not make yourself a subject for idle gossip.'

'Indeed?' Sebastian rasped. 'I was given the impression when the three of us spoke together yesterday that my methods were to be my own.'

Gray shot a concerned glance towards the grove of trees before turning back to Sebastian. 'Seb, do you not see that the Countess is the worst possible woman for you to fall in love with?' he muttered in concern.

'I am not falling in love with her, damn it!' Dark eyes glittered dangerously at the mere suggestion that Sebastian's emotions were becoming engaged. The Countess, like all his previous women, was a diversion—nothing more. She meant no more to him than any of the other numerous women he had made love to over the years.

Gray's gaze became searching. 'I believed this to be a good plan when Bancroft first suggested it, but now—now I fear for you, Seb.'

'I have no idea why you should do so.'

'Because I know you, Seb. I am well aware of the St Claire sense of honour and pride. And beneath the façade of charming rake you choose to present to the rest of the ton, it burns as strongly inside you as it does inside your siblings.'

'You do not know me as well as you think you do, Gray—otherwise you would never have colluded with Bancroft in suggesting I play Lady Boyd false,' he stated. 'Do not concern yourself. You will have your proof of the lady's innocence before I am done,' he added scornfully as the other man paled. 'And, once you do, I suggest that you take yourself out of my sight for the foreseeable future!'

Gray winced. 'Seb—'

'Why did you come here, Gray?' Sebastian cut in. 'What was so urgent that you felt the need to interrupt my efforts to charm Lady Boyd?' Although, in truth, Sebastian was unsure as to who had been seducing whom, when it was *his* loins that still throbbed and ached from the need for release…

The other man looked at him searchingly for several long seconds before sighing deeply. 'I cannot tell you how much I regret that this business appears to have damaged our friendship.'

'No doubt I will overcome my distaste for your company at some future date, Gray,' Sebastian said wearily. 'For now, I think it best if we just concentrate on the matter in hand—do you not agree?' The challenge in his gaze left the other man with no other option.

Gray gave a reluctant nod. 'I came in search of you because another guest has arrived, and has been persuaded to stay overnight at least—so that he might attend the ball this evening. I thought, as he is related to you, that you might wish to be amongst the first to greet him.'

Sebastian gave him a scathing glance. 'You also thought it a good excuse to try and save me from myself, did you not?' A member of Sebastian's own family was the last thing he needed to add to a situation that was already fraught with tension!

'I told you, I am concerned for you—'

'And I have assured you there is no reason for your concern. Lady Boyd means no more to me than any of the other women I have seduced and bedded these last ten years,' Sebastian growled.

Juliet, her appearance now returned to some semblance of order, was about to leave the protection of the trees and join the two men on the quay when she heard Sebastian's last remark.

His last painful remark!

Oh, it wasn't painful because she had thought Sebastian genuinely cared for her—neither of them had admitted to feeling any emotion for the other apart from insidious desire—it was the fact that he was talking with another man of the intimacy of their relationship that upset her so. Quite clearly Sebastian was not a gentleman if he felt no hesitation in discussing her in this way with one of his friends. Nor was he a man it would be wise for Juliet to continue being alone with.

Sebastian might have seduced her, but as yet he had not succeeded in bedding her—and, after the conversation Juliet had just overheard, neither *would* he!

* * *

'Your Grace.' Sebastian gave Lord Darius Wynter, Duke of Carlyne, a distracted bow as the two men greeted each other a short time later in the Bancrofts' drawing room, where many of the other guests had also gathered for tea.

'St Claire.' The older man bowed, the sunshine streaming in through the windows behind them turning his hair to gold and picking out the shadows and hollows of an arrogantly handsome face dominated by hard blue eyes.

Despite Gray's earlier claim, Sebastian considered the kinship between himself and Wynter to be of a tenuous nature, to say the least; the man was a half-uncle-by-marriage to Lucian's new wife, or some such. The other man was some years older than Sebastian—nearer his brother Hawk's age of two and thirty—although the two of them had met frequently over the years at their clubs, or across the gaming tables. Wynter had been something of a rake and a gambler until inheriting the Dukedom from his older brother some months ago.

Sebastian's distraction was for an entirely different reason than the arrival of Darius Wynter.

And that reason was seated with several other ladies at the other end of the long drawing room.

Juliet was seemingly deeply engrossed in conversation with the Duchess of Essex when Sebastian glanced at her. She had been coolly withdrawn the whole of the time while Sebastian had rowed them back to the side of the lake before he'd stepped ashore to help her alight from the boat. Her nod had been one of gracious dismissal, and she'd raised her parasol before turning to walk unhurriedly back to the house.

Admittedly it had been a little awkward to have Gray interrupt them, but that in no way explained Juliet's coolness towards him now—after all, Sebastian was the one who had been caught with his pants down…literally! No, there had to be some other reason why Juliet was avoiding his company…

Could she have overheard his conversation with Gray? Was she now aware of Bancroft and Gray's suspicions about her? Worse, did she know that Sebastian had been asked to establish or disprove her innocence?

'I trust your family are all well?'

Sebastian brought his attention back to the new

Duke of Carlyne with effort. 'As far as I am aware, Your Grace.'

'I believe Darius or Wynter will do.' The other man gave a grin that took years off his age and made him look more like the unprincipled rogue he had been considered for so many years. 'I am afraid I am still not thought to be quite respectable in the eyes of the ton,' he added dryly, and he gave a hard glance at their fellow guests. The ladies, old as well as young, were flushed in the face, their gazes over-bright, as they obviously gossiped about him behind their raised fans.

Sebastian relaxed slightly as he remembered that his lack of approval by the ton had been the reason he had always rather liked the older man. 'Hawk assures me that inheriting the title of Duke allows for a certain blindness where a man's earlier indiscretions are concerned,' he said.

'Does he indeed?' Wynter drawled, his eyes glittering deeply blue. 'So far I have not found that to be the case, I am afraid.' He raised his quizzing glass to glance about the room. 'Can that possibly be the lovely Countess of Crestwood I see, conversing with the Duchess of Essex…?'

Sebastian did not at all care for the calculating

look that had appeared in the other man's shrewd blue eyes. 'I believe she still mourns the loss of her husband,' he bit out stiffly.

'That dry old stick Crestwood? Oh, I think not, St Claire.' The Duke tapped him lightly on the arm with his quizzing glass before allowing it to drop down against his muscled thigh. 'If you will excuse me...' He didn't wait for Sebastian's reply before turning to stroll the length of the room.

Sebastian's mouth tightened as Juliet turned and greeted the Duke with a smile as he bowed before her.

Juliet had been aware of Sebastian's conversation with the Duke of Carlyne from the moment she had entered the drawing room a few short minutes ago, having retired briefly to her bedchamber in order to tidy her appearance before joining the other guests for tea. She was still hurt at hearing Sebastian discuss her with Lord Grayson in that ungentlemanly way, but one thing Juliet was decided upon: hurt or not, she had no intention of hiding or cowering in her bedchamber for the rest of her stay here.

What would be the point of that when she

knew Sebastian was more than capable of invading her privacy there if he felt so inclined?

She allowed the wickedly handsome Duke of Carlyne to take her hand and raise it to his lips, her cheeks warming as she found herself the focus of knowing blue eyes. 'I had not realised you were to be a guest here too, Your Grace,' she said, delicately but firmly removing her hand from his grasp.

Those blue eyes gleamed with amusement as he allowed his own hand to drop back to his side. 'Only overnight, I am afraid, Lady Boyd. I merely called to conduct some business with the Earl of Bancroft, and now find myself in the midst of a summer house party.' He did not look displeased by the fact as he flicked out the tails of his blue superfine before making himself comfortable beside her on the sofa. The black band about his arm was evidence of the recent death of his eldest brother. 'I understand there is to be a small ball this evening?'

From the number of guests Lady Bancroft had informed Juliet had been invited, the grandeur of the decorations in ballroom she had seen earlier, and the mountain of food apparently being prepared downstairs in the kitchen, Juliet did not think it was going to be a *small* ball at all. But the Duke of Carlyne's older brother had been dead only a few months, so perhaps Dolly had decided to downplay the size of the event slightly, in order to secure the social feather in her cap that would be the appearance of the Duke of Carlyne at her ball this evening?

According to the gossips, Carlyne had been as socially elusive as Juliet since inheriting the title a few months ago. Much to the chagrin of all the marriage-minded mamas!

'Perhaps you would do me the honour of reserving the first waltz for me?'

Juliet's eyes widened warily on Darius Wynter. Wildly handsome, an acknowledged rake and a gambler, he was yet another man that Crestwood had not included in his close circle of acquaintances. As such, he was not a man Juliet knew at all well.

He chuckled as he saw her obvious uncertainty. 'I assure you that my attentions are purely innocent, Lady Crestwood.'

'Indeed?' she said coolly.

He nodded. 'But imagine how seeing the two

of us together will set the tongues a-wagging, dear lady!'

The Black Widow and the Notorious Rake?

That would certainly be a cause for gossip. It would also, Juliet decided shrewdly, show Sebastian that he was not the only man here who found her attractive enough to pursue. Or beddable. Yes, perhaps Lord Darius Wynter was exactly the man Juliet needed to flirt with in order to show Sebastian St Claire that she did not at all care for his conversing about her with other men!

'You will have no teeth left at all if you continue gnashing them together in that way, Sebastian!' Dolly Bancroft murmured, coming to stand beside him as he stood on the edge of the dance floor, watching the other guests twirling about the room in a waltz.

Watching Juliet dancing a waltz with Darius Wynter, of all men!

Sebastian's jaw clamped tightly as he glanced down at his hostess. 'Are you concerned that I may have lost the Countess's interest?'

Dolly arched blond brows. 'Surely more to the point, are *you*…?'

Sebastian had no idea what he felt at this moment. He had found no opportunity during tea this afternoon to speak privately with Juliet, and then she'd retired to her bedchamber with the obvious intention of resting before she had to change for the ball this evening. Excusing himself minutes later, with the intention of joining her, Sebastian had found the doors to Juliet's bedchamber—both the one in the hallway and those on the balcony—locked to bar his entrance. Neither had Juliet responded to his knock on either door.

As if that were not bad enough, he had been slightly late arriving downstairs—only to find Juliet already dancing the first set with Gray. To be followed by Bancroft. Then the Duke of Essex. Now, worst of all, she was dancing the waltz—a dance still considered one of the most risqué by many of the ton—with that rake Wynter!

In Sebastian's opinion the other man was holding Juliet far too closely, and his conversation was causing a becoming blush in her cheeks. What was he saying to her? It was all Sebastian could do to prevent his teeth grinding together again!

Juliet's gown of ivory silk, with only that string

of pearls once more adorning the darkness of her hair, gave her the appearance of a beautiful swan set amongst a gaggle of overdressed peacocks; the other ladies were all dressed in the brighter colours so much the fashion at the moment, with outrageously large feathers in their hair.

'They make a becoming couple, do you not agree?' Dolly jibed slyly as she easily followed the direction of Sebastian's brooding gaze.

'No, I do not agree!' He glowered down at her. 'If you will excuse me, Lady Bancroft?' He bowed briefly, before turning on his heel and striding from the room in search of some stronger refreshment than was currently being served.

Allowing himself to over-imbibe alcohol was probably not a good idea, Sebastian appreciated, but at the moment it was certainly an appealing one!

'Has St Claire done something to offend you?'

Juliet stumbled slightly in the dance and looked up to give the Duke of Carlyne a startled glance. 'I am at a loss to understand, Your Grace,' she said.

He easily corrected her stumble before he continuing to twirl Juliet about the room, his grin rakishly teasing. 'I believe that you and St Claire were out boating on the lake together when I arrived this afternoon?'

'Yes…'

'Alone?'

Juliet bristled. 'There was nothing improper in it, Your Grace,' she defended—not quite truthfully. Her behaviour in the privacy of the grove of fir trees had been completely improper!

'Perhaps that is the reason for your annoyance?' the Duke drawled mockingly.

Juliet felt the colour warm her cheeks. 'Your Grace?'

Darius Wynter chuckled softly. 'A handsome rake alone with a beautiful woman, and St Claire did not even *try* to seduce you? How disappointing for you!'

Sebastian had not needed to 'try' to seduce her, Juliet acknowledged with self-disgust—she had already been seduced willingly several times!

She gave a reproving shake of her head. 'You are talking nonsense, Your Grace.'

'Am I?'

Juliet gave him an irritated glance. 'I am a

widow of almost one and thirty, Your Grace, and I have no interest in having a young man such as Lord St Claire attempt to seduce me.'

'No?'

'No!'

'Then perhaps you can explain why is it that you have been aware of St Claire's every move this past hour?'

Juliet stumbled again, allowing the Duke no opportunity to cover the stumble this time. She came to an abrupt halt in the middle of the dance floor. Much as she was still angry with Sebastian for his behaviour this afternoon, much as she might wish to ignore his very presence, Juliet knew that she had indeed been aware of his every move for the last hour—just as the Duke had said…

How could she *not* be aware of Sebastian when he looked so magnificently handsome in his black evening clothes and snowy white linen, with the bright candle-light bringing out those golden streaks in the darkness of his hair?

'You are drawing attention to us, Lady Boyd,' Darius Wynter pointed out, with a distinct lack of concern.

'I have a headache, Your Grace. Perhaps some

air will be beneficial. If you will excuse me…?' She attempted to extricate herself from his arms, but failed as he refused to release her. Instead he took a firm hold of her elbow in order to walk with her towards the French doors opened out onto the terrace. 'Release me, sir.' Her eyes flashed up at him in warning as she realised it was the Duke's intention to accompany her outside.

'I fear I have offended you.' There was genuine regret in his tone as he did as she asked.

'I cannot think why you might imagine I should be offended at having been accused of allowing Lord St Claire to seduce me!' Juliet said haughtily.

'I believe my intimation was that you were offended because you had *not* been seduced!' The Duke looked down at her and raised an imperious eyebrow. 'Perhaps you would benefit from a change of companion?'

Her mouth firmed. 'Yourself, perhaps?'

'I fear you would be more disappointed than ever, dear lady,' he drawled ruefully.

'In what way, Your Grace?'

He shrugged. 'My recent experiences with women have soured my regard towards relationships somewhat.'

Juliet's eyes widened at the bitterness she detected in his tone. As Lord Darius Wynter this man had certainly earned his reputation as a rake and a gambler. As the Duke of Carlyne he was still an unknown quantity.

She arched dark brows. 'One experience in particular…?'

He gave a weary sigh. 'Perhaps. But how amusing,' he murmured as he glanced briefly over Juliet's left shoulder. He grinned wickedly and turned back to her. 'I do believe St Claire is about to attempt to save you from what he perceives as my lecherous advances!' he confided with a certain glee.

'What?' Juliet turned just in time to see a thunderous-faced Sebastian bearing down on them, a look of grim determination in his eyes.

'This is our set, I believe, Lady Boyd.' Sebastian didn't wait for Juliet's agreement or refusal, but took her hand in his before accompanying her onto the dance floor and leaving her with no choice but to follow his lead. 'You are making an exhibition of yourself, madam,' he bit out stiffly as they came together for the first time.

Her eyes widened indignantly. 'How dare you?'

Sebastian continued to hold her gaze with his as they parted, before once more coming together again. 'Wynter is not a man on whom feminine wiles should be practised. Not unless a woman wishes to find herself flat on her back and naked in his bed!'

Juliet gasped at his deliberate crudity. 'You are insulting, sir!'

'I mean to be.' Sebastian was so angry with her he was beyond caring whether or not any of the other couples dancing could overhear their argument.

Not only had Juliet completely ignored him since they'd left the privacy of the island earlier today, but he had returned to the ballroom—after helping himself to a fortifying glass of brandy from the decanter in Bancroft's library—just in time to see Juliet being escorted from the dance floor by Darius Wynter, the intimacy of their conversation evident for all to see.

'You have led me to believe that you value your reputation,' Sebastian continued furiously as they came together for a third time. 'But perhaps you now consider the possibility of en-snaring a duke as your second husband worth the risk of losing that reputation entirely?'

'Sebastian!' Her eyes were full of reproach as she looked up at him, and her fingers trembled slightly against his.

Sebastian remained unmoved as he returned her gaze. 'You will go to Lady Bancroft once this dance has ended and make the excuse of a headache before retiring to your bedchamber. I will join you there shortly.'

'You will join—? I most certainly will *not* excuse myself!' Juliet gasped indignantly before they were forced to part once again. 'How dare you speak to me in this way?' she hissed, as it became their turn to move together down the centre of the other dancing couples.

'How dare I?' He gave a cynical laugh. 'I am your lover, madam, not some irritating youth you can just discard when a bigger catch arrives to take your fancy.'

Juliet really did have a painful pounding at her temples as she looked about her, to see if any of the other couples were actually listening to this conversation. If they were, then they were too polite to show it. Which did not mean they had not overheard every word spoken!

Sebastian really thought— He truly believed—

'For your information, *Lord St Claire*,' Juliet told him fiercely beneath her breath, 'the Duke of Carlyne spent the majority of his time quizzing me about my relationship with *you*!'

He gave a hard smile of satisfaction. 'Indeed?'

'Indeed,' Juliet snapped. 'I had just finished assuring him that the two of us do not *have* a relationship when you dragged me away in what I can only describe as a proprietorial manner!'

Perhaps because—to Sebastian's surprise—he *felt* proprietorial where Juliet Boyd was concerned!

She was *his*, damn it, and the sooner she realised that the better he would like it. The sooner he claimed her completely the better it would be for both of them!

'Make your excuses, Juliet,' he advised softly as the music came to an end and signalled the finish of their dance together. 'Or I will make them for you,' he warned, and he kept his hand firmly beneath her elbow to guide her to the side of the brightly lit ballroom.

He could clearly see the sparkle of anger in

Juliet's eyes as she glared up at him. And something else… There was another emotion besides anger in that green sparkle and the flush to her cheeks. Could it possibly be excitement…?

'I think that would be most unwise, Sebastian.' She gave a slow shake of her head as she continued to look up at him with those glittering eyes. 'If the Duke's questions are any indication, then people are already speculating that there is a relationship between the two of us.'

'I do not care for other people's speculation. Do you?' Sebastian frowned down at her broodingly.

Her chin rose challengingly. 'What *I* do not care for, My Lord, is hearing myself discussed between you and another gentlemen as meaning no more to you than any of the other women you have bedded these last ten years!'

Ah….

Chapter Eleven

Sebastian grimaced. 'I meant you no insult, Juliet—'

'I assure you, My Lord, insult was *definitely* taken.' Her tone was brittle, her gaze hard and unyielding.

Sebastian knew from the frostiness of her manner that Juliet was not going to make this in the least easy for him. He also knew that his cutting response earlier to Gray's concerns that he might be falling in love with her had been a purely defensive one.

Sebastian was not—absolutely *was not*—falling in love with Juliet Boyd!

Admittedly, he had wanted her for a long time now, but since coming here, and since having that talk with Bancroft yesterday morning, Sebastian's main concern had become that of Juliet being accused of treason and murder unjustly. But he would have felt the same way about anyone who was not being given the opportunity to defend themselves. It was that St Claire honour and pride coming into effect once again, along with his innate sense of fair play. Gray had annoyed him intensely earlier today by suggesting that there was any more to his feelings for Juliet than that.

Just as Sebastian had perhaps annoyed—hurt?—Juliet by making such a cavalier remark in her hearing…?

'Let us go upstairs, Juliet.' His voice had lowered. 'And I will endeavour to show you how sorry I am for speaking of you so inelegantly.'

She arched dark brows. 'By bedding me, My Lord?'

Sebastian drew in a sharp breath. 'Juliet—'

'In future, sir, you will address me as either Lady Boyd or the Countess of Crestwood,' she informed him coldly.

He winced at that coldness. 'I would much rather *un*dress you….'

Her eyes glittered furiously at his levity. 'I realise

now how foolish it was of me to have allowed someone such as you to take liberties with me!'

'Someone such as me?' Sebastian echoed. 'What exactly does that mean?'

Juliet was only too happy to elaborate further. 'You are obviously a young man who cares only for indulging his own wants and needs—'

'Was that what I was doing last night? And again this morning?' He scowled darkly. 'Forgive me, madam, if I have quite a different memory of those occasions!'

Two bright spots of colour appeared in the paleness of her cheeks. 'Believe me, Lord St Claire, when I tell you there will be no other such incidents for you to either discuss or laugh about with your equally rakish friends!'

Sebastian straightened at this insult to his honour. 'I have *not* laughed—'

'Then perhaps that comes later?' she suggested disdainfully as she looked down her haughty nose at him. 'Or perhaps you have won your wager, after all?'

'For the last time—*there is no wager*!' Sebastian bit out between clenched teeth, his hands equally clenched at his sides. 'I am a gentleman, madam. The son and brother of gentle-men. We do not discuss the women we are involved with. Neither do we laugh about them with our friends.'

'Really?' Juliet scorned, far too angry now to even try to check her temper. 'Then I must have been the exception to your rules. Or perhaps you just assumed, as the rest of the ton refer to me as the Black Widow and think me responsible for killing my husband, that those rules of gentle-manly behaviour do not apply to me?'

She was absolutely mortified at the thought of Sebastian discussing the intimacy of their rela-tionship with another man. So much so that it was all she could do not to slap him across his arrogantly handsome face!

She had trusted this man. Foolishly, perhaps. But nevertheless she had trusted him. With her honour. With her friendship. With her vulnerability. With her inexperience of physical pleasure….

Because of those things Sebastian St Claire now knew her nature more thoroughly, her body more intimately, than any other man ever had. Or would!

Juliet set her shoulders stiffly. 'It would be foolish of me to attempt to deny that you have hurt me with your lack of concern for my—my vulnerability, Lord St Claire.' Her voice was husky as she fought back the threatening tears. 'But you may be assured it has been a lesson well learned. And not one to be repeated, either.' She turned away blindly.

Sebastian had been rendered speechless by Juliet's tirade, by her inference that he had treated her with less respect than other women because he considered her reputation to be already lost.

But that speechlessness left him as abruptly as Juliet was now attempting to leave him. 'We have not finished talking yet, My Lady,' he said grimly as he grasped her arm in a vice-like grip to pull her along beside him as he strode forcefully across the ballroom.

'People are staring, Sebastian!' Juliet hissed, as she almost had to run to keep pace with him.

His smiled humourlessly. 'Let them.'

'Lord St Claire?'

Sebastian came to a sudden halt in the cavernous hallway to turn sharply, his expression darkening thunderously, and watch the Duke of Carlyne stroll forward to stand pointedly, challengingly, between

Sebastian and the staircase. 'What do you want, Wynter?' he demanded impatiently.

The Duke bowed politely to Juliet, before turning back to the younger man, his smile one of lazy unconcern. 'I believe the Countess is promised to me for the next set....'

'The Countess,' Sebastian grated harshly, 'is promised to *me* for the rest of the night!' He met the challenge in the other man's gaze.

The Duke appeared completely unruffled by Sebastian's obvious anger. 'Is that not for the Countess to decide?'

'Would you kindly get out of my way?' Sebastian ordered. 'Otherwise I will be forced to rearrange certain of your much-admired features.' He barely heard Juliet's gasp of dismay as he continued, 'This is none of your concern, Wynter.'

Instead of answering him, the Duke turned to Juliet. 'Lady Boyd...?'

Juliet chewed on her bottom lip as she worried about which course she should take. If she asked the Duke of Carlyne to take her back to the ballroom, then she knew that Sebastian, in his present mood, was quite capable of carrying out his threat of physical violence against the other man. If she did not ask for the Duke's aid then she would have no choice but to accompany Sebastian up the stairs.

She didn't want to do either of those things….

To accompany the Duke back into the ballroom when all of the ton had seen her leave with Sebastian—no, seen Sebastian all but drag her from the room!—would make her the object of further curiosity. To disappear up the stairs with Sebastian, no doubt to her bedchamber, was unthinkable….

She moistened the dryness of her lips. She spoke quietly. 'I believe, Your Grace, that what I would like most of all is some refreshment.'

'Indeed.' Those blue eyes had darkened in sympathy for her plight. 'St Claire?' His voice became steely as he glanced at the hold Sebastian still had upon Juliet's arm.

Juliet chanced a glance at Sebastian's face, not at all reassured by the stubborn set of his features. His eyes were so dark as he stared at the other man it was almost impossible to distinguish the pupil from the iris. His cheekbones were starkly visible against the hard contours of his cheeks and his mouth had thinned. His clenched jaw was thrust forward aggressively, and a nerve pulsed rapidly in his throat.

Juliet hoped Sebastian would restrain himself from attempting physical violence against the Duke of Carlyne. She knew from past memories of the other man before he had inherited his dukedom that he was more than capable of returning any blows he might receive. In fact, he might relish them!

'My Lord.' She turned to Sebastian, her gaze beseeching. 'You must release me.'

That nerve in his jaw pulsed more rapidly as he continued to look at the other man rather than at Juliet. 'Must I?'

'Yes—'

'Ah, there you are, St Claire!' A completely unruffled Dolly Bancroft left the ballroom and came smilingly towards them. 'Have you forgotten we are promised for this set?'

Juliet was not fooled for a moment by the other woman's apparent lack of concern. She was sure that Dolly could not be unaware of the tension that existed between Sebastian and the Duke of Carlyne. No one could be anywhere near them and *not* be aware of it!

Sebastian spared their hostess a scathing glance. 'Interfering again, Dolly?'

'Not at all.' She gave him a reproving frown. 'I am simply avoiding having fisticuffs at my ball. Bancroft would be most displeased to have blood spilled on one of his beautiful Aubusson carpets!'

Sebastian was torn as to how to proceed. What he wanted to do was continue up the stairs, dragging Juliet with him if necessary, and have this out with her once and for all. To tell her everything—Bancroft's suspicions of her traitorous behaviour during the war against the French, her involvement in Crestwood's death, that damning letter signed simply 'J'—and demand that she proclaim her innocence in all of those matters.

Yet by doing so he would lose Juliet's good will for ever.

For, whether she was innocent or guilty, she would hate him for his part in the conspiracy against her—regardless of how unwilling he had been to undertake it in the first place….

Damn, damn, *damn*!

'Very well, Dolly. You and I shall dance.' He released Juliet so suddenly that she stumbled slightly, although she was cautious enough, after a glance at Sebastian's tautly set features, not to accept the arm that the Duke of Carlyne immediately offered her.

Until these last few days Sebastian was aware he had been known for his amiable temperament. His lazy good humour. His charm and ease in any given situation, and especially with women of all ages.

Until these last few days....

Sebastian had been in a rage of emotion of one kind or another ever since his arrival at Banford Park. Desire for Juliet. Fury towards any other man who even looked at her. Even now he knew he would not be responsible for his actions if Darius Wynter so much as laid an unnecessary finger upon her...

Juliet gave Dolly a grateful glance, relieved that the other woman's intervention had prevented the two men from actually fighting each other. 'Shall we, Your Grace?' She avoided looking at Sebastian again as she placed her hand on the Duke's arm and allowed him to escort her to the refreshment room.

But Juliet would have been deceiving herself if she had not admitted to being aware of that narrowed golden gaze of his as it followed every step of her departure....

Juliet had never felt so emotionally drained as she did three hours later, as she made her way wearily up the wide staircase to her bedchamber.

There had been no more scenes involving Sebastian St Claire and the Duke of Carlyne, thank goodness. Mainly because, following dancing a set with Dolly Bancroft, Sebastian had disappeared from the ballroom completely. And had not returned.

The evening had dragged by so slowly after his departure that Juliet had dearly wished she might follow his example. But propriety had dictated she could not. To be seen retiring to her bed-chamber so soon after Sebastian had left the ballroom would only have led to further specu-lation about the two of them.

And so she had remained in the ballroom, dancing every set with one or another of the Bancrofts' male guests. The last set of the evening, danced only few minutes ago, had once again been reserved by the Duke of Carlyne.

Juliet found him to be a strange, unpredictable

man. In the company of others—and especially in front of Sebastian!—he gave every appearance of being the rakish flirt he was reputed to be. But when talking to Juliet he proved to be a man of impeccable manners and high intellect, that flirtatiousness nowhere in evidence.

All of which succeeded in proving to Juliet that she did not understand men at all!

Before their marriage Crestwood had appeared to be a serious and honourable man her poor deceived parents had so approved of. Once Juliet had become his wife—in the privacy of their bedchamber most especially—Crestwood had become a monster.

She had found Sebastian St Claire to be the opposite: concerned only for her pleasure and comfort in the bedchamber, but totally unpredictable outside of it.

The Duke of Carlyne was another man of contradictions. A man who had obviously once been hurt by love himself somewhere in his disreputable past, and who still suffered from that disillusionment.

Juliet dearly hoped that Helena would not be waiting in her bedchamber in expectation of helping her to undress and prepare for bed. She knew that her cousin would demand a minute-by-minute account of the ball, and its guests, before allowing Juliet to retire.

It was a habit the two women had fallen into over the years—due mainly to Helena's social inability to attend such grand occasions herself, but partly to a young woman's interest in all things to do with the ton. But tonight Juliet was just too weary, too disheartened by the events of the day, to have the patience to describe such tedious inanity.

So it was with a heavy heart that Juliet opened the door of her bedchamber and found the room brightly lit by several candles, rather than just the one on her nightstand—an indication that Helena did indeed wait for her.

Not just several candles, Juliet realised with a frown as she stepped reluctantly inside the bedchamber. Dozens of them. On every conceivable surface. So many that the room was as well lit as a bright summer's day.

What on earth…?

'Close the door, Juliet.'

Her shocked gaze moved to the bed, her brows rising, her eyes widening incredulously as she saw Sebastian St Claire lying in the bed, the covers about his waist revealing that his chest was completely bare.

Sebastian sat up against the downy pillows, his heart plummeting as he saw Juliet's initial shock replaced by outrage. She did indeed close the door—no, slam it!—before turning back to glare at him with blazing green eyes.

'How dare you?' she demanded indignantly. 'After our conversation earlier this evening, I cannot believe you have the temerity, the sheer *nerve*, to assume I would welcome your presence in my bedchamber ever again!'

Now was not the time, Sebastian appreciated ruefully, to tell Juliet how beautiful she looked when she was angry. Even if it happened to be the truth. The darkness of her hair was in slight disarray from her hours of dancing. Her eyes glittered like twin emeralds. Her cheeks were flushed. Her lips full and pouting. The fullness of her breasts quickly rose and fell above the low neckline of her gown as she breathed agitatedly.

Juliet wasn't just beautiful in her anger—she was magnificent!

And, far from assuming anything where she

was concerned, Sebastian knew exactly the risk he had taken by waiting for her in her bedchamber in this way. A long and tedious wait it had been, too. Hours and hours of it.

All spent with the added apprehension that Juliet might not be alone when she did eventually retire for the night—that the arrogantly handsome and no doubt completely willing Duke of Carlyne might have persuaded her into allowing him to accompany her....

Not that Sebastian believed Juliet made a habit of bringing men to her bedchamber. He knew she did not. But she had been angry enough with him earlier, disgusted enough with him over the overheard remark to Gray, that she might just have considered the idea of bringing Darius Wynter to her bed as a suitable punishment for Sebastian's behaviour.

That she was alone after all gave Sebastian some hope, at least, that Juliet might eventually be persuaded into forgiving him. 'One of the things you said earlier was that I have taken advantage of your vulnerability,' he reminded her huskily. 'I am here now to make you a present of my own vulnerability.'

Juliet frowned fiercely. 'I have no idea what you are talking about—' She broke off abruptly as Sebastian threw back the bedcovers and rose slowly to his feet.

He was completely naked!

'Sebastian…!'

Juliet's protest did not come out as strongly as she would have wished. How could it when she was almost overwhelmed by his physical beauty? Tall, and leanly muscled, he had not an ounce of superfluous flesh upon his body! His hair fell onto the broadness of his shoulders in dark waves shot through with gold. The muscled contours of his chest were covered in silky hair that thickened about his nipples, then thinned out over the flatness of his stomach before thickening again about his—

Juliet's shocked gaze moved back to fix determinedly on the beauty of Sebastian's face. 'I see no vulnerability, Lord St Claire, only a naked man!' A naked man who, as she had already observed, was magnificently aroused!

He held his arms out from his body. 'Considering all the mores and inhibitions of our society, is that not the best vulnerability one person may offer another?'

Juliet's gaze became uncertain and she looked at him searchingly. What did he mean?

Sebastian's expression softened as he saw her confusion. 'I am giving you leave to do with me as you will, Juliet. To touch me. Caress me. Arouse me,' he said gruffly. 'Do exactly as you wish with me, Juliet. I will not speak, or touch you in return, unless you bid me do so. Neither will I attempt to stop you in anything you wish to do to me. Earlier this evening you accused me of boasting to my friends of bedding you.' His mouth compressed in memory of that conversation. 'I am now offering you the opportunity of bedding me. Or not,' he added evenly. 'It is your choice, Juliet. For you to decide. For you to claim the victory of bedding me, taking me for your own pleasure before discarding me, if that is what you choose.'

Sebastian had thought long and hard as he waited for Juliet to return to her bedchamber, before finally realising that the only thing he had to offer as proof of his genuine regard for her was exactly what he was now offering her. Would she take it? Would she take *him*? Or would she simply dismiss him from her bedchamber and completely ignore him for the rest of her stay here? Either way, Sebastian's offer had ensured that the victory would be Juliet's alone.

Juliet's thoughts were a complete contradiction. The wisest thing to do would be to tell him to leave her bedchamber now. To just go and never approach or address her ever again. The alternative was to accept his offer of doing with him as she would. Of taking him for her own pleasure….

There was no denying she was filled with a trembling anticipation at the thought of having Sebastian St Claire completely at her mercy. Of caressing each and every hard plane of his beautifully sculptured body. Of indulging her earlier curiosity until she was satisfied. Of this time caressing that hardness with no interruptions. To taste him as she had so longed to do this afternoon….

Sebastian had to be insane or drunk—or both—to make her such an offer!

Surely a woman could not seduce a man against his will?

Yet he had not said it would be against his will. In fact, his words had implied the opposite. He had invited her to touch him, caress him, arouse him, take him for her own pleasure, and in return he would neither speak nor touch her unless she asked him to do so. He was giving her free will to explore his body exactly as she chose.

Sebastian wasn't insane—*she* was!

For her to treat him merely as an object for her own sexual gratification would surely make her behaviour no better than Crestwood's had been towards her all the years of their marriage.

'I did not say that I would not enjoy it, Juliet,' Sebastian remarked softly, as if he could easily read the thoughts racing so rapidly through her mind. The initial glow of anticipation in her eyes. Then the self-doubt. Quickly followed by the realisation that he really was offering her free will to do with him as she chose. Before her pained frown told him that her thoughts had in all probability turned to Crestwood's treatment of her during their marriage. 'I assure you, Juliet, whatever you do to me I will enjoy it,' he encouraged, and he took a step towards her.

'Would you break the agreement already, Sebastian, by moving when I did not bid you do so?' She held up a defensive hand to ward him off. 'You—' She broke off as the door to the bedchamber suddenly opened behind Sebastian and she saw her cousin Helena standing there.

'I am so sorry I was not here when you retired—'

Juliet stared wide-eyed across the room at the shocked Helena as she stood transfixed in the doorway, her gaze riveted on the lean length of St Claire's naked back, hips and thighs!

This was shocking. Worse than shocking. It was, without a doubt, the most embarrassing moment of Juliet's entire life.

'Get out!' Sebastian instructed harshly, without turning round.

'I— Yes. I will leave you now and come back in the morning, Juliet.' An obviously flustered Helena shot her an apologetic grimace, before backing out of the room and closing the door hastily behind her.

Juliet closed her eyes, willing all of this to be a dream. A nightmare from which she would soon awaken and—

No. When she opened her lids, Sebastian still stood naked in the middle of her bedchamber. Naked and rampantly aroused.

Juliet felt the return of some of that anger she had experienced towards him earlier. How dared Sebastian invade her bedchamber in this way? How dared he make wild erotic suggestions about her taking her revenge upon him by seducing him? How dared he make a show of himself like this in front of her young and impressionable cousin? Something Juliet would no doubt have to explain fully on the morrow!

More importantly, how dared Sebastian order Helena to leave Juliet's bedchamber in that arrogant fashion?

Juliet's mouth firmed and she snapped. 'I do not remember giving you permission to talk!'

Sebastian relaxed slightly as he realised Juliet's reprimand meant she was accepting his offer of seduction after all.

Only to tense again as the glitter in Juliet's eyes promised retribution of some kind for his high-handed behaviour just now in ordering her maid from the room. That sensuous gaze held his for long, timeless seconds, before moving deliberately down to watch the response of Sebastian's hard arousal as she slowly, delicately, began to peel one of her gloves down her arm, to pull it from her fingers one by one....

Sebastian groaned low in his throat as he realised his torture had just begun....

Chapter Twelve

He had been wrong, Sebastian very quickly realised; torture did not even begin to describe the torment he was very shortly to suffer at Juliet's hands. And lips. And tongue!

She placed her gloves carefully down on the dressing table and moved to stand behind him, her fingers as soft and fleeting as the touch of butterfly wings as they became familiar with the hard tension of Sebastian's shoulders, before moving caressingly down the length of his spine. His buttocks tensed. Waiting for a caress that never came, as Juliet ceased touching him altogether.

Sebastian couldn't see her as she stood behind him, could only hear the rustle of her gown as she moved. Doing what? Sebastian cursed the promise he had made as seconds, minutes passed, without his having any idea what Juliet was about. Was she just standing there, looking at him? Was that to be his punishment?

'Dear God…' he groaned as suddenly he felt the firmness of naked hard-tipped breasts against the curve of his spine, the brush of her loosened hair against his sensitised flesh, before warm lips and a moist tongue began to seek out the muscled contours of his back.

Once again those caresses stopped suddenly.

Because he had broken his promise not to speak?

Juliet was standing so close to him that Sebastian could feel the warmth of her breath against his back. So close, but no longer touching him.

Fine beads of moisture appeared on Sebastian's forehead as he forced himself not to speak again, knowing that he could not if he wanted Juliet to continue to touch him, to caress him. If he wanted to know release from the hell of arousal that the last twenty-four hours of making love to this woman without taking her had induced so achingly.

Sebastian stiffened, his arousal throbbing, pulsing, as the softness of Juliet's breath moved lightly, hotly against his parted thighs and told him that she was on her knees behind him.

Dear God, what was she going to do next?

It was all he could do not to cry out as her hands moved delicately along the length of his thigh before moving forward to curve hotly about his arousal.

His back arched involuntarily even as he gritted his teeth in order not to move against that disembodied hand. Slowly it stroked the length of his aching shaft, from base to tip, the soft pad of her thumb briefly pausing to seek out the beads of moisture released from the intensity of his arousal.

Sebastian had never experienced, never *seen*, anything as erotic as Juliet making love to him in this way. He knew that if she didn't soon stop those caresses he was going to climax before they had even begun!

'Juliet…!' he pleaded.

'Yes, My Lord?' Juliet replied huskily.

'I so desperately need to kiss you!' Sebastian gasped hoarsely, and he turned to pull her to her feet and take her in his arms before fiercely claiming her mouth with his.

He kissed her hungrily, deeply, the thrust of his tongue into the hot cavern of her mouth telling her of his need. Of his desperation to be inside her.

Juliet returned the hunger of Sebastian's kiss, her arms up about his shoulders. Her fingers became entangled in the silky thickness of his hair, those fingers tightening to pull his head back and break their kiss as one of his hands moved to cup the thrust of her breast. 'Not yet, Sebastian. I have not finished my own…explorations yet,' she reproved, and she took his hand to sit him on the side of the bed.

'What—?' Sebastian's question ended in another tortured groan as Juliet knelt before him, her hand moving about his throbbing arousal before she bent her head and began to pleasure him in the way she had so longed to do this afternoon, totally emboldened, made wanton, by the licence Sebastian had given her to do with him as she wanted.

Juliet's actions were instinctive rather than knowledgeable, but she knew her caresses pleased Sebastian when she felt his arousal pulsing beneath her hand as she ran her tongue lightly across the head of that shaft, cupping him lower down as she explored the length of that hardness from base to tip. He was so big, so swollen with need as she continued to tease and taste him with her tongue.

Sebastian believed he might truly go insane as he looked down at Juliet pleasuring him, the darkness of her loosened hair silky across his thighs. 'Juliet!' he gasped as she finally took him into her mouth. That heated moisture was almost his undoing. 'No more, Juliet!' he entreated weakly as he threaded his fingers into the long length of her hair and pulled her away. 'I will not be able to hold if you continue to do that,' he explained painfully, when she looked up at him with sultry green eyes.

She moistened her lips with the tip of that wicked tongue. 'But have you not told me that a man may make love all night with the right woman?'

He swallowed hard. 'Yes, I did say that—'

'Are you saying I am *not* that woman, Sebastian?' She sat back on her heels to look up at him challengingly, her bare breasts full and pouting, the nipples hard and thrusting.

'Of course you are—'

'And did you not say I may do with you as I will?' She arched dark brows.

Yes, Sebastian had said that. But twenty-four hours of making love to this woman and taking no release for himself meant that his control was already at breaking point. 'I need to be inside you—'

'And you will be,' she assured him as she stood up.

Sebastian's breath caught in his throat as he looked at her slender nakedness: silken legs, that tantalising thatch of dark curls between her thighs, her hips gently curvaceous, her waist slender below the fullness of those beautiful breasts. Her lips were full and swollen from the force of the kisses they had shared, her green eyes dark and enticing as she moved, so that Sebastian lay beneath her on the bed. Now she could straddle the hardness of his thighs.

'Just not yet,' she added naughtily.

Sebastian lay unmoving as her hands moved to press his own hands on the pillows either side of his head. Her breasts were jutting forward just beyond the reach of his mouth as she began to move against his thighs without quite taking the throbbing length of him inside her. And all the time those green eyes gazed seductively into his, tormenting him almost beyond his endurance.

He had created a monster, Sebastian acknowledged wildly to himself, as he realised that Juliet intended driving him quietly but most assuredly out of his mind!

Juliet was punishing herself as much as Sebastian. She longed, ached to have his lips about her breast as she took him deep inside her.

'I *need*, Juliet,' he whispered hoarsely.

'What do you need, Sebastian?'

'For God's sake, woman—*take me*!'

She held his gaze as she slowly lowered herself towards him. Her breasts were no longer just beyond his reach—an advantage Sebastian took full advantage of as he latched on thankfully, his lids closing as he drew the hardened nipple into his mouth to suckle hungrily.

Juliet felt a new rush of hot moisture between her thighs and knew that it was time—that she couldn't wait any longer, either. She had to have Sebastian inside her, filling her. Except, for all her earlier daring, Juliet wasn't quite sure how to go about achieving that….

Luckily she was saved having to admit that as

Sebastian, obviously goaded beyond endurance, turned suddenly on the bed, taking Juliet with him, so that she now lay beneath him. He parted her thighs and entered her in one long, slow thrust before resting there, his weight on his elbows, as he allowed her to become accustomed to having the thick length of him inside her.

'Do not move!' Sebastian pleaded gruffly, resting the dampness of his forehead against Juliet's. Just being inside her threatened to shatter all his earlier control. She was so hot and moist, her inner spasms telling him that she, too, was on the point of release.

Sebastian held Juliet's gaze with his as he rolled onto his side, taking Juliet with him, so that they lay side by side. One of his hands moved in between their joined bodies in search of the centre of her pleasure. One caress of his fingers against that swollen aching flesh and Juliet's body shattered into fierce release, the whole of her body shaking with the force of it.

It was too much—far, far too much for Sebastian to withstand after Juliet's earlier teasing, and as her inner convulsions pulsed hotly around him he knew his own release could no longer be held at bay. He surged up and over her to thrust fiercely, wildly inside her, continuing those thrusts long after he knew himself drained, and the aftershocks of their pleasure continued remorselessly, endlessly, until Sebastian collapsed weakly against her.

He couldn't breathe. Couldn't move. He just wanted to stay buried deep inside Juliet, connected to her, a part of her.

Except he couldn't do that. He knew his weight alone was enough to crush her.

Sebastian moved to gently disengage himself. 'Stay there,' he murmured, before getting up and crossing the room to where a jug of water and a bowl stood on the washstand. The water was only lukewarm, but it was better than nothing, Sebastian decided as he dampened a cloth and returned to Juliet's side.

Her eyes opened wide in alarm as he gently drew back the bedclothes she had pulled over her nakedness. 'What are you doing?'

'Gently, Juliet,' Sebastian soothed, much as he might a young filly in his care. 'I will not hurt you.' He wiped her with the damp cloth, easing whatever soreness she might be feeling at the same time as he cleansed her.

She gasped, her cheeks flushing brightly red. 'I am not sure you should be doing that!'

'I am,' Sebastian insisted. 'Let me care for you, love,' he insisted, and he parted her thighs to continue that gentle cleansing.

He still hungered! He had just made love with this woman, had climaxed until he felt as if he had nothing left inside him to give, and yet Sebastian could once again feel the stirrings of his body as he looked down at Juliet's loveliness.

He pulled the bedclothes back over her before moving away from the bed to replace the bowl and cloth on the washstand, his thoughts racing as he tried to make sense of his burning hunger to take her for a second time. How could he possibly want her again so quickly?

What was it about Juliet alone that brought him to his knees with aching want? That made him want to take her again and again, until only exhaustion prevented him from continuing? What made her so different to any other woman Sebastian had ever known…?

Juliet lay silently in the bed as she watched Sebastian move restlessly about the bedchamber, his gaze studiously avoiding meeting hers. For which Juliet felt grateful; she was achingly, painfully embarrassed by his gentle ministrations to her comfort.

She had absolutely no idea what thoughts were behind his harshly hewn face as he collected up his clothes, but her own were thoughts of turmoil and confusion.

She felt pleasure and wonder at the joy she had once again experienced as Sebastian made love to her. And surprise, because Sebastian had not hurt her—not once. Not even when he had been buried so deeply inside her Juliet had felt as if he touched the very centre of her being.

She felt hatred towards Crestwood, because he *had* hurt her, time and time again, and she knew now that he need not have done so. A little patience and kindness on his part, and Juliet knew those painful years of being his wife need never have been. Sebastian St Claire, a man she had known only a matter of days, had shown her the kindness, the consideration and care, that her husband had not. *Would* not…

'I should go,' Sebastian said abruptly as he sat down to pull his pantaloons over his nakedness.

'It would not do for your maid to return and find me still here.'

'No,' Juliet agreed huskily—painfully.

Helena had taken one look Sebastian's nakedness earlier and said she would not return until morning. Sebastian was leaving now because he wanted to—not because propriety dictated he must.

Because Juliet had been a disappointment to him? Because he had found little pleasure in her inexperienced caresses?

Tears of humiliation burned her eyes. Tears Juliet hoped would not fall until after Sebastian had departed her bedchamber!

Sebastian stood up to pull his shirt over his head, his hair a dark tumble of mahogany and gold. 'We will talk in the morning.' He carried the rest of his clothes and his boots as he moved to the door out onto the balcony.

Somehow Juliet doubted very much that she and Sebastian *would* talk in the morning. Or indeed at any other time. He had taken what he had come here for, and now, hard as it was for Juliet to accept, his interest in her, in the chase, was over.

'Of course,' she agreed evenly.

Sebastian paused in the open doorway, his gaze narrowing on the paleness of her face. 'Juliet…?'

She roused herself with effort. 'Yes?'

He frowned darkly. 'It *is* for the best if I leave now. It really would not do for your maid to return, either tonight or in the morning, and find me still here.'

Her gaze did not meet his as she nodded. 'I have already said that I understand, Sebastian.'

Then Juliet understood a damn sight more than Sebastian did—because he had no idea what had happened tonight! Between the two of them or inside himself. And until he did know Sebastian felt it wiser to put some distance between himself and Juliet….

'I do not wish to talk about it, Helena,' Juliet told her cousin stiffly, when she entered the bed-chamber the following morning.

Helena looked disappointed as she crossed the room, hardly limping at all now, to where Juliet sat listlessly in the chair beside the window. 'But—'

'I said no, Helena.' Juliet stood up, her face as pale as the nightgown and robe she had quickly pulled on after Sebastian's hasty departure the night before. 'There are some things that are…too private to be discussed even with you, dear Helena. Sebastian St Claire is one of those.' Her frown was pained as she remembered the way he had left, immediately after the two of them had made love together.

Because he, like Crestwood, had ultimately found her a disappointment in bed…?

'So that is the handsome Lord Sebastian St Claire the other maids have been twittering about the last few days…' her cousin murmured speculatively as she moved about the room, collecting up Juliet's clothes from where she had discarded them so carelessly the evening before. 'They say he is the brother of a duke.'

Juliet frowned at Helena's persistence. 'I really cannot talk about this now, Helena!' Her voice broke emotionally.

Although she doubted there were any more tears left inside her. She had cried so long and so hard the previous night, after Sebastian had left, that her throat now ached and her eyes were red and swollen.

What could have possessed her to accept the challenge that Sebastian had thrown down when he'd invited her to do with him as she would? What madness had driven her to tease and torment him in that utterly shameless way? To behave with a wantonness that had so obviously shocked Sebastian he had left her as soon as was politely possible!

'Being the wife of just a lord would not be as grand as being a countess, of course, but—'

'It is not my intention to marry the man, Helena!' Juliet interrupted sharply.

Her young cousin gave her a teasing look. 'I seem to recall, before coming here, it was not your intention to take a lover, either.'

Juliet closed her eyes as she drew in a deep breath in an effort to control the roil of emotions coursing through her. There was no longer any doubt about it. Last night Sebastian St Claire had become her lover in the fullest sense of the word. Even thinking of the wonder of the pleasures he had introduced her to made Juliet feel weak at the knees.

As for how intimately she had touched and kissed him in return…

How could Juliet ever look at him again and not remember her wanton behaviour? How would she ever be able to face him again and not remember the disgust he had felt afterwards…?

'I am not in the mood for your speculations or innuendos this morning, Gray,' Sebastian warned the other man harshly, when he strolled into the breakfast room to find Sebastian sprawled in a chair, scowling into the bottom of his empty teacup.

He had been sitting there for some time, completely alone—apart from the footman who occasionally came in to ask if he could serve Sebastian breakfast. Considering even the tea Sebastian had drunk was still churning uncomfortably inside him, he had refused all offers—even the idea of adding food to that discomfort made him feel ill.

Gray, completely unperturbed by Sebastian's surliness, poured himself some tea before moving to occupy the chair directly opposite Sebastian's at the table. 'Am I permitted to observe that you look like hell?' he murmured dryly.

Sebastian felt like hell, too, after making love with Juliet for half the night and then lying awake and restless in his own bed for the remainder of it! 'No, you are not,' he bit out curtly, well aware that, although his valet had assured him that his appearance was as impeccable as usual, there was nothing to be done to hide the dark circles beneath Sebastian's eyes or the pallor of his skin. 'And if you have nothing better to do this morning than irritate me, Gray, then might I suggest you go away and find something?'

His friend raised dark brows. 'Am I irritating you…?'

'Intensely.'

Gray gave an unconcerned smile. 'I have some business in London that requires my attention this morning; I wondered if you would care to accompany me?'

His mouth twisted. 'And would this *business* have anything to do with the Countess of Crestwood?'

Gray gave him a reproving glance. 'I assure you, my movements and thoughts do not revolve solely around the activities of the Countess of Crestwood.'

Sebastian's scowl deepened. His own movements and thoughts did not revolve solely around the activities of the Countess of Crestwood, either—but enough so that he found the idea of leaving Banford Park for some hours, possibly overnight, deeply appealing.

Last night had been a revelation. Of what, Sebastian was still not sure. That he had lain sleepless in his bed, continuing to desire Juliet long after leaving her bedchamber, was in no doubt. That it had taken every ounce of his will-power not to return and make love to her again was also in no doubt. Why she, of all women, should have such a profound effect on him was what continued to mystify him.

Something else had happened last night to disturb him. But while Sebastian's thoughts were so centred on Juliet he could not recall what that something was. Or why it was. Perhaps time away from Banford Park, away from Juliet, would help him to remember....

Chapter Thirteen

"You have decided not to leave this morning after all, Your Grace?' Juliet's expression was politely interested as, after making his bow, Darius Wynter lowered his elegant length onto the seat beside Juliet's own where she sat on the terrace, watching the other guests participate in a riotous game of cricket.

The Duke shrugged. 'I am in no hurry to leave now that I have completed my business with Bancroft. Are you desirous of another boating trip on the lake, my lady?'

Juliet gave a rueful shake of her head. 'I fear my interest in boating has waned, Your Grace.'

As her interest in Sebastian St Claire had waned….

Or perhaps a better way of putting it was that

Sebastian was no longer at Banford Park for her to be interested in!

Juliet had lingered in her bedchamber this morning, long after Helena had helped her dress and style her hair, delaying the moment when she would have to face him again; she still blushed to the roots of her hair to remember her wanton behaviour of the night before!

It had been yet another blow to Juliet's shaky self-esteem, once she had finally come downstairs, to be informed by an obviously ruffled Dolly Bancroft that two of her guests—Lord Gideon Grayson and Lord Sebastian St Claire— had decided to ride to London this morning. Dolly had added waspishly that she had no idea when they would return. Her tone had implied *if*…

Having thought long and hard through a disturbed and sleepless night, Juliet had come to the decision to make her excuses to her hostess and depart for home herself this morning. Helena's ankle had made an excellent recovery, so there was nothing standing in her way. She certainly had not expected that Sebastian would already have made his own departure from Banford Park, without so much as a word of farewell!

'I see,' the Duke murmured softly, that blue gaze narrowing on her shrewdly. 'I take it that boating with someone else does not hold the same…appeal as it did with St Claire?'

'It no longer holds appeal with or without Lord St Claire,' she said coolly.

Darius Wynter steepled his fingers together before turning that piercing blue gaze onto the other guests, as they rampaged about the grass with an enthusiasm that would no doubt rival that of the children they had left at home in the nursery. 'Country pursuits such as these have never particularly interested me,' he said, with obvious distaste for the antics of their fellow guests.

'Or me,' she acknowledged ruefully.

'Even so, the constraints of the widowed state can be a tiresome business, can they not?'

Juliet instantly remembered that this man's wife had died the previous year. Although rumour had it amongst the ton he had not suffered too badly at the loss….

'Very tiresome where no love existed, yes,' she admitted.

That blue gaze became even sharper. 'As so often it did not.'

Juliet turned away. 'I would not advise involving oneself in another relationship that might prove just as disastrous, either,' she said bleakly.

'I assure you I have no intention of doing so,' the Duke said firmly.

'Nor I,' Juliet said.

'St Claire left for town earlier this morning, I believe…?'

Juliet's spine stiffened defensively before she answered. 'Lady Bancroft mentioned those were his plans, yes.'

Blond brows rose over those incredibly blue eyes. 'He did not tell you so himself?'

'I can think of no reason why he should have done so, Your Grace.' Juliet gave a lightly dismissive laugh—utterly unconvincing.

'No?'

Had Juliet's budding relationship with Sebastian been as obvious to the Bancrofts' other guests as it had to the Duke of Carlyne? Following Sebastian's arrogant behaviour the evening before, when he had all but dragged Juliet from the ballroom, then the answer was most probably yes. The fact that he had now left so unexpectedly for London only added to Juliet's public humiliation.

Sebastian's invitation for her to do with him what she would had resulted in Juliet behaving in a quite shameless and wanton way. A wantonness that had so obviously disgusted Sebastian he had decided to go back to town this morning.

She stood up gracefully. 'If you feel so inclined, I am sure that the…constraints of our widowed state do not prevent us from strolling in the garden together, Your Grace.'

The Duke smiled up at her, those blue eyes crinkling at the corners as he stood up, too, a tall and elegant figure in brown superfine, gold brocade waistcoat, white linen, beige pantaloons and brown black-topped Hessians. 'I would be more than happy to walk with you for a while before taking my leave.' He offered her his arm.

Sebastian felt a cold rage such as he had never known before when he stepped out onto the terrace at Banford Park and saw a happy and smiling Juliet, strolling about the garden arm-in-arm with Darius Wynter.

He and Gray had been halfway to London

before the other man had admitted that he was, after all, going to London at Bancroft's behest— that he would be bringing back information from other agents because the older man could not go to London to collect it himself when he had a houseful of guests.

No matter what Sebastian's private reservations might be concerning the continuation of any sort of relationship with Juliet, this disclosure had made him realise that he could not, after all, desert her in this way, when he had made a promise to himself several days ago not to abandon her to Bancroft's suspicions.

Sebastian had instigated his meeting Juliet at Banford Park with the intention of indulging in a light-hearted flirtation with her. Followed by a short-lived seduction. He had flirted. He had seduced. He had been seduced in return.

As with his other affairs, that should have been an end to it.

Instead, Bancroft and Gray's continuing suspicions concerning Juliet dictated it could not end here. Honour—that damned St Claire honour, taught to him on his father's knee!— dictated that Sebastian could not simply just walk away and leave Juliet to deal with those suspicions on her own.

Gray's negative response to Sebastian's sudden decision to return to Banford Park had been predictable, if irritating. The other man had reminded Sebastian that the Countess was a widow, several years older than himself and, worst of all, a woman of questionable character where the death of her husband was concerned. Sebastian's response to those insults might have been less easy for Gray to predict, but no doubt the bruise upon his jaw would fade in time!

To then return and find a happy and contented Juliet, strolling about the garden in the company of that rake Wynter, looking cool and oh-so-beautiful in a gown of pale green muslin, carrying a matching parasol, made a nonsense of Sebastian's earlier concern for her.

'I would not advise another scene like yesterday evening, St Claire.'

Sebastian turned narrowed and glittering eyes upon his host as the Earl moved to stand at his side. 'I have already received quite enough advice from my so-called friends this morning, thank you, Bancroft!'

The older man gave an unperturbed grimace. 'I do not believe that you and I have ever considered ourselves as friends, St Claire.'

Nor were they ever likely to do so once this fortnight came to an end. Just as Sebastian believed his friendship with Dolly had been damaged beyond repair. As for Gray…! That friendship might never recover, either.

'Neither are Wynter's attentions to Lady Boyd anything for you to be concerned about,' Lord Bancroft assured him.

Sebastian turned sharply to the older man. 'Explain yourself!' he demanded.

'I am not in the habit of explaining myself to anyone!' the older man rasped back.

Sebastian looked at Wynter as he once again caused Juliet to laugh huskily at one of his softly spoken remarks. 'He is another of your spies?' he said, outraged.

'Hardly,' Bancroft drawled dryly. 'I merely wished to reassure you that Wynter is no more interested in a relationship with the Countess than I am!'

'Am I supposed to feel grateful for your assurances?' he said sarcastically.

The older man gave a weary shrug. 'Do with them what you will.'

What Sebastian wanted was for this whole charade to be over and done with! 'Are you expecting the papers Gray is to collect today to bring you any closer to learning the identity of the person or persons who have spied for the French?' he asked Bancroft.

The other man seemed unperturbed by Sebastian's knowledge of Gray's purpose for going to London. 'Perhaps. But my investigation here continues.'

The very reason Sebastian had returned so hastily. 'And has it provided you with anything new?'

'I have...further information, yes,' the older man allowed grudgingly.

Sebastian's eyes sharpened. 'Did something else happen last night?'

Bancroft raised grey brows. 'Why do you ask?'

Sebastian winced inwardly at the lack of discretion he was about to reveal. 'If it did, then I believe you should know that Lady Boyd was with me.'

'I do not believe you can account for *all* her movements last night, St Claire,' Bancroft said pointedly. 'Nevertheless, I agree that she did not leave her bedchamber after retiring,' he allowed.

It was not too difficult for Sebastian to guess how the other man might know of Juliet's movements the night before. And the thought of some faceless person—one of the servants, perhaps?—spying on Juliet in this way was totally repugnant to him. 'Then perhaps you would care to enlighten me as to this "further information"?'

'And perhaps I would not.' The older man easily met the challenge in Sebastian's gaze.

Sebastian scowled darkly. 'This whole business seems a lesson in futility when we are no longer at war with France!'

William Bancroft frowned. 'Perhaps you would like to tell that to the families of the many people who died as a result of the information passed to the French by this agent J?'

Sebastian's jaw clenched. 'I simply do not believe that Juliet could ever be involved in such deceit!'

'Then find me evidence to support your claim,' the Earl advised harshly. 'Prove to me beyond a shadow of a doubt that the Countess is innocent, and I will gladly call off my men.'

'Your *spies*, you mean!' Sebastian corrected.

The Earl frowned again. 'As Grayson has already pointed out, would you still feel this way if it had been Lucian who had perished at Waterloo?'

Sebastian knew that he would not. It was because Gray's own brother had been killed there that he allowed his friend even the grudging benefit of the doubt.

'What a pleasant surprise to see you so unexpectedly returned, St Claire.' The unmistakable voice of the Duke of Carlyne sounded behind Sebastian. 'And so quickly, too!' he mocked.

Sebastian schooled his features into an expression of boredom before turning to face the older man, glad of that composure when he saw Juliet standing beside the Duke, her gloved hand still resting upon his arm. 'Wynter,' he greeted him tersely. 'Lady Boyd.' He gave her a stiffly formal bow.

Juliet had been stunned when, as she and the Duke strolled back to the house, she had recognised Sebastian standing on the terrace talking with the Earl of Banford, knowing he could not possibly have ridden to London and back again so quickly. Which begged the question: why had

Sebastian returned without reaching London, as he had originally planned?

'Lord St Claire.' Juliet curtseyed, her lashes lowered as she refused to meet the intensity of his searching golden gaze. Sebastian had departed Banford Park this morning without so much as a single word of goodbye. Such behaviour after their night together was unforgivable. 'If you will both excuse us…?' She smiled at the Earl of Banford. 'His Grace has suggested taking me boating on the lake,' she added, with a pleading glance at the Duke for having changed her mind without consulting him. He gave a silent, but gracious acknowledgement with his head in reply to her plea.

Her chin lifted determinedly, green eyes sparkling with challenge as she turned back to Sebastian and saw the blaze of scorn that darkened his face. After leaving her so suddenly the night before, and his abrupt departure this morning, how dared Sebastian look at her in that contemptuous way? How *dared* he!

'Did you not see enough of the wildlife on the island yesterday?' he asked insultingly.

Juliet felt the bloom of heat in her cheeks even as she continued to meet his derisive gaze.

'Admittedly, our little excursion yesterday was…informative. But I am sure that another visit to the island today in the company of His Grace will prove to be as much if not more so.' Her eyes glittered in triumph.

Sebastian was left in no doubt, during this conversation of *double entendres*, as to Juliet's anger towards him. Indeed, she had every reason to be angry, he acknowledged painfully, after his behaviour in leaving her last night. But was she really angry enough with him to allow the Duke of Carlyne to row her over to the island and then seduce her?

Sebastian had a sinking feeling that she just might be…

'I am sorry if you found my own…knowledge to be so limited.' Sebastian's mouth thinned as Juliet's gaze continued to battle silently with his own. 'Perhaps I should accompany the two of you this morning, so that I, too, might learn from His Grace's experience?'

Juliet had never felt so much like striking someone as she did Sebastian at that moment. His whole demeanour was intolerable. Inexcusable. Totally unacceptable when he had made it more than obvious by his behaviour last night, and again this morning, that she was no longer of interest to him now that he had finally succeeded in bedding her!

It was also totally ridiculous to even suggest that Sebastian might learn anything from the Duke of Carlyne on the subject of 'experience' when their own lovemaking the night before had proved so exquisite Juliet still trembled at the knees just thinking about it.

'I very much doubt that the row-boat is big enough to accommodate three people, My Lord,' she told him sweetly. 'And, even if it were, you have already explored the island once—so rendering it of no further interest to you.'

Sebastian's jaw clenched. 'In *your* opinion.'

'In my *considered* opinion, yes,' Juliet corrected him, with a gracious inclination of her head. 'We really should go now, Your Grace.' She turned to the Duke. 'Otherwise we will have no time for our excursion before luncheon.'

Those wicked blue eyes laughed down at her appreciatively. 'Your wish is my command, dear lady.'

Juliet gave Sebastian a challenging glare as

she answered the Duke. 'You are everything that is accommodating, Your Grace.'

'Where ladies are concerned I find it wiser to be so,' he drawled dryly, before turning to the other two men. 'No doubt we will see you later, St Claire, Bancroft.'

Juliet would most definitely see him later, Sebastian decided furiously as he found himself left with no choice but to stand on the terrace and watch her as she accompanied the reputedly fickle but equally seductive Duke of Carlyne down to the lake....

'Did you find Wynter's *experience* as *informative* as you had hoped it would be?'

Juliet came to a stunned halt in the doorway of her bedchamber as she saw Sebastian's elegant figure once again sprawled on top of her bed, his head resting against the raised pillows as he looked across at her with narrowed eyes. Thankfully, he was fully dressed this time!

As it happened, boating with the Duke of Carlyne had proved a more pleasant experience than Juliet could ever have imagined as once again, away from the curious gaze of the other members of the ton, he had proved himself to be a pleasant and intelligent companion, with no hint at flirtation. He had also been polite enough not to mention Juliet's decision to accept his invitation, after all. Or the reason for it….

Sebastian's arrogance in invading her bedchamber once again was intolerable. 'I found His Grace most knowledgeable, yes,' she returned coolly as she strolled into the room and closed the door behind her. 'I do not recall giving you leave to come and go in my bedchamber whenever you please, Sebastian,' she added firmly.

'No?' Sebastian drawled as he sat up to swing his legs over, so that his booted feet now rested on the floor. 'I had believed last night gave me that right.'

'Considering the haste with which you left my bedchamber once you had succeeded in what you came for, I cannot imagine why you should do so!' She raised scornful brows.

Sebastian bit back his angry retort. 'I warn you not to push me any further today, Juliet.'

'Do not attempt to threaten me, Sebastian,' she returned frostily, those green eyes glittering like twin emeralds between thick dark lashes, and her cheeks flushed with temper.

She had never looked more beautiful, Sebastian acknowledged heavily. If they were to make love now he had no doubt that Juliet would be utterly magnificent. But their earlier conversation, and the challenging look in Juliet's eyes before she disappeared to the lake with Darius Wynter, warned Sebastian it would be a grave mistake on his part to even attempt to make love with her in her present mood. A mood his own cavalier behaviour the night before had no doubt created.

He drew in a controlling breath as he forced himself to relax. 'Juliet—'

'Would you please leave, Sebastian?' she cut in impatiently. 'I wish only to forget what transpired between us last night.'

'I doubt very much that you are any more able to forget it than I am!' Sebastian rasped harshly.

Her chin rose. 'You think too much of yourself, My Lord. I assure you that the attentions of a man such as Duke of Carlyne are more than adequate to banish any thoughts of our own time together completely from my memory!'

Sebastian became very still, breathing deeply, his hands clenched at his sides as he fought to control the urge he once again had to either kiss

Juliet into stunned silence or put her over his knee and spank her little bottom until it was warm. But he knew that to do either was guaranteed to alienate her even further. If that were possible…

He sighed, making a monumental effort to relax. 'Juliet, I apologise if any of my actions have offended you—'

'Neither you nor your actions have offended me, Lord St Claire,' she said waspishly. 'Obviously I have little experience in such matters, but I believe it is the way of the ton to—to enjoy a flirtation at gatherings such as these, before both parties move on to other amusements?' She gave a dismissive trill of laughter. 'Heaven forbid that you should find me any less sophisticated than the women you usually consort with!'

A nerve pulsed in Sebastian's jaw. 'I do not believe I have ever given you reason to believe I regard you in that casual way—'

'And I do not believe you gave regard to me at all when you deserted my bedchamber so abruptly last night or left Banford Park so suddenly this morning!' Her eyes flashed furiously.

'I have come back.'

'And am I supposed to feel grateful for that?' she snapped.

'You might have waited a day or so, at least, before taking Carlyne into your bed in my place!' he retorted jealously.

'The Duke will not be here in a day or so.'

'So you thought to take your chance with him today, while there was still time? Now that you find yourself sexually liberated, who is to be next, I wonder? Bancroft, perhaps? Or Grayson? Or perhaps you might like to try your newly found experience with the Duke of Essex? I doubt a man of his years has been capable of satisfying his wife in bed for some years now, but it may be different with a woman so much younger than himself.'

'You are *despicable*!' Juliet cried, and she slapped Sebastian hard against one rigid cheek. She gasped, her eyes wide with distress, as she realised what she had done. 'Please leave, Sebastian,' she choked as she raised her hands to the heat of her own cheeks. 'Leave now, before we succeed in hurting each other any more than we already have.'

Sebastian closed his eyes briefly, the stinging

slap to his cheek having succeeded in bringing his emotions back under his control, at least. He raised his lids to look at Juliet. 'We should not be hurting each other at all,' he admitted wearily.

'And yet we are doing so.'

'And yet we are doing so,' Sebastian acknowledged heavily. 'I should not have left you so abruptly last night.'

'You should not.'

'Or again this morning.'

'No.'

Sebastian sighed. 'I can only apologise again, Juliet.'

She gave a stiff inclination of her head. 'Your apology is accepted.'

He nodded. 'It would go some way to cooling my anger if you would assure me that you have not been foolish enough to succumb to Carlyne's brand of seduction?'

'Foolish, My Lord?' Juliet echoed sharply.

Sebastian grimaced as he easily heard the return of indignation to her tone. 'Perhaps I chose my words badly…'

'Perhaps?' The scorn was evident in Juliet's eyes. 'Tell me, My Lord, why should it be any more foolish of me to allow the wealthy and eligible Duke of Carlyne to seduce me than Lord Sebastian St Claire? I seem to recall that you told me yourself that a duke is much more of a social catch than a lord? I believe that must apply to a lover as much as a husband!'

Yes, he had said that, Sebastian recalled with disgust. He had said and done a lot of things, hurtful things, to this woman that he now wished undone and unsaid....

It was one of the reasons he had lain awake most of the previous night, trying to find the answer to those questions, only to be left with another question he had no answer to: why was it that Juliet brought out such possessiveness in him as Sebastian had never encountered before? Or felt comfortable with...

'Is Wynter now your lover?' he pressed.

Juliet raised dark brows. 'I believe His Grace is in his bedchamber even now, preparing to leave Banford Park.'

'You did not answer my question!'

'Neither will I!' Juliet told him impatiently. 'It really is past time you to left my bedchamber, Lord St Claire,' she insisted.

Sebastian's mouth thinned at her formality. 'Juliet—'

'Now,' she ordered. 'I am currently undecided as to whether or not I intend remaining at Banford Park or taking my leave. But you may be assured that if I *do* decide to stay then I will be asking Dolly Bancroft to move me to another bedchamber as soon as is possible!'

'Perhaps the Duke of Carlyne might be persuaded into staying after all if you were to move into the bedchamber next to his?' Sebastian jeered.

Colour brightened her cheeks. 'Perhaps he might!'

Sebastian once more drew in a controlling breath before slowly releasing it again. 'We appear to be having our first lovers' quarrel, Juliet.'

'You are quite wrong, My Lord,' Juliet assured him coolly.

He raised dark brows. 'How so?'

She gave a brief nod. 'This is our last quarrel, not our first.'

Sebastian scowled. 'You are ending our relationship?'

Juliet gave a weary sigh. 'I believe you have done that quite effectively already. You came to

Banford Park, bent on seduction. You have more than succeeded.' Beyond Juliet's wildest dreams! 'Let that be an end to it.'

'And if I do not wish for it to end?'

'If that should be the case—'

'It is.'

Juliet grimaced. 'Then I am sorry. It is over,' she added with finality. Whatever madness had possessed her, whatever attraction Sebastian still held for her, Juliet knew that if she were to retain anything of her pride then it must cease. Now.

'You—'

'I am late again, Juliet…'

Juliet turned to see her obviously embarrassed cousin once again standing in the open doorway of her bedchamber. 'Please come in, Helena,' she said. 'Lord St Claire was just leaving.' She turned to him and raised a challenging eyebrow.

Sebastian was filled with frustration as he returned that gaze, knowing by the determination in Juliet's expression that if he left now she would do everything in her power to make sure they were never alone together like this ever again. Neither could he continue this conversation in front of her maid.

'Come back later.' He dismissed the younger woman without so much as a glance.

'I do not think so, My Lord,' Juliet was the one to answer him firmly.

His mouth thinned. 'We need to finish this conversation *now*, Juliet.'

'It is finished, Sebastian.' Her voice was husky. Final.

Sebastian looked at her searchingly, knowing by the calmness of Juliet's gaze and the proud tilt to her chin that she was not referring only to their conversation. That she *really* meant this to be an end their relationship….

Chapter Fourteen

Sebastian's eyes narrowed to chilling slits as he turned to Juliet's maid. 'I believe I told you to leave,' he said to the unattractive stick of a girl. Only to see her wide pale blue gaze turn to Juliet. '*I* am the one who has instructed you to go,' Sebastian ordered harshly.

'Fortunately, My Lord, *you* do not have the authority to say yea or nay to any member of my household.' Juliet's tone was positively starchy. 'Therefore, *you* are the one who will leave my bedchamber. Before I need to ask Helena to summon Lord Bancroft so that he might have you forcefully removed.'

He was behaving more like his arrogant brother Hawk than himself, Sebastian thought with disgust—and he was seriously annoying

Juliet into the bargain. When all he wanted to do was talk to her. No, he would be lying if he claimed that was *all* he wished to do with her! Just being in the same room with her was enough for Sebastian to want to make love with her again. Something, in her present mood, she would obviously welcome as warmly as a dip in the ice-cold water of the lake!

He forced the tension from his shoulders. 'Perhaps if I were to politely request that you dismiss your maid?'

'It would not make the slightest difference to the outcome when it is Helena I wish to stay and you to leave,' Juliet insisted.

Sebastian scowled at her stubbornness. 'Then might I have your promise, at least, that you will not think of leaving Banford Park until we have had the opportunity to speak again?'

'I will give no such undertaking.' Juliet snapped her impatience with his persistence. Why could Sebastian not just leave? Could he not see that there was nothing left for them to say to each other? That for him to be here at all was only causing her discomfort? 'My decision to stay or to go will be set against my own needs and not those of Lord Sebastian St Claire!'

A nerve pulsed in his jaw. 'You—'

'It really is not acceptable for you to continue to bully Jul—My Lady in this way,' interjected Helena, obviously completely forgetting the role of maid she had chosen to play.

Dark brows rose above an expression of incredulous disdain as Sebastian slowly turned to look at Helena. Juliet very much doubted that, as the son and brother of a duke, he usually deigned to notice household staff at all. Or had ever been spoken to by one of them like that! That Helena had done so would have been laughable under any other circumstances.

As it was, there was nothing about this present situation that Juliet could find in the least amusing. 'I am sure Lord St Claire was about to take his leave…' She frowned her irritation as Sebastian made no move to go, but instead continued to glower at Helena. 'Sebastian?' she prompted sharply.

He drew his attention back to her with an effort, that scowl still darkening his brow as he spoke. 'If that is your wish. But I should not make too hasty a departure if I were you, Lady Boyd,' he added. 'The Duke of Carlyne might be leaving later today, but Lord Grayson has informed me that he fully expects to return this evening, once he has dealt with the necessary business matters that so urgently required his attention in London.'

Juliet eyed him warily. 'Lord Grayson's movements are of little interest to me, I assure you.'

'How so, when he is another of your admirers?' Sebastian taunted her.

Juliet could see exactly where he was going with this conversation, and the thought of spending even one more night at Banford Park was becoming less and less appealing to her. 'Whether he is or he is not, Lord St Claire, I have now definitely decided that this evening shall be my last at Banford Park,' she informed him.

'Is that not a little…precipitate on your part, Lady Boyd?' he jeered.

'I find the company here not at all to my liking,' she said coolly.

Sebastian eyed her ominously for several long seconds before giving a token bow. 'Until later, then, Lady Boyd.' He completely ignored the existence of her maid as he strode forcefully from the room.

'Oh, Juliet, I do most sincerely apologise!' Helena instantly turned to give Juliet a rueful grimace. 'I did not realise until it was too late that, as your maid, I should not have spoken to Lord St Claire in that familiar way!'

'Do not give it another thought, dear Helena,' Juliet said tiredly as she moved to sit before her dressing table. After all, Helena was not really a maid, and her only purpose in speaking as she had had been to defend Juliet.

Helena winced. 'It was only that I could not stand silently by while he bullied you like that. It reminded me too much of how Crestwood always treated you.' She frowned.

Juliet could not imagine two men more unalike than her husband and Sebastian St Claire! She had found Sebastian to be full of laughter where Crestwood had been dour. Sebastian warm where Crestwood had been cold. Sebastian a considerate and satisfying lover, whereas Crestwood—

Juliet broke free of those disturbing thoughts. Crestwood was dead. Dead, dead, *dead*! As dead as her relationship with Sebastian now was… 'As

I have every intention of leaving in the morning, Helena, Lord St Claire's behaviour does not signify,' she said dully.

Helena moved to stand behind Juliet and began tidying her hair. 'I would not allow a man such as Lord St Claire to force *me* into leaving if I did not wish to go.'

Juliet gave a rueful smile. 'I assure you it *is* now my dearest wish to leave here as soon as is politely possible!'

Her cousin looked wistful. 'He did not seem at all as charming as the other maids claim him to be.'

Juliet eyed her cousin teasingly. 'Perhaps you preferred what you saw of him last night?'

Helena cheeks coloured warmly as she met that teasing gaze in the mirror. 'Was he as formidable a lover as his body promised?' she asked eagerly.

'Formidable indeed,' Juliet murmured with a self-conscious laugh.

Her cousin chuckled softly. 'Then perhaps the handsome lord might succeed in persuading you into staying on here after all?'

Juliet sobered. 'I am afraid not, dear Helena. My mind is quite made up. Is your ankle fully recovered?' When her cousin nodded in the affirmative, she continued, 'Then I will inform Lady Bancroft later tonight of our departure tomorrow, and you must prepare to leave first thing in the morning.'

And once returned to Shropshire, Juliet hoped that she would be able to put all thoughts of Sebastian St Claire completely from her mind.

If her memory would allow her that luxury....

'Laurent...'

'Milord?' his valet answered distractedly.

Sebastian watched their reflection broodingly in the cheval mirror later that evening, as his dapper little valet flicked imaginary pieces of lint from Sebastian's exquisitely tailored black evening jacket. Laurent had been with him for almost five years now, and Sebastian had always found the other man to be as quiet as he was efficient, with no inclination to gossip as Sebastian's previous valet had been wont to do. Not altogether a helpful circumstance in his present situation!

'Laurent...' he started again.

'*Oui*, milord?' The older man stopped fussing over Sebastian's appearance long enough to look up at him with quizzical brown eyes.

Sebastian turned away from his reflection in the mirror and straightened the lacy cuffs of his shirt so that they showed just beneath his jacket. 'Your accommodation here is…comfortable?'

Laurent looked shocked that his employer should even ask such a question. 'Yes, milord.'

He nodded, avoiding the older man's gaze. 'Is there much gossip below stairs?'

The older man grimaced. 'There is always gossip below stairs, milord.'

'Of course,' Sebastian allowed dryly, still unable to meet the other man's puzzled gaze. 'Such as…?'

Laurent's brows disappeared beneath the grey fringe brushed so meticulously across his receding hairline. 'Milord…?'

'Oh, for goodness' sake, man!' Sebastian gave up all attempt at casual uninterest in their conversation. 'I wish to know what is being said below stairs concerning the guests!'

His valet looked stunned. 'Milord, a good servant would not *dream* of discussing—'

'Poppycock!' Sebastian dismissed. Sebastian was fully aware that valets and maids—household staff in general—usually knew *exactly* what was going on in the lives of their employers.

Especially in their bedrooms! 'Now, get on with it and tell me some of the gossip, before I decide to send you to my estate in Berkshire for a month to deal with my wardrobe there!'

Laurent looked suitably dismayed at the idea of being banished to the wilds of Berkshire. 'Well, milord, Lady Butler—having attempted and failed to attract a certain gentleman…'

'If you mean me, man, then say so!' Sebastian said, suddenly amused.

'Yes, milord.' Laurent looked uncomfortable. 'Failing to engender your interest, she has now turned her attention to Lord Montag—'

'I have absolutely no interest in knowing who Lady Butler is currently attempting to seduce into her bed,' Sebastian interrupted.

His valet gave him a searching glance. 'Perhaps if you were to tell me which of the guests you *are* interested in…?'

Sebastian sighed, hating this conversation, but knowing it was necessary for him to act quickly now that Juliet had informed him she had every intention of leaving here on the morrow. 'I wish to know if there has been any gossip concerning the Countess of Crestwood.'

His valet's brows rose even higher. 'The lady in the bedchamber next to this one, milord?'

Sebastian grimaced. 'Exactly.'

'Gossip about the Countess and whom, milord?'

'Me, of course!' he said.

'*You*, milord?' Laurent looked suitably—genuinely—surprised.

Sebastian's eyes narrowed. 'Her maid has not…gossiped with the other servants concerning my…interest in her mistress?'

'Miss Jourdan is the epitome of discretion, milord. As am I,' Laurent added stiffly, making Sebastian aware that this topic of conversation was as painful for the other man as it was for him. 'Perhaps Miss Jourdan's reticence is because she is unaware of the existence of such an…interest?'

Somehow Sebastian doubted that very much, considering that he had been completely naked the previous evening when Miss Jourdan had entered her mistress's bedchamber! 'I assure you, Miss Jourdan's silence on the subject is much more likely to be because she does not like or approve of me,' he drawled ruefully.

'Surely you are mistaken, milord?' Laurent

looked shocked at the mere idea that a lowly lady's maid should approve or disapprove of anything his lordly employer did. 'Perhaps you have mistaken shyness for disapproval?'

'Perhaps,' Sebastian allowed—although he somehow doubted that very much after the girl's outspokenness earlier!

His valet nodded. 'In our own conversations I have found Miss Jourdan to be very quiet and unassuming.'

Sebastian nodded. 'No doubt the two of you have enjoyed talking together of your mutual homes in France?'

'Not really, milord.' The older man shook his head regretfully. 'I left France many years ago, as you know, and Miss Jourdan, although she enjoys listening to and talking with the other members of the household staff, hardly talks of herself at all.'

'No?'

'Nor her employer,' his valet assured him firmly.

Sebastian smiled grimly. 'Meaning my secret is safe in the hands of yourself and Miss Jourdan?'

'What secret, milord?' Laurent responded discreetly.

'Indeed!' Sebastian gave a chuckle. 'Thank you, Laurent, you have been most helpful.'

'You are welcome, milord.' The valet hesitated, and Sebastian looked a question at him. 'I have just recalled, milord, something that Miss Jourdan said which was rather curious.'

'And what was that?' Sebastian asked.

'Once she said "my cousin" instead of "My Lady"—I considered it a slip of the tongue at the time, but as you have shown such an interest in the maid I thought I should mention it.'

'Very good, Laurent,' Sebastian said thoughtfully.

The valet took this as the dismissal that it was, and collected up the clothes Sebastian had worn that day before quietly leaving the bedchamber.

Sebastian stayed in his bedchamber for some time after Laurent had gone, a dark frown marring his brow. Time was quickly running out to either disprove Juliet's guilt or claim her innocence.

Which meant that Sebastian needed to follow up every piece of evidence, however small. He should speak to Bancroft right away….

* * *

'As we are both in disgrace with Dolly, it is perhaps politic that the two of us engage in conversation together!'

Juliet had been doing her utmost to ignore Sebastian's presence in the drawing room as she chatted with some of the other guests gathered before dinner and he engaged in a lengthy conversation with their host. Although that did not mean she was not completely aware of his imposing and handsome presence across the room in tailored dark evening wear and snowy white linen.

'My Lord?' Turning to look at him, seeing the candle-light highlighting the gold amongst the darkness of his hair, his face arrogantly handsome, was enough to make Juliet's mouth go dry, her cheeks become flushed and her body suffuse with heat. He, on the other hand, looked as self-confident and amused as usual. Almost as if their disagreement earlier today had not happened, damn him!

He gave that lazily seductive smile. 'Now I have informed Dolly that I intend leaving tomorrow, she has accused me of attempting to ruin her house party.'

Her eyes widened. 'You too are leaving…?'

He shrugged. 'I see little point in staying on here once you have left.'

Juliet felt a jolt in the region of her heart. Although why she should be in the least concerned at Sebastian's claim that the timing of his departure was due solely to her, she had no idea. Especially as she had every intention of not even thinking of him again once she left here tomorrow!

She gave him an irritated frown. 'I am sure there are plenty of other ladies present who would welcome the attentions of the handsome and eligible Lord Sebastian St Claire.' She would also guess that the departure of both of them on the morrow would engender even more unwelcome gossip!

He shrugged those broad shoulders. 'But none he has any interest in showing attention to.'

'Really, Sebastian,' she huffed, 'can you not see that any further attempt on your part to charm me is a complete waste of your time and energy—not to mention my own?'

His mouth tightened. 'Perhaps you are so dismissive of our relationship because you and Wynter have made an assignation to meet elsewhere?'

'The Duke and I—!' Juliet gasped at the directness of Sebastian's attack, her face paling. 'You are being ridiculous, Sebastian,' she breathed raggedly.

'Am I?'

'Most assuredly,' Juliet told him firmly. 'The Duke was only being kind to me today.'

'Wynter is not known for his kindness!'

Her eyes flashed deeply green. 'And you are?'

As it happened, Sebastian was indeed known for his agreeable temperament and his lazy charm. It just seemed to desert him every time he came anywhere near Juliet! Why that should be—when Sebastian wished only to be with her, to kiss her, to hold her, to make love with her— was still a mystery to him.

'I would like to think so, yes,' he bit out.

'We are not good for each other, Sebastian.'

'On the contrary, Juliet, we are very good together,' he murmured.

She shook her head. 'That was not the impression you gave me last night, when you left my bedchamber so abruptly.'

Sebastian stared at her blankly. What? 'Juliet, I did not leave you last night because of any disappointment on my part in our lovemaking!' On the contrary, he had left because their lovemaking had been so unlike, so much more than, anything Sebastian had ever experienced before!

Her stance was defensive. 'No?'

'Of course not!' he insisted. 'Was that what today was about?' His eyes narrowed. 'Did you encourage Carlyne's attentions earlier as a means of punishing me because I did not stay with you last night?' If she had, then the punishment had worked; Sebastian's emotions towards Juliet today had been fluctuating between frustration, desire and sheer bloody anger!

She drew herself up proudly. 'You think far too much of yourself, sir.'

'Juliet—'

'If you will excuse me, Lady Boyd, there is a matter I urgently need to discuss with Lord St Claire…?'

Sebastian turned his furious gaze upon his host at his untimely interruption. 'Can it not wait, Bancroft?'

'I am afraid not.' The older man held his gaze steadily. 'Lord Grayson has returned from London, and there are some things we need to discuss with you urgently in my study before we all dine. If you will excuse us, Lady Boyd?' His smile was apologetic as he bowed to Juliet.

She gave a gracious inclination of her head. 'I believe my own conversation with Lord St Claire was at an end.'

Sebastian did not care for the finality in Juliet's tone. And their conversation was far from over! 'I will join you shortly, Bancroft,' he told the other man, even as he reached out and took a firm clasp of Juliet's arm to prevent her moving away.

Even that light touch was enough to make Sebastian completely aware of the silkiness of her skin. To remind him of how he had caressed and kissed every inch of her the night before. And the instant hardening of his thighs was enough to tell him how much he longed to do so again....

Sebastian almost groaned out loud at the need, the hunger he felt, to put his lips against her skin and feel the heat of her blood pulsing beneath.

Dear God, his desire for this woman was going to drive him out of his mind!

Lord Bancroft looked at him for several seconds from beneath hooded lids, and obviously saw the implacability in Sebastian's expression. 'Very well. I will expect you to join me shortly, St Claire,' he capitulated. 'My dear.' He bowed briefly to Juliet.

Juliet waited only as long as it took their host to walk to his wife's side before turning back to Sebastian and attempting to release her arm from his grasp. She looked about her uncomfortably, sure that they must be the cynosure of all eyes. These elite members of the ton were, as usual, studiously looking the other way—at the same time no doubt totally aware of the intensity of the exchange between the Countess of Crestwood and Lord St Claire!

'Sebastian, you must cease drawing attention to us in this way!'

His mouth tightened as he refused to release her. 'Why must I?'

'Because I do not like it.' Her frown was pained. 'I hate having everyone look at me in this way. For them to think—to know… Sebastian, it would be far wiser for you to attend Lord Bancroft in his study,' she pleaded.

'Lord Bancroft can go to the devil!' Sebastian rasped as he stared down at her intently. 'Juliet, I need to talk to you,' he begged. 'There are things I need to tell you. To say to you—'

'Can they not wait?'

He turned to glance briefly in William Bancroft's direction before muttering, 'No, I do not believe they can.'

Juliet shook her head, even as she looked up searchingly into his heartbreakingly handsome face. 'I do not know what you want from me, Sebastian… Another night like last night, perhaps?' she choked. 'I cannot do it, Sebastian. I thought last night that I could. That, like some of the other ladies present, I could take a lover and enjoy the encounter before returning to my quiet life in Shropshire with no regrets.' She gave another shake of her head. 'But I cannot. I do not condemn or judge those who do. It is simply not the way I wish to conduct my own life.'

Sebastian could see by her determined expression that Juliet meant what she said. And he knew by the firmness of her tone that she wanted no more to do with him or their so far turbulent relationship.

He had wanted this woman, desired her, from the first moment he had noticed her at some otherwise totally forgettable ball a long time ago. That desire had increased to the point of madness during these last few days of closer acquaintance. The thought of simply letting her leave him tomorrow morning and go back to Shropshire was totally unacceptable to him.

Only the resolve in her face told Sebastian that she did not intend giving him any choice in the matter....

His hand moved reluctantly, caressingly, down the length of her arm as he finally, slowly, released her. 'We will talk again before you leave.'

'I do not think that wise, Sebastian.'

'To hell with what is wise!' He scowled down at her darkly. 'Juliet, we have been unwise any number of times in the last few days.' His voice softened as he saw the alarm that suddenly appeared in her eyes. 'What possible harm can it do if it happens one last time?'

The harm, Juliet knew, was that it *would* be for the last time....

During this conversation—a conversation that had battered and then stripped away all Juliet's defences as she tried to hold Sebastian at arm's length and failed!—she had realised something so profound, so disturbing, that she could barely think at all.

She was in love with Sebastian St Claire!

Not lightly. Not in the way of some young girl's infatuation with a handsome and charming man who had flattered and beguiled her. But totally, irrevocably, completely in love with him….

Chapter Fifteen

'Juliet…?'

Juliet's mouth had become dry, her breathing shallow and laboured, as she tried to deal with her momentous discovery. She was in love with Sebastian St Claire. Utterly. Futilely!

'Juliet!' Sebastian pressed sharply when she seemed totally lost to him, her face pale, her gaze dark and guarded as she finally looked up at him. 'Tell me what is wrong!' His eyes moved searchingly over the delicate loveliness of her face.

'Wrong?' She gave a broken laugh and seemed to collect herself with effort. 'What could possibly be wrong, Sebastian? I have been seduced. You have allowed me to seduce you in return. Now we are to part ways. Is that not the usual outcome of relationships formed at parties such as these?'

Sebastian had never before attended one of these summer house parties—had always in the past considered them the height of boredom. But, from the little he had observed of the behaviour of their fellow guests, no doubt Juliet was right in her surmise....

His mouth firmed. 'We do not have to part. Instead of returning alone to our respective homes when we leave here tomorrow we could both go to London—'

'I have responsibilities in Shropshire that are in need of my attention.'

'Then I could accompany you to Shropshire.' Until he spoke the words Sebastian had had no idea that he wished to accompany Juliet to her home in Shropshire! But, having made the suggestion, he now fully appreciated the benefits of such a plan. The members of the ton who returned to London for the Little Season would not start arriving back in town for several weeks yet. Weeks he could spend in Shropshire with Juliet....

Her eyes were wide. 'I think not, Sebastian.'

'Why not?' He reached out to take one of her gloved hands in his, and stroked the soft pad of his thumb against the warmth of her skin through the lace. 'We could continue to explore and enjoy this passion we have discovered we feel for each other.'

Juliet's knees felt weak at the thought of spending hours, days, weeks alone with Sebastian in the privacy of her estate in Shropshire, the two of them indulging fully in the physical delights she had so recently discovered in his arms….

But that weakness was quickly followed by thoughts of her recently realised love for this man. Of the increase in pain she would suffer when the time came for them to finally part from each other. As they inevitably would.

Her smile did not reach her eyes when she looked up at Sebastian once more. 'Pleasurable as these days may have been, I assure you my own desire for you is completely spent,' she lied, and removed her hand from his before stepping away. 'Please do not attempt to speak to me on this subject again,' she added, as Sebastian would have done so. 'This has been a…pleasant interlude, and I thank you for it, but now you must return to your own life and I to mine.' She gave him a cool nod before turning away to cross the room to where several ladies stood in conversation. Juliet's smile was polite as, completely contrary to her reception a few short days ago by the other guests at Banford Park, she was warmly welcomed into their circle.

Sebastian ignored William Bancroft as the other man indicated he should now follow him to his study, and instead watched Juliet as she walked away from him. He knew himself well and truly dismissed, and was unsure who he was most angry with. Himself for allowing himself to become embroiled in a situation that was surely going to blow up in his face, or Bancroft and Gray for embroiling him in it in the first place!

He was still consumed with that anger when he left the drawing room and finally joined Bancroft and Gray in the Earl's study. He thrust the door open without first knocking, glaring at the two men seated there as they turned to look at him. 'This had better be good, Bancroft,' he barked. 'I assure you I am in no mood for more of your theatrics!'

'No theatrics, St Claire, but irrefutable proof of guilt. Helped by the information you gave me earlier today,' the Earl announced as he rose to his feet behind the desk, his expression grave. 'If you would please join us, so that we might talk in private…?'

Sebastian's heart felt heavy in his chest as he slowly entered the room and closed the door softly behind him.

Juliet, having been quietly and discreetly summoned to Lord Bancroft's study as soon as the lengthy dinner came to an end, had absolutely no idea what she was doing there. Or why Sebastian and Lord Grayson were also present— Lord Grayson standing in front of the curtained window, Sebastian standing behind the chair in which she sat, his expression grimly unapproachable despite that almost protective stance.

She looked quizzically at Lord Bancroft as he stood in front of her before the unlit fireplace. 'Perhaps you would care to tell me why I have been brought here?'

The prolonged dinner had been something of a trial for Juliet to get through, as she'd tried to engage in polite conversation with the two men seated either side of her, all the time aware of Sebastian's broodingly silent figure seated on the opposite side of the table. The tension she could now feel emanating from the three gentlemen present was doing little to ease that sense of disquiet.

William Bancroft gave a grimace. 'It is rather a—a delicate matter we wish to discuss with you.'

'Yes?'

'Very delicate.' Her host looked distinctly uncomfortable now.

Juliet turned to glance sharply up at Sebastian, where he stood with one hand resting on the back of her chair, but she could still read nothing from the remoteness of his expression. Surely he had not discussed the intimacy of their relationship with these two gentlemen? And even if he had, of what possible interest could it be to either of them?

Sebastian's mouth tightened grimly as he saw the look of confusion on Juliet's face. 'Perhaps you should tell Juliet the good news first, hmm, Bancroft?' he suggested. 'Or perhaps *I* should.' He stepped away from Juliet's chair to move so that he was standing beside her. 'The good news, Juliet—contrary to what Bancroft and Grayson initially believed—' he swept the two men a contemptuous glance '—is that you are no longer suspected of being a spy for the French!'

She gasped, her face paling, those green eyes deep pools of bewilderment. 'I— What *are* you talking about?'

'Perhaps you should allow *me* to explain matters to the Countess, St Claire.' Bancroft shot him a reproving frown.

Sebastian remained totally unmoved by that disapproval, and continued to look down piercingly at Juliet. 'You were invited to Banford Park for one purpose, Juliet, and one purpose only,' he revealed. 'So that Bancroft and his fellow agents of the Crown might ascertain the necessary evidence that would convict you of both treason against your country and the murder of your husband!'

'That is enough, St Claire!' the older man warned coldly.

'Not nearly enough,' Sebastian countered furiously. He was in the grip of a totally impotent fury because Juliet, once made aware of how Sebastian had been privy to the suspicions against her almost since his arrival here, but had done nothing to prevent them, would never forgive him. As she should not.

It did not signify that he had told Bancroft and Gray he believed they were wrong to accuse

Juliet. That he had insisted there had to be some other explanation for the evidence the two men had gathered against her. That even if she had killed her husband he believed she would have had good reason for doing so—a reason that had nothing to do with treason.

Ultimately, despite the deepening of his intimate relationship with Juliet, Sebastian had done nothing to stop or hinder Bancroft's investigations. In his own eyes Sebastian's silence damned him completely. In Juliet's he would become nothing but a cheat and a liar.

Juliet's bewilderment with this situation had only worsened at Sebastian's furious outburst. 'I— The suspicion of my having somehow been involved in Crestwood's death is nothing new,' she exclaimed. 'But why should anyone think me guilty of *treason*?'

'Because that is why Crestwood died,' Sebastian explained. 'For a number of years he had been giving information to the French concerning the movement of English troops and ensuing battles. Including the necessary information that resulted in Bonaparte escaping from his confinement on Elba.'

'*Edward* had?' Juliet gasped. 'You are mistaken.' She shook her head in disbelief. 'Edward was totally loyal to the Crown. Always. He would *never* have done the things you are accusing him of.'

'Not knowingly, no,' Sebastian agreed.

'What do you mean?' Juliet asked.

He drew in a deep breath. 'It is now known that the information was…gathered…encouraged from Crestwood during and after times of intimacy.'

Juliet felt the colour drain from her cheeks at the memory of her own times with Crestwood during and after intimacy. They had never spoken. Not before. Not during. Not after.

She swallowed down the nausea that had risen in her throat at just thinking of those nights when Crestwood had come to her bedchamber and invaded her body, taking his own pleasure before leaving again, without so much as a word—kind or otherwise—having been spoken between them.

Sebastian St Claire, more than any other man on this earth, knew of her complete inexperience with physical intimacy, let alone the seduction of any man. Including her husband!

What part had Sebastian played in Lord Bancroft's investigations? Could it be that he had deliberately set out to seduce her in the hopes of ascertaining such evidence as was needed to—?

'It was your cousin Helena.'

'What?' she cried, a hand brought up to her throat in utter shock.

'The French spy was your cousin. Helena Jourdan.' Lord Bancroft was the one to speak gently after giving Sebastian another censorious glance. 'She was also responsible for killing your husband when he finally realised and confronted her with what she had done.'

Juliet was so pale Sebastian was concerned she might actually faint. 'You are mistaken, sir,' she insisted shakily. 'Helena's parents were killed by the French six years ago. She herself was held captive for over a week before she managed to escape and find passage to England and safety at Falcon Manor. She—'

'Your cousin was confronted earlier this evening and has admitted to being guilty of all the charges made against her.' Lord Bancroft looked down at her sympathetically.

Juliet stood up abruptly, two wings of colour appearing in the pallor of her cheeks. 'Then she is doing so in some mistaken belief that she is protecting me. Because she believes you think me the one guilty of these crimes. Helena would *never* do the things you are accusing her of. Her own parents—my aunt and uncle—were killed by Napoleon's army.'

'Juliet, Helena was the one responsible for bringing those soldiers to the farm of your aunt and uncle, after she gave them information concerning her parents' sympathies towards the English cause.'

Sebastian hated with a passion what they were doing to Juliet. Hated it, but could do nothing to change it. Could do nothing to change the accusation he could see in Juliet's eyes as she turned on him angrily.

'Helena would never have done such a thing! She hates Bonaparte and everything he stands for; anyway, she was only sixteen at the time.'

Bancroft interrupted her outburst. 'Her lover was the French captain in charge of the soldiers the day her parents were killed and the farm ransacked.'

Sebastian sank down wearily into the chair

placed in front of the desk, relieved that Bancroft had taken over the conversation, knowing he could not bear to cause Juliet any more hurt himself. To completely devastate the life she had so carefully constructed for herself since Crestwood's death.

Juliet became very still as she looked from William Bancroft to Lord Grayson, and then finally to Sebastian. 'And you, sir? You have implied that these other two gentlemen are agents of the Crown. What part did you play in this charade? Or needn't I ask?' she added contemptuously.

A nerve pulsed in his tightly clenched jaw. 'Juliet—'

'You have St Claire to thank for clearing your name,' Bancroft interjected.

'Indeed?' Juliet's contemptuous gaze did not waver from Sebastian's, and he could only guess at the thoughts, the memories, that were going through her mind. Sebastian's relentless, single-minded pursuit of her almost from the moment of his arrival. How he had seduced her...

'Certainly,' Bancroft continued, ignoring the knife-edged tension between Sebastian and Juliet. 'It was he who brought to my attention earlier today the fact that your maid was in fact not your maid at all, but your French cousin, Helena Jourdan. That being so, she could easily have carried out the earlier misdeeds, as well as the search of my study yesterday—'

'Your study was broken into yesterday?' Juliet interrupted.

The Earl nodded. 'The drawer to the desk had been unlocked and my private papers were disturbed. That, along with St Claire learning your maid's identity, and the information Grayson brought back with him from town, was enough for me to question your cousin earlier and so ascertain the truth.'

'I see.' Juliet turned back to Sebastian. 'No doubt your name will be mentioned favourably in Lord Bancroft's report of this affair?'

The strength of Juliet's anger was the same as his brother Hawk's, Sebastian realised with an inward groan: one tenth of it on the surface, and ninety per cent of it hidden beneath an icy contempt! The contempt she obviously now felt for him and his involvement in this investigation....

Her shoulders firmed determinedly. 'I wish to talk to Helena.'

'I doubt that would be a good idea,' Lord Bancroft said quietly.

'Oh, but I insist, Lord Bancroft, since you have accused my cousin of such heinous crimes.' Juliet stood firm, sure that there must have been some mistake—that Helena could not possibly be guilty of any of the things these men were accusing her of.

Or Crestwood. Her husband had been many things, but a traitor to his king and country had not been one of them. He— Her thoughts came to a sickening halt as she suddenly remembered something Lord Bancroft had said earlier.

'You implied that Crestwood passed along information during and following intimacy?' she whispered, her face once again deathly pale. 'Are you saying—? Are you implying—?'

'Juliet, your cousin has admitted that she and your husband were lovers almost from the time she entered your household six years ago,' Sebastian told her gently.

'*No!*' She shut her eyes in horror. 'That cannot be. Helena would never— Crestwood was not a sensual man. He was cold. Unfeeling. Totally lacking in all warmth.'

Lord Bancroft looked uncomfortable. 'Crestwood *was* a sensual man—but perhaps not in the way you imagined. For years before your marriage Crestwood, whilst he was in the navy, was attracted to very young, immature females.' His gaze did not quite meet Juliet's. 'Young girls completely lacking in—in the fullness of a womanly figure, shall we say. It did not take your cousin long to discover these preferences, and once she realised his weakness she exploited it to the full.'

Juliet stared at the Earl blankly as she tried to comprehend what he meant. Then she realised what her own figure had been like twelve years ago, when Crestwood had married her; she'd still retained the slimness of her girlhood, before the passing of the years had given her more alluring womanly curves…exactly the sort of womanly curves that Lord Bancroft claimed would not have been at all attractive to Crestwood.

Oh, dear God…!

'These preferences were apparently not seen or recognised whilst Crestwood was away at sea,' Lord Bancroft continued evenly. 'But once he left the navy and took up his seat in the

House, became adviser to the government, such things were not acceptable. Hence his late marriage, apparently, to a woman much younger than himself.'

To Juliet. At eighteen years of age. With a figure that had barely begun to blossom and with no knowledge at all of physical relationships—let alone those as unnatural as Lord Bancroft described!

Juliet felt ill, sick, as she relived every horror of her marriage to the Earl of Crestwood.

'Lady Boyd, I am so sorry—'

'Do not!' Juliet flinched as Lord Grayson would have reached out and taken her trembling hands in his. At that moment she could not bear to be touched. She felt unclean, sullied by the things Lord Bancroft had told her of the man who had been her husband for so many years.

Crestwood had been a man of perversion. A— Juliet could not even think the word, let alone say it. 'I wish to talk to my cousin now,' she told Lord Bancroft flatly.

If Sebastian had not already had reason to admire this woman, then he most certainly did so now, as she stood so erect in the centre of the room, looking at the three men with a proud bearing that refused to be bowed by any of the horrors she had been told.

Juliet Boyd was without a doubt the woman most deserving of being regarded as a lady that Sebastian had ever met.

A lady now totally out of his reach….

'Have you come to gloat?' Juliet snapped miserably, turning to face Sebastian as he stepped from her balcony into her bedchamber.

'Never that.' He gave a weary shake of his head, his expression grim. 'Juliet—'

'Do *not* touch me,' she bit out icily, as Sebastian would have reached out and taken her into his arms.

Juliet could not bear for him to touch her. Could not bear for anyone to touch her. She knew that if anyone did so the brittle shell she had erected about her emotions these last two hours would surely shatter and break, leaving her completely exposed to the pain she was trying so hard to keep from totally overwhelming her.

The pain of having Helena admit—no, proudly claim!—to being guilty of all the charges Lord

Bancroft had made against her in the face of overwhelming evidence against her.

The Helena that Juliet had spoken to an hour ago had been a stranger to her—no longer the child she had once played with, nor the friend and confidante of these last six years.

Helena had betrayed her parents, England and Juliet. All without remorse, as far as Juliet could tell.

God knew all of that was difficult enough to bear—and would still have been impossible to believe if Helena had not so defiantly admitted her actions. But for all those things were so horrendous, so numbing, Juliet suffered from a disillusionment even worse than that....

A pain worse than anything she had ever suffered before. Worse than the hell of her marriage to Crestwood. Worse even than Helena's betrayal.

Sebastian's deceit and duplicity these last few days were beyond bearing. To know that he had flirted with her, charmed her, made love to her—all in an effort to discover whether or not she was guilty of heinous crimes. That was more humiliating than anything else Juliet had suffered, either at Crestwood's or Helena's hands.

To know that she had fallen in love with him while he had only been playing a game in the hope of possibly entrapping her…!

She drew in a deeply controlling breath. 'I wish for you to leave, Lord St Claire.'

His worst fears had been realised, Sebastian thought in despair as he heard and saw the utter contempt in Juliet's voice and expresion as she looked up at him. 'Juliet, please let me explain—'

'There is nothing left to explain.' Her tone was icy. 'Impossible as it still seems, my cousin has admitted to me that she is guilty of all Lord Bancroft accuses her of.' Her voice wavered emotionally. 'There is nothing more to be said. Either on that subject or any other,' she added more firmly. 'My only wish now is to leave here and return to the privacy of my estate in Shropshire.'

Sebastian grimaced. 'Your cousin's confession does at least clear you of any involvement in your husband's death. It means that you will be able to return to Society—'

'I do not *wish* to return to Society!' Her eyes flashed deeply green. 'Helena is my cousin. She has been my constant companion and confidante these last six years. To now discover that she had a hand in her own parents' deaths, as well as that of Crestwood, is beyond endurance!' Her breasts quickly rose and fell as she breathed agitatedly. 'I almost wish I *had* been the one to kill Crestwood rather than Helena—if only so that it would banish the hurt and betrayal I now feel so deeply!'

Sebastian did not need to hear Juliet say that she felt the same hurt and betrayal where he was concerned. It was there in her gaze as she looked at him, in the twist of her lips. 'Juliet, you have to believe me when I say I never believed you guilty of any of Bancroft's accusations.'

'I no longer choose to listen to, let alone believe anything you have to say to me, Lord St Claire!' she declared. 'I am leaving here at first light tomorrow. The two of us will not meet again.'

'Juliet—'

'We will *never* meet again, Sebastian,' she repeated with finality.

A finality that Sebastian knew Juliet meant with every fibre of her being....

Chapter Sixteen

Two months later. The Countess of Crestwood's house, Berkeley Square, London.

Juliet looked up from her embroidery as the elderly butler at her home in London stood hesitantly in the doorway to the family parlour. 'What is it, Haydon?' she prompted, when she saw how uncomfortable he looked.

'I— You have a visitor, My Lady.'

'A visitor, Haydon?' Juliet asked warily.

The butler nodded stiffly. 'A Lord St Claire.'

Juliet swallowed hard. Sebastian! It could be no other. Was she ready to see him yet? That she would have to see him before returning to Shropshire she had already accepted. But did it have to be this morning? Could it not wait until

Juliet felt more able to face, deal with, such a confrontation?

'I am afraid the gentleman is refusing to leave until he has spoken with you, My Lady.' Haydon looked even more uncomfortable at relating this information.

Apparently it could *not* wait…

'In fact—' the butler gave a pained wince '—Lord St Claire—'

'Has stated that it is his intention to sit in your hallway until such time as you will agree to see me!' Sebastian finished as he strolled into the parlour to hand his hat and cane to the butler before turning to hold the door open and quirk an imperious brow to indicate the other man should leave. Now.

Such was Sebastian's forceful arrogance that Haydon did so without a single murmur of protest, Juliet noted with a sinking feeling as she carefully laid her embroidery aside.

'Ah,' Sebastian drawled in satisfaction as he shut the door firmly behind the other man. 'It is something of a relief to know that the St Claire air of authority is still fully functional!'

Juliet stared at Sebastian as she slowly rose to

her feet. Although how she managed to do either of those things was beyond her when her heart had ceased to beat. When every part of her was alive and sensitised to every part of him!

Her memories of Sebastian these last two months—those vivid memories Juliet had known she would not be able to put from her mind, haunting as they had been—had not done him justice.

The darkness of his hair shot through with gold was longer than she remembered, and slightly tousled, as if he had been running agitated fingers through it before coming here this morning.

Those whisky-coloured eyes—Juliet would never be able to look at a whisky decanter again without thinking of Sebastian—gazed boldly into hers, as if daring her to deny him.

His mouth—that wickedly sensual mouth that knew and had kissed every inch of her body— was curved into a humourless smile.

As for the muscled strength of his body…

No, Juliet's memories of Sebastian were nowhere near as disturbing as the flesh-and-blood man himself!

She collected herself with effort as she challenged him, 'Have you ever had reason to doubt your authority?'

'Many times during these last two months,' Sebastian admitted.

Two months since Sebastian had last set eyes upon Juliet. Nine weeks, two days, and almost three hours, to be precise, since he had stood aside and watched her coach departing down the driveway of Banford Park.

And not a waking moment of that time had passed without his having thought of her. Wondering if she was well. If she ever thought of him as he thought of her.

If she still hated him…

Sebastian crossed the room in two long strides so that he now stood directly in front of her. She looked so delicately beautiful, in a gown of the palest lemon that perfectly complemented the darkness of her hair and the magnolia of her complexion, the short puff sleeves leaving her arms, throat and the tops of her breasts bare. It was a delicacy that was completely at odds with the angry glitter burning in the depths of those deep green eyes.

'I have missed you, Juliet,' Sebastian told her huskily.

Juliet's heart stalled for a second time before resuming its beat again, harder and faster. She would not—could not allow herself to be seduced by him again.

Except...

Now that Sebastian stood closer to her, Juliet could see subtle changes in his appearance. Fine lines fanned out from those gloriously golden-brown eyes. There were deep grooves etched beside the firmness of his mouth, and his face looked thinner too—harder, and much less inclined to smile.

'Are you unwell, Sebastian?' she asked, with a concern she couldn't hide.

Sebastian's mouth thinned. 'Other than the fact that I cannot eat, sleep, or make merry as I used to, I believe I am perfectly well.'

Juliet did not know what to make of Sebastian's last statement. Was he implying that *she* was in any way responsible for his insomnia and lack of appetite, either for food or the carnal delights he had once so enjoyed to excess? Or had it been the events of the summer, that insight into the sometimes dark and painful reality of life, that had effected these changes in him? Until she knew the answer to that question, Juliet had no idea what to do or say to him next. Or whether she *should* do or say anything at all, in fact!

'So much so,' Sebastian continued dryly, 'that out of a complete lack of anything else to do with my time I have opened the stables at my estate in Berkshire for stud and training.' He gave an almost embarrassed shrug as Juliet's eyes widened. 'Even my worst enemy would assure you that I have always been a fine judge of prime horseflesh. A stud seemed a logical choice when I looked for something to do with both my time and my money.'

Juliet regarded him quizzically. 'I thought your time and money were to be fully occupied in the pursuit of pleasure?'

He frowned. 'As I said, I no longer have an interest in such things.' Sebastian couldn't even look at a woman nowadays without Juliet's face taking that woman's place. And neither gambling nor drinking managed to banish her from his thoughts, either.

'Really?' Juliet looked far from convinced by his claim.

Sebastian sighed. 'Juliet, will you at least allow

me to ask your forgiveness for what occurred during the summer?'

Juliet bristled into unapproachable stiffness at his mention of the summer. 'Exactly *what* are you asking forgiveness for, Sebastian?' she said coldly. 'My name has been totally vindicated by my cousin's admission of guilt and her subsequent arrest. Lord Bancroft has seen to it these last two months that I am welcomed back by the ton, if I wish it.' She raised an eyebrow. 'I see nothing there to ask forgiveness for.'

Sebastian wasn't fooled for a moment by the logic of Juliet's words—knew by the brittleness of her tone that she was still grieving over the disillusionment she had suffered concerning her friendship and love for her cousin, that none of the things Juliet had mentioned could ever make up for the loss and betrayal she still felt.

He shook his head. 'I deeply regret that I was in any way to blame for causing you hurt—'

'You think altogether too much of yourself, Sebastian!' Juliet snapped. 'You deliberately set out to seduce me, and in that you succeeded. Admittedly, your reasons for doing so were reprehensible—'

'My reason for doing so was because I had

desired you from the moment I saw you, when I accompanied my sister Arabella to the Chessinghams' ball two years previously!'

Juliet eyed him uncertainly. 'What?'

Sebastian began to pace the room. 'I doubt you will choose to believe me—why should you?—but my wanting to see you again this summer, to meet and be introduced to you at the Bancrofts' house party, was strictly to do with pleasure. I went to Dolly in all innocence and asked her to issue an invitation to you.'

'*You* asked Dolly to invite me?' Juliet echoed sharply, still totally befuddled by Sebastian's claim that he had seen and desired her even before they had been introduced at Bancroft Park, when she had still been married to Crestwood....

He nodded. 'She assured me that she had already invited you, at the same time leaving me completely unaware that she had issued that invitation at her husband's request.' His mouth compressed. 'I had no idea of Bancroft's reasons for inviting you until after we had met and I had already begun my pursuit of you. If I *had* known—' He broke off in obvious frustration.

'If you *had* known…?' Juliet prompted softly.

Sebastian scowled darkly. 'I would not have allowed it. As it was, I was put in the invidious position of having to continue to woo you myself or standing back and allowing Grayson to do so.'

'Lord Grayson?' Juliet exclaimed. 'But I had absolutely no interest in being pursued by *him*—' Juliet broke off, realising too late what she had just admitted! She quickly changed the subject. 'Why should I believe any of your claims?'

'Why?' Sebastian became very still. 'Because I do not lie, Juliet. I have *never* lied to you. Except perhaps by omission,' he allowed grimly. 'But that will never happen again, either—no matter what the cost to myself. Ask me anything, Juliet, and on my honour as a St Claire I swear I will tell you the truth.'

'Anything?' she asked doubtfully.

'Anything.'

'Very well.' Juliet drew in a deep breath. 'On your honour as a St Claire, are you lying to me now?'

He met her gaze steadily and clearly. 'I am not.'

'Very well.' She nodded. 'Were you and Dolly Bancroft ever lovers?'

'No.'

'Sebastian—'

'I swear it is the truth, Juliet,' he growled. 'She was kind to me when I first came to London at seventeen. Nothing more than that. Ever.'

'Why was the thought of Lord Grayson seducing me so unacceptable to you?' Was it the same reason Sebastian had not introduced her to Lord Grayson that day? The same reason he had scowled down the dinner table at her on the evening she was seated next to Lord Grayson?

'Not unacceptable, Juliet, but completely abhorrent,' Sebastian rasped. 'And it is not just Grayson; I dislike it when *any* other man dares to come near you!'

Her brows rose. 'Including the Duke of Carlyne?'

'Especially the Duke of Carlyne!' he muttered. 'Arrogant son of a—!' He broke off, a tinge of colour in his lean cheeks.

Juliet almost smiled at his vehemence. 'I believe you misjudge him, Sebastian. Personally, I find him a most attentive and charming companion.'

Sebastian breathed deeply. 'I really do not

care to hear your favourable opinion of other gentlemen.'

'Why not?'

His jaw was clenched. 'For the reason I have already stated.'

Juliet swallowed hard. 'Sebastian, why did you leave my bedchamber so—so abruptly that night after I had…'

'Made love to me?' he finished gently.

She winced. 'You said once it was not because I had disappointed you.'

'You did not,' he insisted forcefully. 'It was my own emotions, my response to you, that I so distrusted that night, that I did not fully understand.'

Juliet looked at him searchingly. 'Do you understand them now?'

'Oh, yes,' he admitted.

'Will you tell me?'

'When you have finished asking your other questions,' he promised.

Her questions? Oh, yes—her questions. 'How did you know I had come to London at this time?'

Sebastian's gaze avoided hers. 'I have been aware of your every move since we parted at Banford Park.'

Her eyes widened incredulously. 'You have had me followed?'

'Not I,' he assured her hastily as Juliet's eyes glittered her displeasure. 'Bancroft is the one who has had you watched. But only for your own protection. In case any of your cousin's associates should decide to pay you a visit. Bancroft owed you that, at least, after the erroneous suspicions he had harboured against you,' Sebastian told her.

Juliet swallowed hard. 'So Lord Bancroft was the one to inform you of my—my visit to London?'

Sebastian nodded stiffly. 'It was the least he could do, in the circumstances.'

'Why were you even interested?' Juliet frowned, not altogether happy with the idea of being watched. What if Sebastian had been informed as to where she had been yesterday morning? 'It has been two months since we last met, Sebastian.'

Sebastian was well aware of exactly how long it had been since he'd last seen Juliet! 'I wanted to give you time to get over the well-deserved anger you felt towards me. To find myself an occupation, so that when I did come to you, you would see that I have at least tried to change from your description of me as being "nothing more than a rake and a wastrel".'

'Why?'

Sebastian had made his promise to answer her truthfully, and he would keep to it, but this was much harder than he could ever have imagined it being. Just seeing Juliet again, being with her, was more painful than he could ever have imagined.

'Sebastian, *why*?'

He drew in a harsh breath. 'For the same reason I left your bedchamber so abruptly that night.'

'Which is?'

'Because I am in love with you! Because I love you, damn it. Every part of you. From your head to your toes. Oh, God, Juliet, I love everything about you!' he groaned huskily. 'Your innocence. Your vulnerability. Your pride. Your courage. Juliet, I have spent the last two months longing, aching to see you again, to be with you again. To tell you how I feel about you.'

Juliet began to tremble even as she felt the wall she had kept so securely about her own emotions begin to crumble and fall.

Sebastian gave a self-deprecatory shake of his

head at Juliet's silence. 'It was not my intention to fall in love with any woman. I did not even recognise the emotion for what it was until it was too late and you had gone from my life. That night I waited in your room for you, and you made love to me so—' He stopped and breathed raggedly before continuing, 'I left your bed-chamber that night because I did not understand my own emotions. Had no idea what was happening to me. I only knew that I had to leave, be apart from you, in order to try to collect my thoughts and feelings.'

Juliet moistened the dryness of her lips with the tip of her tongue. 'And have you now collected your thoughts and feelings?'

'It appears they have collected me,' he said ruefully. 'Juliet, I promise you I have changed in the two months we have been apart. I have found a purpose for my life at my estate in Berkshire. Will you not—could you not give me another chance to prove myself to you?' He reached out to grasp both her hands in his. 'I swear on my honour that I had no part in Bancroft's machinations. Damn it, I only wanted to protect you.'

'I know.'

'And in trying to do so I— What did you say?' Sebastian stared at her incredulously.

She nodded. 'I have had the same two months in which to think, Sebastian. In which to remember. I was naturally upset that last evening at Banford Park. So shocked by what Helena had done that I did not listen properly to what else was being said. But I have realised, from the things you said that night, that you meant me no harm.'

'I would never do anything to harm a hair upon your head,' he vowed.

'I know, my dear.' Juliet squeezed his hands.

'Then you will let me woo you?' he prompted anxiously. 'I do not care how long it takes— weeks, months, even years. I warn you now that it is my intention to woo you until I have worn you down into agreeing to be my wife.'

'You wish to *marry* me?' Juliet gasped breathlessly.

Sebastian frowned fiercely. 'What else have I been telling you? Juliet!' he exclaimed, as he realised she had believed him to be suggesting they simply resume their affair. 'I would *never* dishonour you, what I feel for you, by offering you anything less than marriage!'

'But you have not...'

'I have not what?' he asked.

'Offered me marriage,' Juliet said a little shyly.

Sebastian grimaced. 'But I have not yet wooed and won you.'

'Oh, Sebastian!' Juliet sighed. 'I believe that you won me the moment you first kissed me!'

He stood back to look at her uncertainly, searchingly. 'Juliet, are you sure...?'

She laughed softly, a warm bubble of happiness building inside her and longing to break free. 'Your behaviour in setting out to seduce me at Banford Park was totally reprehensible.'

'I will spend the rest of my life apologising for that if you will only marry me!'

'*Totally* reprehensible,' Juliet repeated huskily. 'But it was also wonderful, Sebastian. Exciting. So pleasurable that even now it makes me tremble to think of it. Oh, Sebastian, I had never known such wonders before as when you kissed and touched me!' She looked dazed just at the memory. 'I did not know that physical love could be so—so beautiful.' She suddenly frowned. 'Crestwood—'

'We will never talk of him, Juliet, if it makes you unhappy,' Sebastian said firmly.

'It does not.' And, strangely, it no longer did.

Juliet had come to realise these last two months, whilst alone in Shropshire, that Crestwood had been a man she could never have understood. Nor pleased. She had always believed the unhappiness of their marriage in the bedroom must have been because of a fault within her. That *she* was the one who was somehow lacking. Helena's revelations of her own twisted relationship with Crestwood had finally proved that to be untrue, and released her from her feelings of guilt and shame.

As Juliet's response to Sebastian's lovemaking had shown her how deep was her own sensuality…

'I will talk of him this once, Sebastian, and then never again.' She removed her hands from his to move away and stare sightlessly out of the window as she began to talk. 'I can say it now— he was a brute of a man. Hard. Implacable. Totally lacking in warmth of any kind.' She swallowed hard. 'He showed absolutely no mercy, no tenderness, when he took my virginity on our wedding night. Or any of the nights he came to me during our years of marriage.' She gripped her hands tightly together. 'I think it was made worse because he—he would always snuff out the candle when he came into my bedchamber, and in the darkness I was never sure where he was or when he would take me.'

'So that is the reason you did not want me to blow out the candle that first night!' Sebastian breathed.

She shuddered at the thought of those other, painful memories. 'On one of the occasions Crestwood came to me I tried to talk to him, to explain that if he would only be a little kinder—' She shook her head. 'He beat me so badly that night I could barely stand afterwards.'

'*Juliet!*' he choked.

'It is all right, Sebastian.' She turned to reassure him shakily. 'Oh, my dear…!' She quickly crossed the room to smooth the devastation from Sebastian's expression. 'It really is all right,' she soothed again. 'Until I met you I had not known what it was to find joy with a lover. To laugh and talk, and just enjoy lovemaking.' She shook her head sadly. 'It is true I did not kill Crestwood—but I wanted to. On several occasions I certainly wanted to!'

'He deserved to die!' Sebastian rumbled, his

eyes glittering darkly. 'If he were not already dead, I would take great pleasure in killing him myself!'

Juliet regarded him warmly. 'That would not do at all, Sebastian.'

A nerve pulsed in the rigidity of his jaw. 'I would have enjoyed making him suffer as he made you suffer all those years!'

Juliet's smile widened. 'But then the father of my baby, the man I love to distraction, would be in prison rather than free to be with the two of us, would he not?'

'Yes, but— *Baby?*' Sebastian echoed sharply, his gaze avidly searching the pale oval of Juliet's face as she gazed up at him. 'Juliet—'

'I am with child, Sebastian!' she announced happily, her face lighting up with joy. 'I came to town yesterday in order that I might have a physician confirm my suspicions.' Tears of joy glistened in her eyes. 'I have been trying to find the courage since yesterday in which to come to you and tell you…! Oh, Sebastian! My darling, wonderful Sebastian, in seven months' time we are going to have a son or a daughter. You are going to be a father!'

Sebastian felt as if someone had dealt him a

severe blow to the chest. He couldn't breathe. Couldn't speak. Could only look down at Juliet in wonder.

He became very still. 'Juliet, did you just call me…? Did you just say that you loved the father of your baby to distraction?'

She beamed up at him. 'I did. I do. I love you, Sebastian. To distraction.' She laughed gaily at his dumbfounded expression.

That Juliet carried his child was a shock. A wonderful one, to be sure. But that she loved him too…!

Sebastian swept her up into his arms and began kissing her as if he never wanted to stop.

Which he did not. He was hungry for Juliet. The taste, the feel of her after two months of not seeing her. Being with her. Of wondering whether or not she still hated him, doing all that he could in order to show her that he had changed.

They were both trembling with longing when Sebastian finally broke the kiss to rest his forehead against hers. 'Have you ever made love on a sofa, Juliet?'

She gave a husky laugh. 'The only occasions on which I have ever *made love* have been with you,' she murmured softly, her expression quizzical as Sebastian released her to collect the chair from in front of the bureau. 'What are you doing?'

'Making sure that we cannot be interrupted,' he explained, as he propped the chair beneath the door handle before returning to her side. 'I hope you do not mind, my darling Juliet, but I intend to make love to you until you scream!' He swept her up into his arms and carried her over to the sofa.

Juliet did not mind at all….

'Why are you smiling?' Juliet was completely naked, as was Sebastian, as they lay in each other's arms upon the sofa much, much later.

His grin widened. 'I am going to have such fun informing my haughty brother Hawk that not only is his reprehensible youngest brother about to take himself a wife, as soon as can possibly be arranged, but that he is also to be a father!'

Fun…

It was something that Sebastian had brought into Juliet's life.

Along with love. And laughter. And the simple joy of being alive.

And of loving and being loved in return....

Epilogue

'How on earth did the Duchess manage to organise such a wonderful wedding supper for us in just a few days?' Juliet said wonderingly, as she and Sebastian began the first dance of the evening in the crowded ballroom at St Claire House.

'Jane is a mystery to us all,' Sebastian agreed admiringly.

All of the ton were there, many of them having travelled from their country estates in order to attend the October nuptials of Lord Sebastian St Claire, youngest brother of the Duke of Stourbridge, and Lady Juliet Boyd, Countess of Crestwood. They had been married earlier that afternoon at St George's Church in Hanover Square, and were now at St Claire House in Mayfair.

Juliet would be eternally grateful for the

warm welcome shown to her by both the Duke and Duchess of Stourbridge. Lord Lucien St Claire and his wife had also been extremely kind to her. As had their sister, Lady Arabella. So much so that Juliet felt as if she had a family again.

Most especially, she had Sebastian for her husband. The man she loved. The man she had no doubt she would always love, and who would always love her. And in just under seven months' time they would welcome their child into that love.

'I wish everyone could be as happy as we are, Sebastian!' She smiled up at him glowingly as they danced together, completely oblivious of everyone else in the room.

'They could not possibly be,' Sebastian assured her gruffly as he gazed down lovingly at the woman who was now his wife. Lady Juliet St Claire. How absolutely, perfectly right that sounded.

'I am so pleased that you were able to forgive the Bancrofts and Lord Grayson enough to invite them to our wedding,' Juliet approved.

Sebastian was not sure that he had completely forgiven any them for their earlier mistrust of

Juliet. Or if he ever would. But it had been Juliet's wish that the three be invited today, and Sebastian loved her so deeply that he was unable to deny her anything that she wished for.

God knew Sebastian had had enough cause to regret those invitations earlier today, when Bancroft had taken him aside to confide that Helena Jourdan had somehow escaped imprisonment and her whereabouts at this moment were unknown…!

Something Sebastian had no intention of Juliet learning today, of all days. This was their wedding day. The beginning of the rest of their lives together.

'I am less inclined to forgive the Duke of Carlyne's obvious pleasure in seeing you again when he arrived earlier.' He frowned as he saw his sister, Arabella, being escorted onto the dance floor by that very same duke.

Juliet gave a trill of laughter at his jealous grumble. 'I am sure he enjoyed annoying you more than seeing me again.'

Sebastian's arms tightened about her still slender waist. 'Now that others are dancing, do you think anyone would notice if we were to slip away and find a secluded and private place where we might make love?' he asked huskily.

Juliet smiled. 'Oh, I think that the disappearance of the bride and groom might be cause for comment!'

He arched quizzical brows. 'Would you mind very much if it were?'

'Not in the slightest!' she admitted happily.

Sebastian grinned down at her. 'You have become shameless, wife.'

Juliet arched a teasing brow. 'Are you complaining, husband?'

'Never!'

Juliet laughed again as Sebastian took a firm hold of her hand to lead her from the ballroom in search of 'a secluded and private place' so that they might make love.

She had no doubt that everything between herself and Sebastian, for the rest of their lives together, would be about love….

HISTORICAL

Large Print

ONE UNASHAMED NIGHT
Sophia James

Lord Taris Wellingham lives alone, concealing his fading eyesight from Society. Plain Beatrice-Maude does not expect to attract any man, especially one as good-looking as her travelling companion. Forced by a snowstorm to spend the night together, these two lonely people unleash a passion that surprises them. How will their lives change with the coming of the new day?

THE CAPTAIN'S MYSTERIOUS LADY
Mary Nichols

Captain James Drymore has one purpose in life: revenge. But when he rescues a beautiful young lady, James allows himself to become distracted for the first time... As he slowly puts together the complex pieces of his mysterious lady's past, James realises he needs to let go of his own. Can he and Amy build a new future – together?

THE MAJOR AND THE PICKPOCKET
Lucy Ashford

Tassie bit her lip. Why hadn't he turned her over to the constables? She certainly wasn't going to try to run past him. She was tall, but this man towered over her – six foot of hardened muscle, strong booted legs set firmly apart. Major Marcus Forrester. All ready for action. And Tassie couldn't help but remember his kiss ...

MILLS & BOON

HISTORICAL

Large Print

THE RAKE AND THE HEIRESS
Marguerite Kaye

Any virtuous society lady knows to run from Mr Nicholas Lytton. But he's the one person who can unlock the mystery surrounding Lady Serena Stamppe's inheritance. Accepting Nicholas's offer of assistance, Serena soon discovers the forbidden thrills of liaising with a libertine – excitement, scandal…and a most pleasurable seduction!

WICKED CAPTAIN, WAYWARD WIFE
Sarah Mallory

When young widow Evelina Wylder comes face to face with her dashing captain husband – *very* much alive – she's shocked, overjoyed…and so furious she's keeping Nick firmly out of their marriage bed! Now the daring war hero faces his biggest challenge – proving to Eve that his first duty is to love and cherish her, forever!

THE PIRATE'S WILLING CAPTIVE
Anne Herries

Instinct told her that Captain Justin Sylvester was a man she could trust. Captive on the high seas, with nowhere to run, curiously Maribel Sanchez had never felt more free. Now she had to choose: return to rigid society and become an old man's unwilling wife or stay as Justin's more than *willing* mistress…

MILLS & BOON

HISTORICAL

Large Print

THE VISCOUNT'S UNCONVENTIONAL BRIDE
Mary Nichols

As a member of the renowned Piccadilly Gentlemen's Club, Jonathan Leinster must ensure the return of a runaway. Spirited Louise has fled to her birthplace, hoping to find her family – but charming Jonathan stops her in her tracks! His task is simple: escort Louise promptly home. Yet all he wants to do is claim her as his own!

COMPROMISING MISS MILTON
Michelle Styles

Buttoned-up governess Daisy Milton buries dreams of marriage and family life in order to support her sister and orphaned niece. But Viscount Ravensworth shakes up Daisy's safe, stable existence. Could a tightly laced miss be convinced to forgo society's strict code of conduct…and come undone in the arms of a reformed rake?

FORBIDDEN LADY
Anne Herries

Sir Robert came in peace to claim his lady honourably. But Melissa denied their love and her father had him whipped from the house. Embittered, Rob sought his fortune in fighting. As the Wars of the Roses ravage England, Melissa falls into Rob's power. He should not trust her – but can he resist such vulnerable, innocent beauty?

 MILLS & BOON

HISTORICAL

Large Print

PRACTICAL WIDOW TO PASSIONATE MISTRESS
Louise Allen

Desperate to reunite with her sisters, Meg finds passage to England as injured soldier Major Ross Brandon's temporary housekeeper. Dangerously irresistible, Ross's dark, searching eyes warn Meg that it would be wrong to fall for him… But soon sensible Meg is tempted to move from servants' quarters to the master's bedroom!

MAJOR WESTHAVEN'S UNWILLING WARD
Emily Bascom

Spirited Lily is horrified by her reaction to her new guardian, Major Daniel Westhaven. He's insufferably arrogant – yet she can't help longing for his touch! Brooding Daniel intends to swiftly fulfil his promise and find trouble-some Lily a husband. Yet she brings light into his dark life – and into his even darker heart…

HER BANISHED LORD
Carol Townend

Hugh Duclair, Count de Freyncourt, has been accused of sedition, stripped of his title and banished. Proud Hugh vows to clear his name! Childhood friend Lady Aude de Crèvecoeur offers her help – after all, turbulent times call for passionate measures…

 MILLS & BOON